DATE

SEE THE WORLD THROUGH HONOR JANE'S EYES

F
K

Anita Clay Kornfeld
In a Bluebird's Eye

AVON BOOKS
A division of
The Hearst Corporation
959 Eighth Avenue
New York, New York 10019

ISBN: 0-380-00672-3

First Avon Printing, June, 1976

AVON TRADEMARK REG. U.S. PAT. OFF. AND
FOREIGN COUNTRIES, REGISTERED TRADEMARK—
MARCA REGISTRADA, HECHO EN CHICAGO, U.S.A.

Printed in the U.S.A.

To my husband,
John Seiferth Kornfeld,
and to my children,
Marcia, Melissa, and Edwin

1

It was on a Wednesday morning in hot August in Margate. Honor's mother was busy in the kitchen canning green beans and tomatoes, flustered and flushed red in the neck from all the activity and the stifling heat. At the sight of the deep-set frown on her mother's face and that tight, stretched-out look on her mouth—a look she usually got before a migraine headache hit her—Honor made a half-hearted, low-voiced offer to help string the green beans or peel the skins off the scalded tomatoes. But her mother was too busy chunking up the coal fire in the big iron stove and pouring boiling water over the last batch of fruit jars; if she had heard the offer, she made no sign of it.

Honor stood in the doorway leading from the kitchen into the back hall and shifted one bare foot slowly across the top of the other, not sure whether she should make the offer again, maybe in a louder, clearer voice. After all, she reminded herself, it had only been that very morning when she had slipped out of her bed at sunrise to make her most solid vow to the magic bluebird, when she had crossed her heart and hoped to die if she didn't go around on a steady lookout for ways of doing good deeds to make up for any bad that might be caught up in the secret plan she was hatching to help Lola run off from Margate so she wouldn't have to spend the rest of her life as Mamie Clark's free maid—or free nigger, as some called it. She couldn't back off so soon from her promise, even before the ten o'clock mail truck had rumbled down the main cinder road on its way to the post office.

"Can I help you out stringing some of those green beans?" she tried again, forcing herself to speak up.

7

"*May* I help you. How many times do I have to correct you, Honor Jane? The school principal's children have to set the example, even in this dinky Tennessee mountain town where most of the white trash running around out there wouldn't know proper grammar if they heard it!" She grabbed a long-handled spoon and stirred vigorously the tomatoes simmering on the back of the stove in a big aluminum pot. "If we ever do get to move off this mountain to a decent town, you're going to have to watch your P's and Q's, young lady!"

"I guess you don't need me then."

Her mother's long sigh seemed to ride the wave of steam coming out of the pressure cooker as it sent out its first hissing noise. "I don't need one blessed thing extra under my feet on a day like this. It's nice of you to offer. It's not that I don't appreciate it. Lord knows I've heard few enough offers out of any of you children." She opened the door to the icebox, poured out a tall glass of water, and sank down wearily at the kitchen table to wait for the gauge to hit its mark. "But don't worry. Just as soon as you grow out of this gawky stage you're going through right now ... I declare, Honor Jane, I never saw anybody who was more all thumbs and who could get more scabby knees than you." She shook her head and took a long drink from the sweating glass of cold water, rubbing her own stiff thumbs up and down, making tiny little rivers on the sides of the glass. "As soon as you're old enough, I'm going to teach you everything I've had to learn the hard way. I never was taught one blessed thing about being a housewife. Why, I wasn't even allowed to set foot in the kitchen, with so many Negro servants running around a dime a dozen to do the housework."

Honor saw that far-off look creeping in and loosening up the frown above the bridge of her mother's wire-rimmed glasses.

"I just hope I get to show you children, once before I die, that wonderful old house where I grew up."

Then, as if her mother had suddenly read her mind and guessed what she was staring at—the exact place where her glasses bore into the bridge of her nose and made a little red ridge—her mother reached up and took off the glasses and wiped them with the corner of her apron. With the glasses off, Honor thought her mother's eyes looked even more empty and watery. Even when they looked right at you, they didn't seem to really be seeing you. She decided it would be the perfect time to back out the doorway and slip down the hall into her special hiding place under the dining room table.

But her mother's voice suddenly cut through the heavy smell of cooked tomatoes hanging in the room. Something in the drifty tone of it made Honor stop in the doorway, just as she had started sliding her feet backward.

"When I was a girl your age, Honor Jane, I had so many privileges." She seemed to be talking more to herself. "Would you believe that I didn't realize it at the time? No, not me, Miss know-it-all Martha Jane Cunningham. Do you think anybody could tell me a thing? Why, I thought Maddoxville, Mississippi, was the tail end of no place. I thought the worst fate in this wide world would be to have to marry a Maddoxville boy and settle down on the Delta. 'I'm not going to bury myself on this hot empty old Delta,' I used to brag, popping off my big mouth. But then who comes along but your father, Mr. Hotstuff himself! Henry Jason Whitfield in all his glory, strutting into my life, spouting off his fancy pipe dreams, and turning my head around so fast I didn't know which way was what!" She made a hollow, dried-out sound that reminded Honor of a grasshopper caught in the middle of the main cinder road, not knowing which way to hop next. "Do you know what I'd do this very minute if some miracle from God would give me a chance! Why, I'd fall right down on my hands and knees and not be the least bit ashamed, right there in front of God and anybody else who cared to look, and I tell you, I'd kiss the very ground of Maddoxville, Mississippi!"

There was a sudden loud whistle from the stove as the pressure cooker topped the gauge.

"*May* I go now?" Honor asked politely, putting special stress on her correct grammar. But her mother was too busy to answer as she darted frantically about the stove, grabbing a dishcloth to protect herself from the steam shooting up toward the gray-planked ceiling, and took the last flurry of steps before putting up the tomatoes.

"You just run along now, Honor Jane. Go find yourself something to do I'd approve of. But you stay in close hollering distance, you hear? I might need you to do something later on."

But Honor scarcely heard. She had already made her favorite exit, a kind of sliding around the doorway, the way their cat, Stonewall Jackson, slid in and out of rooms without anybody noticing. She was running on tiptoe the long way through the house—through the back bedrooms, across the wool rug in the living room, and into the dining room, from the opposite direction.

Her favorite hiding place under the round oak table had become awkward for her. That year she had suddenly grown big for an eleven-year-old; and to fit her gawky frame under the table, she had to sit with her shoulders hunched forward so her head wouldn't bump against the rough iron bolts. She chose a spot under the limply hanging Sunday tablecloth where the shadows swallowed her up as they fell their deepest and darkest, so that if anyone should happen to come into the room, which was highly unlikely on a weekday morning, they'd be less apt to see her. She huddled up into her special sitting position where she could stay as still as a statue and suck in her breath until she didn't make even a hint of a breathing noise to give herself away.

Deftly, her fingers reached out and found the notebook paper and pencil she had hidden under the legs that jutted out from the big fat center pedestal of the table. She had forgotten to resharpen the lead to the fine point she needed for drawing maps. She put the pencil in her mouth and chewed delicately on the wood around the stubby point and then tried to use her front teeth on the newly exposed lead to whittle it down. The lead tasted chalky and bitter, kind of the way coal dust tasted on a hot windy day when little clouds of it would suddenly whip up off the main cinder road and fly straight up her nose and into the back of her mouth.

She pulled her knees up higher, into a more cramped position, to make better drawing room. The movement stretched the place on her right knee where her latest scab was just beginning to crust over into that final healing stage where she could pick it off safely and not make it bleed again. She wanted desperately to scratch at it now, to go after the itch under the scab as hard as their old bird dog, Lucifer, dived after his fleas. Instead, she held

10

her fingers back and made only gingerly picking stabs at the safer, dried-out edges of the scab. She'd show her mother how fast she could grow out of her gawky stage. All thumbs and scabby knees, was she!

She clenched the pencil in her fist. She was going to show the whole town of Margate a thing or two. She knew something they didn't know. She knew who was really running around with killing in their souls, and it wasn't necessarily Lola—even if Lola was the only one, so far, who had been locked up in the state penitentiary. Besides, Lola had paid her dues. She didn't deserve to be still shut off someplace away from her own people, stuck with somebody as grouchy and stingy as Dr. Clark's old wife, Mamie, who was more interested in riding around in her big black Packard than she was in finding out if Lola did or didn't have a good reason for killing that white man in the first place and maybe ought to be turned loose. Wasn't having to stay put and out of sight in that little house in back of Dr. Clark's about the same as being locked up, even if there wasn't an iron bar on the door? But then maybe Mamie Clark wasn't anxious to let her free nigger go.

She squinted her eyes to get used to the shadowy light under the table and studied her first rough sketch of the map of Lola's escape route. The main cinder road wiggled like a snake across the paper. It wasn't going to do at all, she decided, to have Lola try hitchhiking down the main cinder road, being the only Negro in Margate—the only one on that side of the mountain if you left out Suzie Daniels, who wasn't all the way dark-skinned like Lola and had one speckled blue eye like a robin's egg that told the whole world, as she had heard Ruthie Mae Stinnet's mother telling her mother one day when she had slipped under the dining room table and listened to their gossiping, that it wasn't by a long shot, all *nigger* in Suzie Daniels' woodpile. No, anybody who'd bother to stop and give Lola a lift down the mountain, or even as far as DuCasse where the cinder road ran into the paved county road, would probably guess right off that Lola was running away and haul her back and dump her in old Mamie's lap again, maybe turn Lola into a real killer, who might cut loose with her razor in anybody's direction.

She thought for a long moment, chewing on the pencil.

11

Maybe the railroad track would be best. Lola could hike down the railroad bed, which wound its way out to DuCasse too and went on all the way down the mountain through Olympia and on to Nashville. Maybe Lola could even hobo, grab hold of one of those ladders and swing herself up into one of the open boxcars and get a free ride all the way.

But the thought of Lola trying to swing her big bottom up in an easy motion along with a moving freight train—even one that went as slowly as a loaded-down coal car picking up steam—made her bite down harder on the pencil. She didn't think Lola could manage that without breaking her neck. Besides, her mother had warned her too many times about hoboes, how they hid alongside the railroad tracks just waiting for some girl to come along. They'd probably jump out and grab Lola as fast as they'd grab anybody else. It was that white man's jumping out and grabbing her—if what Lola had told her on their last visit was true—that had made her kill him in the first place.

The new cramped position had made her legs start tingling with a sharp sensation that both hurt and tickled at the same time. She slid down, resting her head against the pedestal and stretching her legs straight out so that her feet stuck out from under the tablecloth. She wiggled her toes to try to get the circulation going and wake up her legs.

It was so quiet and the air was so still beneath the tablecloth that she found herself getting drowsy. She was more in the mood for thinking, she told herself, than she was for trying to draw something that wasn't figured out yet.

She let her mind track itself back to the time she and Lola had had their first long talk. Lola hadn't found some quick excuse, like she usually did after a few polite sentences, to duck back inside Mrs. Clark's kitchen behind a closed, unwelcome door. That was also the first time she had gone up the new path she had made for herself so she could sneak around behind Lola's little house by taking the side alley, ducking down low, and easing her way alongside the grape arbor and the fence loaded down with pink rambling roses.

Her new path had been such a good one, in fact, that

she had even caught Lola off guard, and Lola had ears as keen as old Lucifer, flushing a covey of quail out in the field. She smiled to herself, remembering the surprised look on Lola's face and the way her eyes had widened in a flash to the size of quarters, and how she had taken her snuff rag and dabbed with fast, nervous, little dabs at the corner of her mouth.

"God a'mighty, you 'bout scared the living daylights out of me!" Lola had sat up straight in her chair and looked at her with a hard glint in her eyes. "You'd better quit that slipping up on people behind their backs. You're going to get yourself in a whole mess of trouble doing that one of these days. Some people don't like that."

"I wasn't slipping up on you. I was looking for something I lost last time I was up here," she had lied.

"Must've been your shadow you lost then." Lola had looked at her with that digging-down kind of look where she wouldn't settle for anything short of the truth. She had tucked one of those secret-looking smiles at the corner of her mouth where she kept the dip of snuff and had looked as if she knew more than anybody else in Margate—more than even Preacher Pullum, who got his information out of the Baptist rendering of the Bible. "Well, don't just stand there burning the soles of your feet on the hot ground," Lola had finally said, dropping her accusing look. "If you took all the bother to slip around a country mile to get here, you must have something more on your mind than just standing there with that fraidycat look all over your face."

"I'm no fraidycat!" She had set Lola straight on that right away. "I'm not afraid of nothing or nobody! And I ain't afraid either of things like . . . oh, snakes, lizards, getting typhoid shots . . . haunted houses, or graveyards. And I ain't afraid of even getting a hairbrush whipping from my mother if I get caught slipped off up here talking to you!"

"But you're still afraid of Lola, now ain't you?" Lola had that bearing-down look again, but there was something about the way the sun had bounced off Lola's skin, making it shine like the brown satin band on her mother's Sunday hat, and a kind of soft, understanding droop to her bottom lip, even if it was tucked in to hold the snuff, that made the butterflies beating inside her stomach slow

13

down some. For the first time, she found her deep-rooted fear of Lola easing up in her stomach and in the palms of her hands, which always started grabbing and sweating when she was face to face with Lola.

"Maybe I ought to be afraid," she dared Lola, staring her back in the eye. "Preacher Pullum told everybody in his congregation that Sunday morning when Dr. Clark drove off down the mountain to Nashville to get you out of the penitentiary on loan—"

"On *loan!*" Lola interrupted her with a loud kind of laugh that didn't sound as if she thought it was very funny. "Is that what they call it? That's somethin', ain't it, when they told me down at the pen that it was letting me out on my good behavior. But then I guess as how you could call it a loan at that. 'We'll loan you a free nigger maid if you'll see to it that she's kep' well out of sight and she don't get herself into no more trouble.'"

"Preacher Pullum didn't say all that," Honor had corrected, trying to get the friendly look back on Lola's face. "He just said that God might bring down his wrath on the whole town—that it wasn't meant to be to mix up people with different skin colors and all. And he mentioned something about Suzie Daniels' speckled blue eye being a sign of the devil. Do you know about Suzie Daniels?"

"I heard tell," Lola said, dabbing at her mouth. "But come on, you ain't scared of Lola because of this here dark color under my skin?" She pointed at her arm.

"I told you I ain't scared of nothing, even if Stuart and Buford—they're my brothers—told me you'd as soon slit anybody's throat with a razor if they pestered you the wrong way, just like you slit that white man's throat." She had felt her heart pumping hard against her ribs. That had been the first time she had ever talked about the killing with Lola, and she didn't know how Lola was going to take to it. She got her feet in the tiptoe position to run her fastest if she had to.

But Lola was looking at her with a funny far-off look. Then she smiled her secret, knowing look again. "So that's why you always stand there staring at me so funny. You're wondering where I keep my razor hid, ain't you?"

It seemed that Lola could look straight into her mind. "I know you don't have a razor." She tried to sound easy and slow-talking above the awful racing of her heart. "I know all you keep in your apron pocket is your snuff rag."

"You look for more than razors, don't you then?" Lola chuckled. "You notice lots of things while you staring at me with that silly look on your face."

"I don't mean to be staring at you," she said, ducking her gaze downward to the line she was drawing in the dust with a stick she had picked up next to Lola's porch. "It ain't polite, my mother said, to stare at anybody ... even if you *are* the first Negro I ever got to look at up close."

"I guess that ought to make Lola kind of special then," Lola had said, narrowing her eyes and looking off in the direction of two blue jays squawking in the top of a sycamore tree over by the shed where Dr. Clark kept his old Ford V-8, which he used for making house calls way back in the mountain. Then Lola stood up, stretched, and put her hands in the small of her back at the place where her behind made that hump that Stuart and Buford were always laughing about. "I guess you'd better scoot off back down that alley and head out for home before your mother catches you up here and gives you that hairbrush whipping you was talking about."

"Oh, there ain't much hurry, being as how she's off with Mamie Clark at the Missionary Society meeting. If Mamie Clark wasn't off there, you wouldn't be taking time off to sit on your front porch and take a dip of snuff and prop your feet up for a rest, would you?"

"Lord, if you ain't the funniest little girl," Lola had said, looking down at her. "What you always trying to hang around me for? Where'd you learn to ask all them questions—slipping up on people asking questions?" She sat back down again and took out her can of Bruton's snuff and put a fresh dip under her bottom lip, and then dabbed at the corners of her mouth. "Listen, Lola's going to give you some good advice. It ain't no disgrace to be afraid of something. Ain't nobody I ever met wasn't scared of something. Now, you take what you said about not being afraid of snakes. It's something mighty big not to be afraid of snakes. If Lola here sees a snake, she's going to yell at the top of her lungs, you can bet your little ass—'scuse me, I didn't mean to let that bad word slip out."

"Oh, ass ... shit, that word ain't nothing. I know lots of

words like that. I bet I get my mouth washed out with soapsuds least once a month, sometimes more'n that! Why, I guess I've known ass—shitass—since I was around about five years old."

"If I was you, I wouldn't go bragging around about it, which happens to be part of the advice I aim to give you." Lola had shaken her head back and forth and let out a big laugh that seemed to come out of her belly. "You are some other kind of little girl. . . . Listen to Lola now. This is the only time I'm going to say it 'cause it's the last time I want you to come slipping round up here. You hear? You going to get me and you both in a big mess. Now, like I said, it ain't no disgrace to be scared. It's how you act when you are scared that matters. There's times you don't need to let on to the whole world."

"But you said you'd yell at the top of your lungs if you saw a snake. That's letting the whole world know, ain't it?"

"I'm not talking 'bout things like snakes, things you can see out in broad daylight so's you know where your enemy's at. That's the easy kind you can holler 'bout and somebody'll come running. I'm talking 'bout the kind where somebody ain't being honest with you—or with hisself. That's when everybody kind of shuts their eyes and plays like it ain't there and first thing you know you've done got your tail caught in a crack. You've gone and done something dumb when if you'd thought around the corners of being scared you might've outsmarted whatever it was scared the shit out of you."

"I'm always getting my tail caught in a crack," she had said, trying to put a look on her face that would make Lola think she understood everything Lola was saying. "Lola, speaking of tails, what makes yours stick out so big and funny in the back? I never saw so big a tail."

"Is that the kind of question your mama taught you was polite, asking somebody about something they can't do nothing about, something they was born with?"

"I didn't mean to make you mad, Lola. It was one of those questions I just let slip off the tip of my tongue."

"An' that's another thing! You don't have to be always saying the first thing comes to your mind. You learn to stand back and wait a spell. The world ain't going to rush off no place and leave you behind while you're waiting. It

16

sure ain't going to rush off nowhere up here on this mountain top!" She dabbed at her mouth and shook her head again. "Learn how to hold your tongue—not just the tip of it but the whole thing. Wait for the other person talking to let out how dumb or how smart *he* is. Then you got yourself a kind of measuring rod to go by, to maybe tell you what you *ought* to say instead of what's maybe riding heavy on your mind."

"I reckon I see what you mean."

"Well, look. Sometimes words don't mean nothing. They kind of bounce around playful-like, like a rubber ball in that game of jacks you was trying to play last time you came slipping up here. Sometimes words get heavy as a ton of bricks. They can smash up things too, just like a brick can break a glass window if you throw it at it."

She had not been exactly sure of all that Lola meant.

"And there's one more thing, little girl . . ."

"My name's Honor—Honor Jane Whitfield."

"Suits me—Honor Jane Whitfield. But you tuck this under your busy little bonnet too. Now you take them dirty words you was bragging about knowing so many of—sometimes one or two of 'em will go a long way with the right person. But it's just plain dumb to say 'em just to prove you know 'em and let the wrong people get hold of what you're saying. That is—'less you like the taste of soapsuds."

Lola had stood up then, with all signs of lingering gone from her face. "I reckon them clothes done boiled out white enough in that iron pot over there. Reckon it's 'bout time for the Missionary Society meeting to let out."

"Pretty soon," Honor had answered, trying to decide how she could keep Lola talking a little while longer. She had watched Lola shuffle over to the iron pot, rubbing the small of her back, and then bend over and pick up her special washing stick and start stirring the clothes around in the big iron pot, which was propped up on three bricks and had a log under it sputtering down into hot, red ashes.

She had started to walk around the corner of Lola's house and head back down her secret path, but just as she turned the corner she had caught sight of a black crow sitting on a fence post down by the grape arbor. Black crows meant bad luck in her book of beliefs. She cocked her stick, pretending it was a twenty-gauge shot-gun.

Fall dead, black crow, she told it with her mind's commanding voice. But the crow hadn't budged and seemed instead to be looking straight at her. Besides that, the blue jays had been tracking her down all day. Putting the black crow and the blue jays together meant bad luck in the air for sure.

She pretended not to be afraid. She forced her bare feet on down toward the fence, as far as the rambling roses. Behind her back she could hear the blue jays still fighting and fussing around in the tops of the sycamore tree.

She pretended to be picking a bouquet of roses, tucking the stick between her knees for safekeeping, as she tried to pick off the pink roses without getting stuck with a thorn. She could outsmart a blue jay or a black crow any time of the day, she told herself firmly.

> *Way up yonder above the sky*
> *A jaybird built in a bluebird's eye . . .*

She hummed the song to herself as she picked off the fifth rosebud.

> *Go limber Jim, you can't go*
> *Go weave and spin, you can't go Buckeye Jim . . .*

She looked down just as the crow lifted its wings and sailed off down the hill. And she hadn't even gotten to the second verse, she told herself smugly. It'd be no problem at all then to drive out the blue jays.

> *Way up yonder above the moon*
> *A jaybird lived in a silver spoon*
> *Go limber Jim, you can't go*
> *Go weave and spin, you can't go Buckeye Jim . . .*

She tucked the roses into a fist bouquet. Maybe she ought to take them back and give them to Lola to put in her little house for some bright color, she had told herself, forgetting for a moment her mission to drive away the bad-luck omen of the blue jays.

She was so used to walking in a picking kind of bare-

18

foot way to keep the soles of her feet from burning where they were tender that she had not realized she hadn't made a noise. She sat down on a tree stump, all that remained of the big oak that had been struck by lightning in the spring. She clenched the roses in one hand and, with the other, churned at the ground with the stick, trying to poke a doodlebug on its way around the root of the stump. Lola was in the middle of hanging up a big double-bed sheet and had her back turned.

"You sure do know how to get clothes washed out all nice and sanitary looking," she said as Lola snapped on the last clothespin.

Lola whirled around. "Lordie help me! I thought you'd done gone. See, here you are sneaking up on me, slipping around behind my back again and it ain't been five minutes."

"I just picked you some roses to put beside your bed," she said, holding out the bouquet. "They smell good, and pink is my favorite color in roses."

"Black and blue is going to be the color of your little white ass if your mama catches you up here hanging aroun' me. You just begging for that hairbrush whipping."

"I figure I got a good ten more minutes."

"Then, in that case, would you lay them roses down over there on my chair. That's a right nice thing, you thinking 'bout flowers for old Lola." She reached down in the basket and pulled out a second sheet, whipped it out in the air to shake out the wrinkles where she had wrung it out, and started hanging it up on the clothesline. "You are 'bout the funniest little girl ever lived. Lordie, Lordie, I wonder what's going to come of you in this world. What things is going to happen."

"One thing is going to happen," Honor said, grabbing hold of the chance to continue the conversation. "Henry Jason Whitfield is taking his family off this mountain!" She banged the stick against the sides of the stump. "He's getting himself a new teaching job, and he's moving us all clear out of Margate and Bragg County! We might even move all the way off the mountain, out of the state of Tennessee even. We might move to Maddoxville, Mississippi. Do you know where Maddoxville, Mississippi, is, Lola?"

"Nope, I can't say I do. I don't know nothing about no

place in Mississippi, 'cept once I had a cousin-removed came from someplace down in Mississippi—someplace on the Delta."

"Why, I bet he might've known my mother's family!" she had cried out in excitement. "My mother grew up in this big old white house on the Delta. She's always telling us about it, how they had niggers—I mean Negro servants—running around a dime a dozen. Every time she tells us, she acts like it's the first time she's ever mentioned it. My Mama really liked growing up in Maddoxville, Mississippi."

"Yeah, I 'spect she did," Lola had answered, taking a clothespin out of her mouth and putting the last pillowcase on the line. "I 'spect she could use herself a servant or two right now."

"Well, when we move off the mountain, and Daddy gets himself a good-paying teaching job again, back in colleges where he belongs— My Daddy used to teach in just colleges."

"Was that 'fore he turned into a drunkard?"

"You got no right calling my Daddy that!" She had jumped up from the stump. "Nobody's got a right calling my Daddy that—and 'specially no nigger—nobody let out of the state pen's got a right!"

"Look, girl, I wasn't calling your daddy nothing that nobody else in this town don't call him behind his back. It ain't no secret—just like it ain't no secret that they calls me a nigger. Nobody got no right to call me that neither, but they all do. I didn't go yelling at you when you called me that. You got no right yelling at me neither, even if maybe you don't know no better. Thank you kindly for the roses."

"I didn't mean to make you mad, Lola . . . but Daddy's quit going out to Bohunk Town buying bootleg. He's on the wagon all the way now. Ever since that last binge when he and Tootie Farber fell in Doe Creek Lake and they both 'bout drowned themselves."

"I'm mighty glad to hear that." Lola bent over and picked up the empty basket and put it on her hip. "Lola don't mean your daddy no harm. He seems to be a friendly, nice man—just finds it hard to stay off the bottle."

"Lola, since maybe Daddy is going to get him a brand new teaching job and we'll be moving away and I won't

20

be slipping off to come see you no more, could you do me one favor? Could you tell me something about Nashville?"

Lola put a match stick in her mouth, tucked her snuff rag into her pocket again. She started walking toward the back door of the Clarks' main house, shaking her head and chuckling to herself. "You just like a gnat—won't go away."

"But see, I don't know one thing about Nashville 'cept what Miss Cora taught us in fifth grade. That it's got the capitol building with the big dome, a city park, the Grand Ole Opry, and WUSM. Tell me what else Nashville's got."

"Well, it's got a big old penitentiary where they lock up people for going around slitting throats. I done slit me one man's throat, and I reckon I'm going to have to start in slitting me a little girl's throat if she don't go on tending to her own business."

"I know you ain't mad. I can tell when you mean it and when you don't," she had dared Lola again. "I was just asking 'cause I've only been down the mountain twice in my life—once to Olympia to get my abscessed tooth pulled by a real dentist, once when Daddy had to catch the L & N train to Chattanooga, when he was trying to get his name cleared on the teaching board so he could get hired back on the college team of teachers. Oh, yeah, I forgot, once we went all the way to Rock Island for a Fourth of July picnic."

Lola had picked up the bouquet of roses and dropped them down into the empty laundry basket. A friendly smile had crossed her mouth before she opened the screen door to the kitchen.

"Since they don't allow much sight-seeing aroun' the state penitentiary, I can't say I knows much more'n you do about Nashville. I came from outside Nashville myself ... down the old Franklin turnpike. I growed up on this white man's place."

"Was that the same white man you killed, Lola?"

"No. Couple of times I thought about it, though." She laughed a deep chuckle. "You asking all them questions again. You asking things ain't none of your business. And Lola ain't telling you nothing more'n this. That white man needed his throat cut. And that white man ain't never going to slip up behind nobody else's back trying to make them do bad things they don't wants to do. That white

21

man is buried six feet under, and even if old Lola is stuck off up here in this no-man's place, she's still got pink roses to smell, a nice open sky to look at, and she can cook herself something 'sides that slop down the penitentiary. She ain't buried no six feet under. That's enough right there to keep Lola going."

"But don't you get mighty homesick for your cousin from the Delta, your own people? Don't you get tired of just being cooped up in your little house smelling pink roses?"

Lola had seemed to look down at her through a skim of water in her eyes. "Jesus knows how tired Lola gets."

"Why don't we figure out a way to get you out of here?" she had asked, the idea to tell Lola about her secret plan suddenly leaping to her mind like a big fat bullfrog leaping out of nowhere when you least expect it. "Why don't you run off, Lola?"

"Questions. You just stuffed full of all kinds of questions, ain't you?" Lola had looked at her with a strange, studying glint in her eye, as if she was suddenly suspicious. She had then opened the door to go in, letting a deep sigh come out of her that seemed to drop down on top of the pink roses in the empty laundry basket.

"Lola, if my Daddy does get us located in a nice new town with lots of people, with maybe a colored town in it too, maybe you could get permission to come and live with us. Daddy could build you a little house better'n this one, out back of our house. Mama's kitchen wouldn't be no worse than Mamie Clark's!"

Lola was looking through the screen door at her, and through the rusty blackness of it, she could not see her full expression. There was a new tone to her voice though, a tone as sharp as a razor's edge. "When Lola gets off this mountain, when Lola finally do makes it out of Margate, honey, Lola ain't going to work in nobody's kitchen! I got better ideas for myself than that!"

They both heard the sound of the big black Packard's wheels crunching into the new layer of cinders on the side alley where Mamie parked it sometimes when she meant to go out again.

"Now you just duck your little ass out of here and Lola don't want you coming aroun' pestering me *no* more, you hear? Lola means business this time. You hear?"

Honor shook her head, caught in that shadowy, drowsy place between being fully awake and asleep. She thought at first it was her remembering mind sending out Lola's voice at full angry tilt.

"You hear me, young lady? Don't you act like you don't hear me calling you, Honor Jane Whitfield! I don't have time for playing hide-and-seek games with you! . . . HONORRR! . . . Come inside this house this minute, wherever you are hiding! You hear?"

Her mother was yelling out the back door, which meant she hadn't guessed where her hiding place was. Honor threw back the limp corners of the tablecloth and darted out from under the table, bumping her head hard as she fled.

2

"Where've you been so long?" her mother asked irritably as Honor came into the kitchen from the back hall. But her mother did not wait for an answer. She was busy wiping steam off her glasses and sweat out of the red ridges in her neck. "I need you to run to the company store for me. I've run out of fruit-jar lids—wouldn't you know! I tell you, this has been the absolute worst canning day of my entire life. Everything that could has gone wrong!"

Honor was rubbing the bump on her head that was fast swelling into a lump the size of a black walnut. "Well, I could've told you this morning it was going to be a bad luck day," she said, trying to squint away some of the pain. "I saw two big fat blue jays perched right over there on the alley fence rail in straight eyeshot of the kitchen. They put the evil eye on you before you even got started."

"That is entirely enough of that silly superstition you've been coming up with lately. Honor Jane, there is no power, none whatsoever, in a bluejay more than its natural ability to fly and do what all birds do." She put both hands on her hips and looked at her with an accusing look. "And another thing—bluebirds aren't magic."

Honor sucked in a quick surprised breath. She hadn't told anybody about the magic bluebird. But she had written it down—how she believed it was as powerful as Preacher Pullum's God—in her secret diary.

"You've got no right reading my diary!" she said, furious with her mother and with the pain in her head from the bump.

"I've got any right I need to keep some degree of sanity in this household—especially with somebody as full of crazy notions as you are lately." She twisted a lid tightly on to a quart jar of green beans and wiped the jar with the dish towel. "I've told you a hundred times that only God has power, God and the Devil. If you'd study your Sunday school lessons the way you're supposed to, you'd know it was a sin to have any false gods. *There shall be no false idols before me.*"

"The Baptist rendering of the Bible ain't the only way of looking at life and religion," Honor said, opening the icebox.

"Don't stand there letting all the cold air out! And would you kindly quit arguing with me? If there's anything I don't need right now, it's more of your sass!"

Honor poured a glass of milk and started to sit down.

"Exactly who gave you permission to go helping yourself to things! We have to pay for that sweetmilk! But you children seem to think money grows on bushes." She came over to check out the icebox to see what else might be missing. "I heard your brothers rummaging around in here when I took time off to go out back to the toilet."

"Out back? Is the indoor commode stopped up again?"

"This time it's the town pump out of whack. It seems to be something all the time. We might as well pay rent on a regular shotgun house, as much use as we get out of our indoor toilet." Her mother sighed again and stopped to line up the row of fruit jars that were finished. "If it's not the pipes freezing in winter or the septic tank backing up on us, it's the town pump going out."

Honor drank down the milk and went over to the sink to rinse out the glass.

"Wash your dirty hands while you're there," her mother said as she sank down at the kitchen table to think out her grocery list. "Honor! How did you rip your dress at the waist?"

"I must've caught it on my knee this morning, early, when I was playing Stuart a game of marbles. It was 'keeps' and Stuart fudged all over the place. He always cheats and takes my marbles away from me."

"I've told you that an eleven-year-old girl is too old to be squatting down wearing dresses and playing marbles— playing where boys can see with their big eyes."

"But it was just me and Stuart." Honor was looking down into the washpan where a bar of Lifebuoy soap had

25

been left in the bottom, and a thick melted film of it made it easy to squish up soap bubbles with her thumbs. She watched as a big bubble floated across the top of the water. She reached out to capture it in the exact spot where the blue stripe of color on the bubble crisscrossed the yellow dab.

"I'm not talking about your brother. I'm talking about that bunch of white trash Northcutt boys who're always hanging around your brother Buford. Don't you ever let me catch you playing marbles with them!"

"They don't ask me anymore," she said. "Besides, Clyde Northcutt can win anybody's marbles without even fudging. He's the best taw-shooter in Margate."

"Don't just stand there dawdling! And go change your dress. I can't let you go to the company store looking like a rag picker." She let out a sigh as Honor came across the room looking for something to dry her hands on. "When are you going to start acting like other young girls your age, Honor Jane? Why don't you play with Ruthie Stinnet—play paper dolls and games girls are supposed to play at your age?"

Honor started drying her hands on a dish towel she found on the back of a chair. "Ruthie and them don't play paper dolls any longer. They used to, but now they just like to play doctor."

"What's that look on your face supposed to mean? You've got that guilty, smart-aleck look spread out like a road map all over your face!"

At the sound of the word "map," Honor held on tightly to the dish towel. She wondered if her mother had been snooping around under the dining room table too. But, then, she hadn't drawn much on the notebook paper that would give it away. Even if her mother had found it, she wouldn't guess in a million years that it was the beginning of an escape map for Lola.

"I ain't looking guilty 'cause I ain't guilty!" she finally said smugly. "But maybe you ought to ask your little pet Stuart a few questions. He plays doctor all the time, and they make Ruthie lay down and they pull up her dress. Talk about boys with big eyes. . . ."

"That is quite enough out of you, young lady! And if you're going to be such a big-britches tattletale, then I suggest to you that the least you could do would be to use

26

correct English! I am sick and tired of hearing you say 'ain't.' And people don't 'lay' down, they 'lie' down." She dropped her head down in both hands. "I don't know what I am going to do with you children! If we don't hurry up and move off this mountain, it's going to be too late for me to do anything. Why, I catch myself all the time lately—when I know better—coming out with things I never dreamed I'd give utterance to. Oh, I was taught better! But when you're surrounded morning, noon, and night with white trash . . ."

"Have you got a migraine headache?" Honor asked, changing the subject. "You want me to get you some aspirin? Some salts? Maybe some Ex-Lax?"

"I want you to get a clean dress on. Go comb your hair and put a ribbon in it and make yourself look like something for a change besides what the cat drug in. And then I want you to go as fast as you can to the company store. The migraine hasn't hit me full yet, but I feel the pain gathering like a dark thunder cloud in the back of my head."

"Why don't you let me rub the back of your neck the way old Mamie Clark gets me to do sometimes when she feels one of her lulus coming on? I know exactly where to rub now. Last time I did it so good—I mean well—she gave me a whole nickel. Usually she just gives me two pennies."

"You should not take payment for doing kind deeds. Now run on. Hurry up!"

When Honor came back into the kitchen, she turned around silently, waiting for her mother to tie the sash to her favorite pink-flowered dress.

"Why did you pick out your only good Sunday School dress?"

"It's got a spot of chocolate on it—from that Baby Ruth candy bar Daddy bought me last Sunday. It needs washing again before I can wear it to Sunday School."

Her mother yanked at the sash ends and straightened the bow to suit her. "I must say, pink is about your best color. It softens you up a little." She fussed with the ribbon in her hair, retied it, pulling a strand of hair as she did. "Where did you get that goose egg on your head, Honor Jane? Have you been in another fight?"

"I bumped it, that's all. Just going through my gawky stage."

"Here, let me pull a little of this hair down to cover it up some. I declare, your hair is already beginning to turn brown, Honor Jane. By the time you're grown, you'll be as black-headed, I bet, as your father. You take after his side of the family anyway. Sometimes I'd swear you weren't my child."

"Who was it in the woodpile then?" Honor asked.

"There wasn't nobody in the woodpile—I mean, anybody!" She went over to the wall cabinet. "Here's a fifty-cent piece, and I guess you'd better take along this extra quarter. The way that J. T. Arnold jacks up prices, you can't tell what things cost anymore. I need a half-dozen fruit jar lids and rubber rings to match. And 'es see . . . we're down to the last of that loaf of bread. It was a jelly sandwich your brothers were trying to sneak in here and make, and they thought I wouldn't find out about it, with them leaving a trail a mile wide behind them—jelly all over the floor and butter smeared on the knife. Not one of you children can fool me!" She thumped her hand on the table, thinking aloud. "That much will just have to do. I've got to stretch every penny these lean summer days. Now don't you go spending one penny of that extra change, Honor Jane. I want every cent back. Tell me what you're going after now."

"A half-dozen fruit-jar lids, rubber rings to match, a dime loaf of light bread."

"You march straight down that sidewalk, and don't stop on the way to talk to anybody. I need to get those fruit-jar lids so I can get out of this kitchen. Don't you go dawdling, getting yourself sidetracked. And put on your shoes. Your feet are going to spread out like nigger feet if you keep going barefoot."

"I broke the T-strap to my sandals last Sunday, when me and Stuart were running."

"Stuart and I . . ."

"Daddy said he was going to fix it for me, but he hasn't had time yet."

"Oh, no, of course not. He's much too busy wearing out the seat of his britches on the banks of Doe Creek Lake with his fishing buddies . . . and his bootleg!"

28

"Last time he caught a five-pound bass ... and a long string of bluegill. You said it helped fill the table."

"I don't intend to stand here arguing with you the blessed day long, Honor Jane Whitfield! You always have to take up for your father, don't you? You just can't resist."

Honor ran light-footed out the front door, the money tied in the corner of a handkerchief and clutched in her hand. When her feet hit the cinder sidewalk, she slowed down to her usual picking kind of walk, with only an occasional skip in those hot dry places worn smooth of cinders where it burned the bottoms of her feet. She hurried along as fast as she could, up the hill past Dr. Champ Clark's house, where Mrs. Clark was sitting in a wicker rocking chair on the front porch, her gold-rimmed glasses dangling on a chain across her big droopy bosom. Honor took a quick, sideways glance, just enough to see Mrs. Clark swat out with her fan, probably at a swarm of gnats or a sweat bee maybe, but not enough so that she could catch Honor's eye and ask her to come up and rub the back of her neck. Even for a whole nickel, it wasn't worth it, Honor thought, hating the thought of her fingers having to rub up and down on that bony, wrinkled old neck.

As she started down the other side of the hill, where the back alley turned in and wound around to Lola's house, Honor lifted her head as straight as she could. Somehow, she always felt Lola's eyes were following her, even if she couldn't see exactly where Lola might be standing, looking out through the cracks in a window shade or from behind a curtain somewhere.

She broke into a faster step. She didn't want to run the risk of added bad luck—not after two blue jays had already put the hex on her mother's canning.

At the foot of the hill, out of sight and hollering distance, she bent over and picked up a stick to have ready to drag along the wire fence that old blue-faced, humpbacked Mrs. Floyd had put up to keep stray dogs from hiking their legs and stunting the growth of her honeysuckle vines, the thickest of any in Margate.

Mrs. Floyd's house was the fourth one in a long row of three- and four-room houses built and owned by the Black Diamond Coal Company and rented out to their employees. This was considered to be the choice row in Margate because it was on the main cinder road and boasted two of Margate's big "white-collar" houses. Unlike the main bulk of company-owned houses, which were painted a dull washed-out red and had outhouses, these were painted white with bright green shutters, and, more impressive to this locality, had built-in toilets that flushed. These were the only houses with indoor toilets in town. Each had been built with rank of importance in mind, the biggest and best going to the company doctor, Dr. Champ Clark. Then, in more or less equal rank, the others went to the mine foreman, Buddy Matthews; the manager of the company store, J. T. Arnold; the bookkeeper, Max Clifty; and last, the school principal—though there were some who thought the company should rent out the Whitfield house, considering the principal's drinking problem, to Preacher Pullum instead.

The row of houses on the main cinder road had the advantage, too, of being a single row, where people could sit on their front porches and look out across the road at the beauty of a long, thick stretch of mountain woods, interrupted in only one small hacked-out place where Dr. Clark had built a special garage for Mamie's Packard.

Honor had been aware of the prestige of living in one of the white-collar houses with a bathroom—even if their toilet was usually on the blink. It was not generally known that the Whitfields had to use their outdoor toilet about as much as anyone else in Margate and that once a year, along with everyone else in town, they had to hire the services of Suzie Daniels' brother, Frank, who came up the mountain from Olympia in his rattling old pickup loaded down with sacks of lye. Certainly she had never volunteered the information, since she enjoyed the priority of being the only girl in the fifth grade who knew what it was to flush a toilet.

But there were times, such as this morning, when a wave of guilt about being special made her feel somehow ashamed, when the only birdcall she could hear from deep in the woods across the way was still the loud mocking squawk of the dirty old blue jay. She ducked her head going by the Hardee's little chicken coop of a house. The five Hardee children were outside playing hopscotch with broken pieces of fruit-jar glass, all of them looking too skinny and hungry to be wasting so much energy jumping

30

around so hard and fast and screaming at the top of their lungs. That family just had no chance in sight of getting off "relief" as long as their father was still put away at the TB sanatorium in Morning Grove.

When she had safely passed the house, she raised her head high, pretending she hadn't seen them, and whistled loudly and shrilly through her teeth, mocking back at the sassy blue jay.

But at that moment she stepped suddenly on a sharp cinder. She grabbed at her heel with her hand, struggling to keep her balance, wincing with added pain at the thought that it might turn into a stone bruise that Dr. Clark would have to lance. The pain gradually eased away, but in its place was another kind of nagging uncertainty. Stepping on the cinder was bound to be another sign. First the goose-egg bump on her head, now the bruise on her heel—she could even smell the bad luck.

She limped, her thoughts spinning. It was time, she decided, past time, in fact, to make her wishes to the magic bluebird, to let him know that she still believed in his power, regardless of what her snooping mother might think. She could make her wishes, even while she was on her way to the company store, if she didn't stop and get distracted and let other kinds of hexes get in the way.

Making the wishes to the magic bluebird was a sacred ritual with her, one she had developed after several months of trial and error. It was secret, too, and she would never write it down in her diary now; they would only laugh at her and accuse her of being in league with the Devil.

Before beginning, she tested to see that the money was safe in the handkerchief. With one finger, she reached up and tried to loosen a tight strand of hair that her mother had wrapped into the ribbon that was pulling at the edges of the goose-egg bump and making it pinch. She didn't want anything to worry about once she started the wishes. The slightest thing going wrong could break the spell.

Don't you dare squawk! she told the blue jay with her mind's fiercest scolding voice.

With a deep, dedicated breath she began:

> *Oh, bluebird, way up above the sky,*
> *Grant me these wishes, by and by.*

But the piercing squawk of a blue jay back up close to Mamie Clark's garage made her stop in her tracks and erase the first beginning. She listened apprehensively until she could no longer distinguish the hateful bird's cry from the mingled sounds of the Hardee children squealing; from the whirring buzz of a horsefly that swooshed low by her right shoulder and angled off sharply toward the road; or from the more muted hum of the woods, which, even on a hot August day when the wind did not stir a leaf on any tree, gave out a gentle, steady, rustling sound.

She repeated the beginning and quickly launched into her first wish, before the blue jay could pipe up again.

Would you please turn all these cracker-box houses here in Margate into big white houses with bathrooms in every single one—bathrooms that won't go out of whack anytime?

She took a deep breath as the stick she was carrying in her left hand jabbed somehow into the side of her leg. But in keeping with the rigid demands of her ritual, she ignored it.

Would you please keep the mines always working so they won't have to shut down or have cave-ins killing people, so people like the Hardees don't have to go on relief and get TB. And don't let little bitty children get abscessed teeth or get scared in the middle of the night over black panthers on the loose or killers with sharp razor blades . . . or the other kind of killer who won't admit the killing in his soul yet. . . .

There were only ten steps to go before she would reach Mrs. Floyd's fence; and just past Mrs. Floyd's, she could already see Mrs. Diddie Ewing squatting down in her flower beds, taming the morning glories with pieces of twine string. Diddie Ewing loved to grab hold of anybody to talk to about her boy Daniel who was off in C.C.C. camp in Cookville, Tennessee; if she let Mrs. Diddie Ewing get hold of her with that big flabby arm and loud "hidy-do," she'd never get all her wishes out or make it to the company store on time to please her mother. She slowed her steps to a dragging motion.

Bluebird, after you've made everybody happy here in Margate, is it too much to ask you to maybe fly on down to Maddoxville, Mississippi, and fix it up some kind of magic way so that my Mama can go home to that big

*house on the Delta and the whole Whitfield family can
move in? There wouldn't be any Bohunk Town in Maddoxville and that would mean there wouldn't be no more
bootleg whiskey for my Daddy, who might get hired in a
big school somewhere on the Delta. If you could grant
this wish, I wouldn't ask for another thing—not even a free
nigger to help in the kitchen. I'd be willing to learn how
to even can tomatoes and green beans and do the housework.*

But as she wound up the last wish, and crossed her
heart and hoped to die on it, instead of having a hope
that took quick little wings like a hummingbird in her
chest, she had a feeling that felt like a sinker on a fishing
line, dropping down to the bottom.

It was hot, and a gnat caught in her eyelashes. She fluttered her watering eyelids, rubbed the gnat away finally
with the knuckle of the fist holding the money.

A nickel's worth of—no, a dime loaf of light bread, she
corrected herself, a half-dozen fruit-jar lids, and rubber
rings to match. That's what I'm going after. She retested
the list as she dragged her stick halfheartedly across the
last section of Mrs. Floyd's wire fence, letting the beats of
it drum into her head, *Rut-a-tut . . . Rut-a-tut . . . Rut-a-
tut.* If she ran with the stick, the beat would change to
tic-a-tic . . . tic-a-tic . . . tic-a-tic.

When she reached the last fence post, she broke the
stick and threw it at the hot sections of the cinder sidewalk that were burning the soles of her feet.

Even the woods, which always promised a cool resting
place, seemed to give off an invisible wave of heat that
rode with the clouds, that caught hold of time itself and
held it above the town of Margate like some kind of storm
that would rain down something much worse than water
or hail.

Mrs. Diddie Ewing had spotted her and was already
waving her arm, but even her flabby skin seemed to be
hanging fixed in the hot air. Suddenly Honor was seeing
not Mrs. Diddie Ewing but her mother with her steamed-
up glasses and her red neck, poking at the coal fire and
sending black soot rolling up to the ceiling like a cloud
that would fade out and leave behind a thin veil of dark
gray. She clenched the knotted handkerchief tighter, re-
dedicating herself to her errand.

33

"Why, I say there, hidy-do, Honor Jane." Mrs. Diddie made a grunting sound as she stood upright from her squatting position. "I seen you a'coming up the sidewalk, poking along like you was lost in a daydream or something. And I just said to myself, 'I can tell that little girl is hot as a firecracker and would just love to sit a spell on my front steps and rest her feet and drink herself a cool glass of lemonade.' I was aiming to stop fussing around with these morning glories anyway. I declare, they've gone plumb wild, bound and determined to climb all over my front porch. Come on, sit yourself down. Won't take me more'n a minute to fix us up a glass. I've got the ice chipped off already."

"No, thank you Mrs. Diddie," she answered, being polite, but keeping a firm toehold on the cinder sidewalk. "I've got to be getting on to the company store for my mother."

"Now what in the world have you got to buy in such a big all-fired hurry that you can't take time out for a cool drink of lemonade on a day hot as this? It won't take me but a minute."

"I can't, Mrs. Diddie, I just can't. I really do have to be getting on so my mother can finish up her canning and get off her feet before her migraine headache sets in full blast."

"Canning! The school principal's wife having to can on a day like this! Poor soul. Bless her heart! Why, I knew you all was having a hard time of it with your daddy out there blowing every dime in Bohunk Town, but I never once thought she'd have to stoop to canning. I mean, the way she's always bragging around about it being nigger work, something that she's too good to lower herself to. Not that some of us don't can, but when you live in one of the big houses . . . well, it ain't exactly . . ."

Honor lifted her head and squared her shoulders and shot a stubborn, proud look straight at Mrs. Diddie who everybody in town knew didn't have a pot to pee in. She could just stand there all by herself blinking her little gopher eyes at the sun and suck on her own chipped-off ice cubes and drink her lemonade that never was sweet enough anyway.

"My mother has to keep her hands busy doing something so she won't have a steady migraine headache—hav-

34

ing to put up with all this white trash morning, noon, and night."

"Well! If that don't beat all! Now I've heard everything, I reckon. It takes nerve, if you ask me, for the wife of the town's biggest sot to go around calling other people white trash—putting on all them airs at the Missionary Society meetings about her sorority sisters from the university and how only niggers did housework where she came from! If she's so high and mighty, looks to me like she could hire herself a nigger from down Olympia or march off and leave her no-good husband stuck out there in Bohunk Town!"

Honor ran as fast as she could down the hill. She tried not to hear everything Mrs. Diddie Ewing was yelling out at her back, though she couldn't resist keeping one ear open. It was the first time anyone had ever come right out and said straight out loud what she had guessed they whispered behind her back, except when Lola had called her father the town drunkard that day.

She'd show Diddie Ewing. She'd show them all! There was some way—there was bound to be some way to get the Whitfield family moved out of Margate! Even being the town's biggest sot was better than being its white trash! Her father could outsmart Diddie Ewing and anybody else in town with his hands tied behind his back and blindfolded!

At the foot of the hill, Honor stopped at the footbridge and looked down at the water, which ran clear and sparkling across the rocks in the bottom of the bed and gurgled its way around the big lumps of stone scattered here and there. Normally, she stopped here to rest her feet and to ease an ache in her side if she had been running all the way. And she stopped because the footbridge was a kind of dividing line in Margate, marking the end of the long stretch of woods and the best row of houses on the main cinder road, and the beginning of other things. Twenty feet beyond, the main road forked. One-half of it split off like a long black racer snake that couldn't wait to wiggle its way around behind the company store and the post office and on through the long, monotonous rows of shotgun houses. These homes lined both sides of the road and were jammed up so close there was hardly room in between to plant a solid row of hollyhocks. This was where most of the real coal miners lived, those who put carbide lamps on their caps and got up before daylight to ride down the mine shafts with their big iron picks and emerge with black rings around their eyes that didn't wash all the way off even after their Saturday baths. Miners' Row was a place she was never allowed to visit. From where she stood she could not see the houses, but she drew them in her mind's eye—gray, flimsy, oversized boxes with pointed peaks of tin called roofs and square little windows, like dwarf eyes, and tall skinny chimneys to tell you people lived there.

The other half of the road narrowed down at the fork and seemed to crawl its way up Black Diamond Hill, past the post office, past the front steps of the company store, past Maude Gate's boardinghouse, and on past the other three white houses with green shutters, until it finally died out at the tip-top of the hill at the steps of the four-room schoolhouse where her father was boss—unless it was Sunday and Preacher Pullum took command of the stage and used the lectern for his pulpit, pounding his fists and shouting to the rafters about the Baptist good and evil. On Wednesday nights the Masons sometimes took over the schoolhouse for their miners' meetings, and the Missionary Society held regular sessions there on Saturday. Behind the schoolhouse was the graveyard, with tombstones standing out like slabs of tree trunks leveled this way and that. Faded crepe-paper wreaths were still left from Decoration Day, and the rambling roses ran so wild in places, they hid the graves; you could step on one and bring on bad luck without even knowing it.

She leaned over the railing of the footbridge and tried to spot her friend, Moses, the crawdad who had lived under the biggest rock since she could remember. Mrs. Diddie's voice was still ringing loudly in her ears.

It seemed that she'd never learn, never get it all straight about what was all right to talk about in a shushed-up way inside houses, but shouldn't be mentioned outside to people like Mrs. Diddie Ewing. Lola had told her to hold back her tongue, to stand back and wait for others to let out how dumb they were or how smart. But she had always known that Mrs. Diddie Ewing was dumb. She knew Mrs. Diddie liked to whip up stories so she'd have something on her mind to talk about with the other ladies, but she hadn't known that Mrs. Diddie Ewing was one of the Baptists with a kind of killing in her soul, too.

She knew it was time to get on with her errand. She brushed her hair back off the goose-egg bump, then decided she'd better cover it up again to keep people from asking nosy ouestions. She straightened her skirt, making sure the hem wasn't turned up, and started up toward the company store.

As she turned up Black Diamond Hill, she saw the dreaded sight of Uncle Dave Blaylock and Tootie Farber sitting on their wooden boxes in front of the post office, heads bent over the checkerboard, legs sprawled out across the narrow sidewalk, taking up so much room there'd be no way to pass without coming up close enough for Uncle Dave to reach out with his long, bony arm, grab her, and pull her up close to pat her on the bottom—unless she wanted to sidestep and walk barefoot through the dried-out Johnson grass where they'd been spitting their tobacco juice all morning.

She tucked the handkerchief holding the money tightly into her fist, and, fighting off the urge to duck her head and run as if she were playing tackle football with her brothers, she squared her shoulders and looked Uncle Dave straight in the eye. "Good morning," she said defiantly, attempting to skirt past him.

But he was too quick for her. "Lookee here, Tootie—I caught me a live one here! If it ain't my little sweetheart!" He grabbed her and jerked her to a halt in the crook of his arm. "Where you trying to squirm off to now? Come on, give your Uncle Dave some sugar. You got me a little kiss saved up, honey?"

"You're not my uncle, and I've got to be getting on to the company store," she said, squirming harder to avoid his patting hands.

"Whoa there! Don't go tearing off 'fore Uncle Dave gives you a little present. Ain't she a honey though, Tootie," he said, as he reached with one hand deep into his overall pocket.

"It's your move," mumbled Tootie, scratching at his scalp through a thick mat of coarse white hair and purposely not looking up. " 'Es get on with this here checker game 'fore Miss Ada puts up the mail and starts in hollerin' at us."

"I'll get on with the game plenty fast enough, Tootie. It

ain't but a matter of a jump for me to have you beat anyways." He held out the palm of his hand filled with pennies and loose change. "I reckon you can wait to lose yourself a game of checkers while I give this little sweetheart some change to buy herself some bubblegum and a jawbreaker. There, honey, pick yourself out some of them pennies. Take that buffalo nickel if you want it … but for the nickel I get me a big juicy kiss."

"Bubblegum and jawbreakers makes my teeth rot out and abscess," she said, ignoring his outstretched hand and looking down at the checkerboard. "'Sides, my mother told me I wasn't supposed to take any more pennies, or any kind of money from you, ever again!"

"Is that a fact?" He let the change slide back down into his pocket. "Then I 'spect you'd better be getting your little britches on up to the company store while I get on to winning this here checker game."

She took a few steps back, out of reach, but where she could watch the next move. When Tootie turned his head to spit tobacco juice, Uncle Dave jumped three of his men.

"How's that for a little checker playing!" he laughed, slapping his legs and leaning back on his wooden box.

"Goddam," mumbled Tootie, scratching his head again. "I was aiming to take that jump myself—next move. Dave, you sure are a mean son of a bitch to play checkers with. Lord if you ain't."

"I see a move, Tootie," Honor said, her fingers itching to take the two RC bottle caps that were Tootie's king and jump a line of orange crush tops of Uncle Dave's that were just ripe for the taking. "Don't you see it, Tootie? You can still beat!"

"Now you just trot your little ass out of here. Go *on!* Checkers ain't no game for little girls no way. What was that you was supposed to get for your mama at the company store?"

"Why you in such a hurry all of a sudden to get shed of her, Dave?" Tootie said, sitting up and motioning for her to come over to his side. Tootie winked at her meaningfully, as if they shared a secret. "She's *my* little sweetheart now."

"She don't know nothing about checkers. Why, she can't even tell you what she was going after at the store,"

38

said Uncle Dave, pointing his finger at her. "Your mama is going to whip your butt if you don't get on about your business."

"I know what she wants at the company store. She just wants a dime loaf of light bread, some fruit-jar lids, and rubbers," she said smugly, sidling over to where she could point the move out behind Uncle Dave's back.

"Did you hear that, Tootie? Sending a little girl after rubbers."

"Dave, you ought to be ashamed, talking dirty-mouthed in front of a little girl like that." He looked at Honor, frowning, asking with his shaggy eyes where the move was.

"The king—that one, Tootie," she motioned excitedly as he toyed uncertainly with the caps on the king row. "You got him! You won yourself a checker game, Tootie," she said, her eyes dancing, as Tootie's fingers finally picked up the right king and started clearing out the orange crush tops.

"Humph! Took the school principal's girl to win it. Tootie's too dumb to beat me on his own!"

"That's a goddam lie, Dave Blaylock! Ain't first time I ever beat you at a game of checkers. You call me dumb again and I'm just apt to beat the living shit outa you."

"You just apt to land bottom-side up back in Doe Creek Lake, if you pick a fight with me," Uncle Dave said, getting up slowly from the wooden box. "It's too damn hot to fight, Tootie," he said, sitting back down again. He turned and glared at Honor. "Get out of here. Go on and buy them rubbers you was talking about your mama needing."

"Don't pay Dave and his big mouth no mind," Tootie called out after her.

But Uncle Dave's glaring laugh and mocking voice bore in deep between her shoulder blades as she hurried on up the sidewalk. She thought she'd heard all the dirty words. She didn't know about "rubbers." She still didn't know how they could make something dirty out of that, unless rubber fruit-jar rings had something to do with that rubber bag with the long hose on it that her mother hid in her bottom drawer along with a sack of funny-smelling powder.

She walked into the company store and waited her turn while Mr. Arnold was slicing a big ring of bologna. She

39

wished there was some way of calling out her list so she wouldn't have to say "rubbers" again.

"And what will it be for you, little Miss Whitfield, all dressed up in your pretty hair bow there? If you don't look mighty pretty today!"

"Thank you kindly," she said, looking down at her feet and taking in a deep breath. She hated it when he said things about how she looked. There was that funny glint he always got that made her know he didn't mean what he said but was just trying to be smart and have some excuse to talk above everybody else's voice and prove how he was the company store manager.

"Cat got your tongue?"

"I was just trying to untie this knot and get out my money," she said, trying to loosen the handkerchief. "My mother said for me to get a dime loaf of light bread and . . . she needs a half-dozen fruit-jar lids . . . and . . ."

"You forgot something? Ain't there something else goes with fruit-jar lids she might find need for?"

"Why, I declare," Honor said, trying to draw up her best manners and stand as tall as she could, "you're right, she does need rubber rings to match."

She tried to race through the rubber-ring part and lower her voice in that Maddoxville, Mississippi, way her mother used sometime when she was trying to impress somebody.

"Speak up, I didn't hear!" Mr. Arnold cupped his hand to his ear and winked at the redheaded Givens boy who was stacking up feedbags in the corner.

"Rub—ber rings to match. I didn't know you were losing your hearing, Mr. Arnold. Mama thought it was maybe your eyesight going bad on you, the way you jack up some of the prices."

"Well, now ain't that interesting! Your mama just might test out her own eyesight! Seems as how she hasn't been looking at those bills she owes us. I notice you ain't asking to charge it today. Tell your mama she'd better come in here and talk to me pretty soon about the big bill she owes."

Honor felt a grabbing, sick feeling in her stomach, as if at any minute she might have to throw up. She had said the wrong thing again—only this time it was worse than with Mrs. Diddie Ewing. Mrs. Diddie always was carrying tales and spreading bad stories. But her mother's voice was ringing in the back of her head with something she had said not long ago to her father: "And tell me just what we're going to do when J. T. Arnold gets the bright idea to bear down hard and dun us for all we owe at the company store? I hear by the grapevine that he's trying to get his brother to apply for job as school principal."

As he dropped the fruit-jar lids and rubber rings and loaf of light bread into the paper sack, Honor's mind was racing in a blind panic. She had to think of something to make him forget about the bill. "My Mama says that even if you do jack up prices, you still keep things down at a cost below most places. She says you're a fine company store manager, and Black Diamond Coal Company ought to be awfully proud of you."

"When did she say that?" He pushed the sack across the counter. His frown seemed to be loosening a little.

"When? Why, she says that so many times I can't tell you exactly. She says it at Missionary Society meetings. She compliments you sometimes so much she makes Daddy wonder if she is a little bit sweet on you." She tried to pucker her mouth in the kind of smile her mother used along with her Maddoxville brogue.

"I declare," Mr. Arnold said, winking again at the Givens boy. "You never know about these Southern belles."

Honor hurried out of the store and saw with relief that Uncle Dave and Tootie had gone inside the post office to stand in line for their mail. Normally, she would have gone inside and stood in line too, to see if she had won a contest or if one of her questions had been accepted by Dr. I.Q., or if a new Sears Roebuck Catalog had come. And then, too, she liked to keep a close check on the Ten Most Wanted Criminals, just to make sure Lola's name wasn't among them.

All the way home she walked at a fast, steady pace, clutching the paper sack in one hand and holding the change in her other fist, keeping her eyes glued to the cinder sidewalk. But it was of no use. Everything had gone wrong. Even her shadow, the way it jerked along tall and slanted and all crooked to one side, seemed just another sign, every bit as ugly and mocking to her as one hundred and fifty blue jays on steady wing.

41

3

With sundown in the mountains there usually comes a breeze that nudges out in gentle waves the lingering pockets of heat that earlier have brought the sweat bees swarming. Rags in tin cans are set on fire to smolder and smoke away gnats. Women, tired from a day's work of cleaning houses gray and grimy from years of collected coal dust, shed their damp, dingy aprons and come to sit on front porches, lifting swollen feet to rest, sometimes chewing on match stems while they absently watch the Big Dipper find its place and listen to the night sounds gather in the woods across the main cinder road. But on this particular evening the breeze was slow in coming. In the Whitfield kitchen a suffocating vacuum of heat and the smell of boiled tomatoes and steam-pressured green beans held the children and their mother in a tight web of mounting discord.

"It's too hot to eat," said Honor, who was making little tunnels with her fork through the pile of macaroni and tomatoes on her plate.

"I hate macaroni," said Stuart, making a face. "Looks more like grub worms floating around—"

"That's enough of that kind of talk at the table, Stuart Lee Whitfield!" said their mother, rubbing her forehead with a corner of her apron. "I've got a little something to talk to you about later on anyway."

Stuart shot a suspicious look at Honor, who very primly lifted one single piece of macaroni on her fork and sucked it slowly into her mouth.

"Eat and quit griping, all of you. There's plenty of tables in this town that would be mighty glad to have this food!"

"You said tables can't be glad. Tables can only hold stuff," said Buford, crumbling cornbread in his glass of milk.

"And I don't need any of your sass either, young man!" Their mother put her fork down beside her plate and took hold of the edges of the table. "Wipe that moustache off your mouth, Buford Jason Whitfield! Decent people don't crumble up cornbread in their milk at the table. I've told you a thousand times."

"I like it that way."

"It's not proper. There's a right way to eat and a wrong way to eat. White trash, common people, do things like crumbling up bread in a glass of milk. Don't act like a mountaineer!"

"But I am a mountaineer," Buford fired back, then calmly drank the milk, leaving the crumbled cornbread soggy in the bottom of his glass.

"I'm going to get up from this table and smack that smart-aleck look off your face. And you're not a mountaineer! Just because you happen to be forced to live here with your family for a period—a period of time, that's all—you are someday going to live in another town, Buford. I want you to know the behavior proper to a school principal's oldest son. A whole lot is expected out of a nearly full-grown fourteen-year-old young man. Especially one who is as big for his age as you are, Buford. All you children can learn the proper way of doing things."

"Where is Daddy?" Honor asked, changing the subject.

Her mother sighed a long, chest-heaving sigh, as she slowly stirred sugar into a tall glass of iced tea. "He left at daybreak with that Clifty Randolph—fishing, he said. He said they were heading for Doe Creek Lake since the bass were supposed to be biting." She rattled the ice in the glass. "But it's no telling where they've ended up by this time of day."

"You mean they've probably landed up in Bohunk Town?" Honor asked, picking at a torn place in the oilcloth.

"I didn't say that. I don't accuse people of things until I've got proof." Her mother started busily picking at her own plate of food. "Your father has been known to end up there, however."

"What does he blow every dime on bootleg whiskey

43

for? Why is it you have to stoop to do the canning when school principals' wives ought to be able to hire themselves a nigger from down Olympia?"

"Honor Jane! You ought to be ashamed of yourself, accusing your father of blowing every dime." Her mother was looking at her over the rim of the iced tea glass.

"Why don't you just march off and leave him stuck out in Bohunk Town? Why can't we move off the mountain where some of your sorority sisters from the university live, or back to the big house on the Delta?"

"You've had a funny look on your face ever since you got back from the company store this morning. I just felt it in my bones that you'd been talking again." Her mother put both hands out flat on the table, and for a moment there was a thick silence hovering over the table. "Who did you go blabbing off to today, young lady? Who got you talking about family affairs again?"

Honor tried to look her mother straight in the eye, but the reflections from the overhead electric bulb made bouncing patterns on her mother's glasses. Her mother was pushing back from the table, and Honor pushed her own chair a little, in case she needed to run away from that first burst of anger.

But her mother stood over her plate, both hands steadying herself on the edge of the table. "Now all three of you children listen to me carefully. I am sick and tired of people with busy tongues going around saying things about your father behind our backs. Jealousy, that's all it is. They're jealous because your father is a highly educated man. He has his degree from the University of Tennessee, and don't you forget that! Just because he doesn't have to go down in the mines and dig for a living, because we don't have to live in a shotgun house . . . because we have manners—upbringing . . . Oh, they're jealous all right! Your father does, I admit, like the bottle, but he's stuck off up here with nobody to really talk to." She rubbed her forehead. "He's a dreamer. Your father's always been full of pipe dreams—poems—foolishness that wouldn't earn a dime in good times, much less in the Depression."

"Chattanooga was a big city loaded down with plenty of people for him to talk to," Honor insisted. "There must've been some pipe dreamers in Chattanooga besides

44

him. Why did he have to drink whiskey there and get kicked off his job?"

"You're talking about things you don't know the first iota about, Honor Jane Whitfield! Chattanooga happened before you were born. It's nothing for you to be asking questions about! And I never want to hear you breathe out loud that your father ever got kicked off his job, and I never want to hear you say 'drink whiskey' again! You hear?"

"Don't talk about it no more," Stuart said, getting up and patting his mother on the shoulder. "You keep talking about Daddy and you'll start off crying. Besides, I saw Clifty with his carbide lamp on his head when they left this morning. They wouldn't have a carbide lamp if they didn't plan on fishing after dark—frog-gigging, maybe."

"I hope you're right, son. Oh, I do hope you're right."

Buford went to the scrap bucket, scooped out his leftovers for Lucifer's supper, and tried to give a signal to Stuart to join him.

"What are you motioning behind my back for, Buford?" their mother yelled. "Stuart Lee isn't going out of this house until I've given him the hairbrush whipping that's due."

Stuart's eyes widened with the look of a surprised deer. "What have I done? It was Honor Jane blabbing off to the town about Daddy. I've been playing here with Buford all day long!"

"I'm not going to whip you for playing with Buford. The score I'm going to settle with you, young man, is about playing doctor with Ruthie Stinnet. I'll teach you a thing or two about pulling up girls' dresses!"

"Tattletale!" Stuart yelled at Honor, tears already spilling down his face. "I'll get even with you!"

A sick feeling hit Honor's stomach with a sudden lump that seemed to settle in the very pit of it. She hadn't meant for Stuart to get a whipping. She couldn't stand the sound of whippings, of any kind of hitting and knocking people around.

"Why don't you wait and give it to him later on?" Honor suggested, her heart thumping like a hammer in her chest. "You might bring your migraine out full blast and you'd end up hurting worse than Stuart Lee's blistered bottom. Besides, it's not as bad for somebody like

45

Stuart Lee who hasn't turned a whole round ten yet to be looking up a girl's dress as it would be if say Buford had been up to playing doctor, would it?"

But her mother had already started marching Stuart toward the bathroom where the hairbrush whippings always took place. "I'll bring you a washrag soaked in ice water. I'll rub the back of your neck and help you get your feet propped up." She ran across the kitchen and grabbed at her mother. "Turn Stuart Lee loose, Mama. Don't take it out on him about Daddy ending up most likely out at Bohunk Town."

The slap on her face hit with a sting that felt as if she might have fallen off Buford's bicycle face down on the cinders. "Don't you ever accuse your father of going to Bohunk Town again! And don't you ever let me hear of you opening up your big mouth and getting pumped dry of information by people like Diddie Ewing and Miss Ada! Which one was it you blabbed to this morning?"

Stuart had seen his chance and ducked across the room. Honor started to run, but decided the full steam had blown off the top of her mother's head. She tried to put the brakes on behind her eyes to keep the tears from sliding down her face. "Can I get you some aspirin for your migraine headache?" she said, pulling herself up as tall as she could.

Her mother seemed to be staring about the room as if she didn't see exactly what was in it. She reminded Honor of a cow being pulled up to the chopping block. "I'll get my own aspirin, thank you. All three of you clean up this kitchen. Wash the dishes. Buford, you sweep and mop the floor. Stuart Lee, you wash every pot and pan in sight, and scrub the stove. You dry and put the dishes away and hang out the dish towels so they won't sour, Honor." She walked toward the bathroom. "I'm going to take a long soak in the bathtub. I'd appreciate it if you children could behave yourselves."

Her voice seemed to have dropped to the bottom of a barrel.

"Yes Ma'am," they answered in unison, staring after her.

"I hope you're satisfied," hissed Stuart between his gapped-open front teeth, as he dipped out fresh hot water from the reservoir at the end of the big stove.

"I saved you from a hairbrush whipping," Honor reminded him, rubbing the red marks on the side of her face.

Buford was leaning on the broom. "Stop it," he ordered, taking command. "We've got to figure out how to find Daddy and get him home before he does make a sight of himself and chalks up more bad marks to give them good reason for firing him. I heard from J. T. Arnold's boy that there was a move on to replace Daddy, maybe even this coming school year."

"But it's too late now to go to Doe Creek Lake. It's already dark and you could get lost in the woods, Buford," Honor said, sudsing up the bar of Oxydol in the dishpan for Stuart. "Remember that time you got lost going after that coon Lucifer had treed and they had to send out a search party for you? You know how fast you can get turned around backwards in the woods after dark."

"I could borrow a carbide lamp and go the shortcut down the railroad track."

"You could get hit over the head by a hobo too," Honor said.

"Yeah, and the Northcutts said a black panther really is loose down by the bluffs." Stuart was dipping the plates down in the hot water.

"There ain't no panthers in this neck of the woods," Buford said, authoritatively. "There's a wildcat now and then, and there's snakes—copperheads. That's about all I'd have to be scared of. I could do it. I could take my shotgun and a carbide lamp."

"If it's dark, then how many people in Margate will see him drunk?" Honor asked, drying a plate. "That is, if he is drunk. Maybe he *is* frog-gigging."

"Yeah, maybe he is. *We* ought to believe in him—even if nobody else does," Stuart said.

"I guess you're right," said Buford, starting to sweep halfheartedly. "But I ain't afraid of going!"

"It's nothing to be ashamed of if you are," Honor said, remembering Lola's advice. "It's how you act about being afraid that makes the difference—and knowing exactly what you ought to be scared of." She stacked the plates carefully on the table. "Are yal afraid of Nigger Lola still?"

Buford bent over and scooped up the dirt with a piece of cardboard. "I wouldn't trust her with my back turned, if that's what you mean," he said, dumping the dirt in the

47

coal scuttle. "They say Lola puts voodoo hexes on people if she gets a chance. That's what Suzie Daniels told the Whitakkers. Junior Whitakker told me himself that Suzie said only black people know how to do voodoo, and she had heard it straight from Lola's Negro cousins in Olympia that Lola had powers."

"Is that why they don't come visit her?" Honor asked.

"They ain't allowed to visit her when she's on parole. She's got to keep a clean record for a long time before she can have company." Buford propped the broom behind the door. "Let me use that rinse water for mopping when you get through," he said, taking on his bossiest tone.

"Well, I ain't afraid of her—even with my back turned," Honor bragged, standing on tiptoe and putting the glasses on the shelf. "And I got ways of stunting anybody's hexes—voodoo or not. I've got good ways."

"You're just a pipe dreamer like Daddy! You ain't got the hexing power to amount to a hill of beans. You ain't got shit." Buford glared at her.

"I got secrets that nobody but me knows about. Nobody! And ain't nobody going to know about it. I'll carry 'em to my grave, and I'll carry 'em off this mountain when we move out of Margate." She straightened out the damp dish towels and started toward the back screen door to hang them on the clothesline on the back porch. Seeing how dark it had grown, she hesitated at the door. "Are you sure there's no black panthers in this neck of the woods?" she asked Buford.

"I thought you wasn't afraid! Where's all that power you talking about?"

"I've got plenty of power!" she said stubbornly, and flung the door open.

The darkness seemed to reach out like arms to grab her. There was a shaft of light that spread out across the back porch in one narrow place. She stayed carefully within its outlines and tried to bring her thumbs in control so she could get the dish towels clipped on the line with the clothespins. Somewhere in the distance a hoot owl had started in, and the tree locusts were sending out a crackling buzz that seemed to swarm like an angry hive of bees through the darkness. She flung the dish towels across the wire and tried to step calmly into the kitchen.

"Clyde Northcutt killed two copperheads this week,"

Stuart was saying, hanging the dishpan on the nail. "He shot one of 'em dead in the eye."

"Clyde Northcutt's the best shot in town," Buford admitted. "He can hit a bull's eye without hardly looking."

"I guess that's everything," Honor said, looking around. "Do you think Mama will be pleased?"

"Not with you," Stuart said, running the cleaning rag across the back of the stove. "I heard her tell Ruthie Stinnet's mother that she never dreamed she'd have a daughter as ugly as you, and she's worried she won't ever get control of you. She says you're going to turn wild, turn out to be like Mildred Matthews who sells it to anybody who'll touch her with a ten-foot pole."

"My mother didn't say all that! She might think I'm ugly while I'm going through my gawky stage, while I'm all thumbs and scabby knees. That's all she thinks!" Honor felt a lump in her throat. "You're just jealous because you wasn't born a girl! You're a big sissy anyway! You'd be a pretty little girl."

"Don't start a fuss!" Buford sternly ordered. "Come on, we'll go sit on the front porch and I'll tell you about the Big Dipper while we watch for Daddy to come home."

They sat in a row on the top step of the front porch, swatting at gnats and looking out into the darkness, the sounds of the mountain night swirling in around them.

After a while, their mother came out, tying a sash to her summer seersucker bathrobe and running a hairbrush through her wet hair. "I feel like a human being again," she said, sitting down in the porch swing. "It's wonderful what a good hot bath and a head washing can do. Honor, I left my bath water for you to use. It's your turn."

Before Honor went into the house, she heard her mother's sigh as she started gently pushing the swing back and forth. "One thing about living in Margate," her mother's voice fell softly across the porch, "it's so quiet and peaceful at night."

4

It was late in the night when Honor awakened to the sound of the old Oakland turning into the lane off the main cinder road. Her heart pounded furiously at the sudden sound of Lucifer barking his welcome and being promptly shushed, of heavy footsteps attempting to tiptoe across the front porch. Would he be drunk and happy, drunk and silly, or drunk and mad? Or would he really have a long string of bass or a live catfish swimming around in the minnow bucket, or a mess of frogs' legs? She pulled the sheet up tight around her chin, listening to the squeaking of the boards of the porch; of the rattle of the front door handle and the door easing open; and of the heavy thump of something as his first footstep fell in the living room. "Goddam, Lucifer. Down! Down, goddammit!"

"Wake up, Buford," she called across the room to the double bed where Buford and Stuart were sleeping. "Daddy's home drunk and mad again. He just kicked Lucifer."

"Hush! Don't say a word, Honor," her mother whispered from the doorway, holding her voice back so that it sounded like the escaping steam from the pressure cooker just before it topped the gauge. "Go back to sleep. And what good would Buford be anyway, if your father turns on me? Only a cyclone could wake Buford."

"Don't start in fussing at Daddy," Honor said, reaching out for the feel of her mother's seersucker nightgown. "If you won't fuss at him, he'll sleep it off on the daybed and won't start yelling back and hitting you."

"Hush! Hush, I said—before he hears us talking. At least pretend you're asleep so he won't accuse me of keeping

50

you children awake to turn you against him more than you are already."

"I'm not turned against Daddy! I love my Daddy," Honor said, trying to hold her mother back in the wrap of darkness.

"That's because you're just like him. You're from his cut of the family." At the sound of her mother's bare feet searching their way around the foot of her bed, past Buford's and Stuart's bed on the opposite wall. Honor knew she had lost her fight to hold her mother back. She slid down in bed, as far as she could go. Her feet pushed hard against the brass rail. As she listened to the fumbling, stuttering sounds of her father pulling off his shoes in the living room and trying to undress in the dark, her heart pounded faster against her hand, which was holding the sheet tight across her chest like a tourniquet. The darkness seemed to take on a swirling pattern, making her feel as if she had been turning round and round and round in circles until she fell down dizzy.

Burning through the center of the swirling darkness were the glaring, glazed eyes of a stranger who looked like her father but who couldn't possibly be the same man who spoke deep in his throat, sometimes in the softest way when he was making up poems for her or telling her story after story about Greek gods and goddesses, who sometimes held her hand and walked with her through the deep-shaded woods until they found a mossy spot by a clear-sparkling branch of water where violets grew. Those eyes bearing down on her now, gleaming with some strange light she did not understand—and could only fear—were not the same blue, shiny eyes that laughed into hers when he picked her up and tossed her high in the air—even now, in her gawky stage—so that she felt as tall as the top of a forest lookout tower.

Back in the deepest dark of her mind, wild fluttering sounds began, like the distant beating of a hundred blue jays' wings. She wrapped her toes in the skirt of her nightgown and crouched lower in the bed, shrinking away from that terrible gathering sound in the back of her head. But the fluttering wings gained steady force until, in one frantic swooping flight, like a covey of quail that Lucifer had flushed taking startled wing overhead, the noise burst

51

through the swirling, dizzying motion to the very open front of her mind.

"Henry, is that you?"

It was her mother's voice splitting the nightmare, bringing her back to a safer place.

"Henry, I said, is that *you*?"

"Henry . . . oh, Henry . . . is that *youuuuu*?" she heard her father mock back in a deep, crackling voice that made his words seem to tumble out through the darkness like coal tumbling down a chute.

"Well, I only asked! I've got a right to ask—somebody stomping into this house past midnight taking the Lord's name in vain and kicking at that poor helpless old dog. I think I have every right to ask who it is!"

"There's one thing you can bet a five dollar bill on—the iceman hasn't cometh! Now, *who* is it? Let me see . . . why, looks like it's Clark Gable in person, but not the way you might've dreamed of him being here . . . since he's already found his lady of the night and he's tired and wants to go to bed."

"Henry Jason Whitfield! If you've been out with that—if you've been in touching distance of that Mildred Matthews, I will never let you touch me again!"

"Leave Daddy alone," Honor begged in one last desperate whisper. "Go back to bed, Mama. Let him sleep it off."

But if her mother heard, she ignored it. Honor tried not to listen as her mother groped her way through the darkness, finding the door to the living room.

"You promised me! The very last thing you promised me this morning when you left this house—this house where I try, God knows, to raise your three children in a decent and civilized manner—was that you would not touch a drop! You said you wouldn't go anywhere except Doe Creek Lake and fishing."

"I went to Doe Creek Lake. And I went fishing. Did I ever go fishing!"

The pressure inside her mother was gathering full steam now, and Honor hoped, for one short-lived moment, that the darkness would somehow absorb it and that her father would drop off in a drunken stupor right under her mother's wagging finger and shrill, pleading cries—cries that died out in time the way an angry mountain wind gets tired tearing at loose boards and flapping loose shingles, and finally skirts on into the night and disappears into some distant waiting emptiness.

"Look at you, sprawled out drunk with your filthy muddy feet all over my cretonne slipcover." From the sudden shaft of light, Honor could tell that her mother had turned on the lamp on top of the Philco radio. "Did you fall in Doe Creek Lake again? What's your big excuse for coming in past midnight this time? Lady of the night, huh? I have warned you about going near that Mildred Matthews, that two-bit . . . Ah! Just as I expected. You *do* have lipstick smeared. I knew!"

Honor put her fingers in her ears and started counting to herself as fast as the numbers would come, until eights ran into nines and thirties got lost and she had to start all over at one again. But even then, their voices would gain a toehold in her listening mind, and she would hear snatches of the storm, until finally it reached its highest pitch and her father's coarse voice was rising up from the coal chute shouting loud and clear: "I warned you, goddammit, to quit hounding me, Martha Jane! You drive me into knocking the jawbreaking hell out of you!"

"Hit me then! Go on, big shot, and prove how strong and mighty you are by picking on a helpless woman, just another dog for you to kick around! A big pipe dreamer you are, Mr. King of Bohunk Town!"

Honor stopped up both ears at the sounds of a chair falling and of her mother's high-pitched wail, a sound that reminded Honor of the time she and Ruthie Stinnet had slipped in the back room at Ruthie's house and listened while her mother was having a baby, until Dr. Clark brought the squirmy, red-faced little boy out squalling. Her hands sweated, and she found herself twisting the sheet back and forth the way Ruthie's mother had done that day.

Then, Honor sensed a strange kind of silence. "Mama, are you there? Are you all right, Mama?"

She heard a soft, low sobbing sound from the living room. There was a different tone to it that made Honor wish suddenly that she could just float away and never have to find out the center of that sound, and what it meant. She pretended she was dead, and waited to be lifted up and up and up.

She heard her mother's voice like a bleating sheep closer to her bed. "He's gone this time. This time I really ran him off for good. Honor Jane, are you still awake? You are awake. I know you've been wide awake listening." She sank down wearily on the edge of the bed. "This time I believe I did it. I sent your poor father out in the middle of the night with nowhere, absolutely not one single place in this wide world, to go." Her voice seemed to be coming up from the bottom of Frog Hollow. "I do nag him. I always have had a tendency toward nagging all my life. Oh, I admit my mistakes."

"Why don't you stop it then?" Honor managed to squeeze out her own small, tight angry voice. "Why didn't you just leave him alone to sleep it off on the daybed, like I told you to do in the first place?"

"As I told you to do," her mother corrected automatically, her voice splitting through a crack in her crying. "You're right. Something just seems to drive me on, and on."

"Well, it drives him to drink!" Honor said, sitting up, furious with her mother. "Daddy's said more than once how you drive him to drink!"

"Honor Jane Whitfield! How could you turn on me like that? How could you take your father's side after you heard what he did to me in there? I know I've got a black eye coming. You know good and well that I am not the reason he drinks!"

"You drive him to drink, by driving him out of the house with no place to go—well, there's always Bohunk Town! Ain't that the same as driving him to drink?"

"I cannot bear your back talk—your desertion of me at this moment—when I need my only daughter's support, with your brothers over there sleeping like hibernating bears!"

She flung herself on the bed, her sobbing starting anew. "I didn't drive him to drink, and I didn't drive him to the town whore either."

"Maybe Daddy just likes Mildred Matthews' big titties."

"Just you wait, young lady! Tomorrow morning, first thing, you are going to get the filth washed out of your mouth! Oh, you are going to get the mouth-washing of your life!"

Honor bit into the twisted sheet the way Dr. Clark had

made her bite into a wooden tongue blade the last time she had a stone bruise lanced. *Hold back your tongue—not just the tip of it, but the whole thing*, Lola had told her.

But her tongue had broken loose. "When I grow up and find me a husband, there is one thing I will never do. I will never nag him or drive him to drink or to go touch whores." If she was already headed for the worst soapsudsing of her life, she might as well get it all said.

But she did not think her mother had heard that last part. From the rattling-around sounds, Honor guessed she was in the kitchen.

For what seemed to be a whole clock-hour, but what was only a matter of a few short moments, Honor stayed as still as she could, letting the jumping inside her head and in her body settle down. An odor drifted into the room, an odor that didn't belong to the middle of the night. She tested it, sniffing hard. Coffee—her mother was going to sit up the rest of the night drinking coffee and waiting for her father to come home.

Suddenly Honor sat straight up in bed. She just remembered that she had not heard the sound of the old Oakland sputtering, chugging up to a start, or of the wheels spinning the cinders as her father drove out of the alley. Maybe he hadn't really gone anywhere. Maybe he had just let off the handbrake and put the car in neutral, letting it coast down the alley and as far as it could down the main cinder road toward Doe Creek Lake, the way Buford had done that time by mistake and got the worst hairbrush whipping of his life.

A new fear gripped her. If he was parked out there along the main cinder road, slumped over drunk, somebody was bound to see him at daybreak. Or the coal miners, on their way to the mines with their carbide lamps strapped on, might look inside and see him. How could she ever convince anybody that her father was on the wagon for good if he was sitting out there in broad daylight where everybody would know before the end of the day, the way the grapevine traveled so fast in Margate.

She scrambled out from under the sheet and light summer blanket and reached for her bathrobe, which she kept tucked across the second railing at the foot of her bed for easy reach in case there was a fire and she had to run out in the middle of the night.

She stood by the side of the bed, tying the sash to the bathrobe and wishing she had not broken the T-strap to her sandals. It was one thing to go barefoot in broad daylight, but in the pitch dark there might be copperheads or lizards—a whole mountain full of things to step on.

Her heart was pounding as she started on tiptoe toward the living room. She knew her way, blindfolded, through the house. Many times she had tied a handkerchief around her eyes and pretended she was blind like her father's brother, Uncle Marshall. She wanted to be as light-footed as she could if the Devil ever decided to put her eyes out for some evil she had done that went too far. In no time at all she had reached the front door and slipped silently onto the front porch.

There was a tiny sliver of a moon and a few patches of stars. The oak trees seemed to be waving their big leafy arms as if they were trying to fend off the sky. She stood there to get her bearings, hoping to quiet the pounding inside her chest that felt as if it would pop right open. *I'm not afraid of anything,* she told herself fiercely. Then she listened intently to every sound she could hear, wanting to pick the gathered rush of the night's noises apart and sort them out so she'd know what she did or didn't have to worry about.

Some of the tree locusts must have gotten tired and given up for the night, she thought. Off in the woods she heard the familiar whooo ... whooo ... whooo of the hoot owl. She was glad old Lucifer hadn't pulled himself out from under the porch where he had ducked after his kicking. Lucifer loved her father most of all. He'd probably stay under there with his tail tucked in between his legs until her father came to coax him out and make up again.

A sudden happy sound caught her ears: a cricket! That was a good-luck sign for sure. You weren't even supposed to kill a cricket that was loose in a kitchen.

She strained to see out through the lumpy darkness, to see if she could spot a shape that looked like the Oakland, and to see, also, if there just might be something like a black panther slinking around. After all, the Northcutt boys bragged that they had seen one. Buford didn't know everything.

Then she made a decision. If she stumbled across some

enemy like a copperhead or a black panther, one she could recognize and scream about at the top of her lungs, she'd just show Margate how loud she could holler bloody murder. She could raise Buford and Stuart out of any sleep. She could raise the dead if she wanted to—if she was scared enough!

She straightened her back as if someone was lacing her into a corset. Very gingerly she made her way across the grass, down the petunia-lined path toward the front gate, which no one used except company coming to call once in a blue moon on Sundays. She eased open the squeaky gate and paused in front of it, feeling the dense woods across the road press in against her with a whole batch of new sounds, like bat wings.

She peered through the heavy darkness, looking for the edges of the cinder road above the drainage ditch. Then she resolutely lifted her gown tail and bathrobe flaps and jumped the distance she thought was needed to clear the ditch. She caught herself with her hands as she fell forward from too much momentum. Then she dusted the cinders from her hands and stood still for a moment to see if any new sounds had cropped up during that flying deaf-and-blind leap.

As she stood there, on the edge of the cinder road, she felt as if a hundred black panther eyes were staring at her through the woods. Panthers were probably like Stonewall, their cat, who could see anything at night.

They'd just have to look! She couldn't turn tail and run back now. She started cautiously down the cinder road, unable to resist looking back over her shoulders and glancing across at the woods. She practically bumped into the back of the old Oakland, which was leaning heavily to one side in the ditch.

Quickly she got around it, stood on the fender, and looked in. Her father was, as she had suspected, slumped into the spaces of the steering wheel. Even in the middle of the night you could see that. She wondered what would be the best way to get him pulled down across the front seat, out of sight. The Northcutt men were about the only coal miners who came up the main cinder road, and they weren't apt to go dawdling away their time or wasting the carbide in their lamps to search the car when they'd already walked three miles up from the bluff and

57

still had a mile to go. The Northcutts weren't the kind to go butting into other people's business anyway, she reminded herself. Everybody knew they were the best shots in Margate. They didn't want anybody trespassing on their business or their land, and they didn't trespass on anybody's in return. As good as she was at slipping around, Honor knew better than to cut across the Northcutt's property. With their good aim, you could get your head blown off with a shotgun and never know which one of them pulled the trigger.

If she could just get her father down out of plain view, she knew the Northcutts wouldn't see him. She would have to work her way from the other side of the ditch, for the front door on her father's side was hopelessly wedged. She made her way around the front of the car, feeling the big headlights and running her fingertips across the radiator vents. She was sure she felt something brush her ankles. The fear of a snake sliding through the weeds made her hurry so fast back to her father's side of the car that she stubbed her toe on the wheel.

She stopped to catch her breath, looking up and down the few feet of darkness she could see shapes through. She had better work fast. Luckily, the back door was open. She climbed into the back seat, following the steep slant of the car, climbed into the front seat, and knelt beside him.

"Daddy," she called out softly, not expecting him to hear. She had seen him sleep one off before. You couldn't budge him with a ten-foot pole, she thought, putting her hands on her hips, and trying to figure out how to get him off the steering wheel and down flat on the seat. For once, she could use Buford and Stuart. Finally, she pulled all the strength she could find from her knees on up through her shoulders and started tugging, yanking, pushing, and shoving. His arms flopped like rubber, and he weighed as much as a ton of coal, she decided. She pushed her hair out of her eyes, and was surprised when her fingertips hit the big goose egg. She had forgotten that she had bumped her head that morning. So much had happened since then. It had been the longest day of her life.

She was running out of room. She climbed into the back seat again and tried to work from there, leaning over and tugging and pulling. Finally, she had him in a twisted position with his head pointed downhill, toward the ditch—all the blood would drain to his head. She felt around in the car for a pillow, the one her mother sometimes propped behind her back when she was driving the car to Missionary Society meetings, if she hadn't got a ride in Mamie Clark's big Packard. She felt in the corners and reached all around on the floorboard, and under the seat. What she found was her father's hunting vest. She felt it to see if any shells were left. Then she folded it up as thick as she could and jammed it under his head. His face felt cold, and she suddenly realized how chilly the night air was. She didn't want him to catch double pneumonia. She quickly took off her bathrobe, spread it across his shoulders, and tucked it in around his neck and up under his chin.

He mumbled and made a moaning sound, as though he might be talking to someone down deep in his drunken dreams. *Don't wake up, Daddy. Don't wake up now until at least six o'clock, and if you do wake up, stay low until after the Northcutts pass.*

For a moment she thought about staying with him, hiding low herself in the back seat of the car. But without her bathrobe, she was feeling a wave of goose bumps run up and down her arms. It was going to be bad enough if she got caught being out of bed, much less spending the night out without permission.

She climbed out of the Oakland and eased the back door shut. A breeze had whipped up and the open night air hit her full force. She felt the darkness fall in on her in jagged lumps and wondered if that's how it was for the coal miners deep in the tunnels. She wondered, too, how they felt if their carbide lamps ran down—or if there was a cave-in. . . .

She ran, blindly, stumbling along and lunging back across the ditch in front of their gate. As she came across the grass and up to the oak tree at the corner of the porch, a sudden darker form hit the night. As she started to open her lungs and her mouth and let out the scream that had already started, Lucifer licked at her ankles, his tail thumping down low between his legs, still feeling his disgrace.

"Oh, God a'mighty, Lucifer!" she whispered, petting him on the head and hugging him tightly. "You just about

59

scared the living daylights out of me. You'd better watch that slipping up on people." She was so relieved that she found her eyes stinging with gratitude tears. "Good old Lucifer," she said, hugging him again. "Daddy didn't mean to kick you. He wouldn't do that in a hundred years if he was sober. Daddy loves you more than any dog in this wide world, okay, old buddy?" she called him by the name her father always used when he was giving Lucifer some reward.

Lucifer seemed satisfied and went over to hike his leg on the oak tree. At least, he knew when to hold his tongue, she thought, wondering how it would have been had he started in barking.

As she slipped the screen door open and stood in the living room by the Philco radio, listening through the sounds of the house for signs of her mother's being on the alert, she felt a sudden rush of love for everything around her—for the creaks and groans in the old house that she knew by heart, for the daybed, the armchair, the Philco radio always in the same places. And even though the Devil's pit did seem to send up its furies to race through their house, stirring up a special hell that belonged only to the Whitfield family for their sins, the Devil didn't stay around forever. There were times when the kitchen was filled with good smells, of brown nutbread baking and chocolate fudge boiling down on the stove. And sometimes she could sit for a long time all by herself on the daybed studying the patterns in the cretonne slipcover, which looked just like a real rose garden out of a storybook when the light hit it just right. There were nights, even after Bohunk Town, when her father had had just the right amount to nip, when he'd be in a silly mood and everybody would gather around the old upright, and her mother would loosen up her stiff fingers and plunk out song after song that she could still remember from her piano lessons when she was a girl in Maddoxville, Mississippi. Sometimes they'd pop popcorn with the old bent wire popper in winter, when it was so cold they even let Lucifer come inside around the fire. When she thought back, there were plenty of long stretches of time when things seemed to go right, when even the indoor toilet would stay off the blink. Margate wasn't all that bad a place, she told herself, thinking how nice and warm it was in the living room.

Then, experiencing a new safe glow, she tiptoed through the dining room, feeling her way around the oak table, and opened the kitchen door a crack to check on her mother and on the streak of bright light shining under the door.

Her mother had drooped her head down into the basket of her arms, which were spread out like chicken wings across the green and yellow plaid oilcloth on the kitchen table. In front of her right hand was a cup of coffee, half-drunk. For a moment, Honor stood there, undecided as to whether or not she should turn off the electric light bulb to save on the light bill, and whether she should cover up her mother's bare arms. But the kitchen was still as warm as an oven, with the smell of cooked tomatoes hanging heavy in the air. Maybe she should just let well enough alone and let her mother sleep it off too.

As she turned to hurry back to her own bed, she noticed that the clock above the icebox said two-thirty.

5

It was a rooster crowing somewhere off in the distance that sounded an alarm and brought Honor into a startled, sitting-up position out of a restless, fretful sleep. She had been dreaming some awful dream about a jaybird pecking a baby bluebird's eye, though she couldn't remember anything else in the dream. She shook it away from her mind and looked over across the room where Buford and Stuart were still asleep, then at the big front window with the little veins of age-cracks in the dark-green window shade, which let in jagged streaks of light, telling her the pitch of night was wearing off.

She reached down under the mattress and pulled out a pair of overalls that her mother had tried to make her throw out and an old plaid shirt of Stuart's that she kept hidden for emergencies. She had to hurry. At this time of morning, just before daylight, Buford and Stuart were coming up out of that hibernating place where they slept so soundly that thunder wouldn't wake them up and were in that lighter sleeping zone where either one could sit up in a flash, wide awake. Her mother might have a stiff neck by now, too, and be up prowling around looking out of windows trying to catch a glimpse of her father. She couldn't let herself get caught now.

She yanked off her nightgown and dressed; then she raced across the living room that was fuzzy looking with the dark fading off, allowing the armchair, the Philco radio, and the daybed shapes to be more clearly outlined.

On the front porch, as she struggled to get the left shoulder strap of her overalls hooked, she saw that a pale flush of daylight was just beginning at the edge of the woods, and the early-morning birds that lived there were starting to shake out their feathers and cut loose with their songs.

She listened a moment for any sounds of her mother bearing down on her heels, but only Lucifer came crawling out from under the front porch and stretched out his long stiff body full length and grunted the sounds of a very old bird dog waking up.

Honor darted across the front yard, with Lucifer trying to gather up enough stiff-legged speed to catch up with her. At the gate, just as she opened it, she looked down in the direction of the Oakland, which was still sitting, side-tilted in the ditch. Then a leap of fear hit her chest as she saw, on beyond, the dim shapes of bobbing, stuttering lights coming from the carbide head lamps of the Northcutt men walking single file on the opposite side of the main cinder road. They were already so close she wouldn't have time to run back to the house. The only place left to hide was down low on the ditch side of the Oakland, she decided.

"Go away!" she whispered to Lucifer, and ducked down to half-run, half-crawl to the tilted-down side of the car.

She tried to calm down the fast beating of her heart and make her breath quit coming out in fast, noisy little spurts. She could hear the low mumble of a deep voice and the steady crunch of miners' boots on the cinders coming closer and closer. She wished desperately that she had had time to peep inside and check on her father's down-low position in the front seat. At least he hadn't been sitting propped up over the steering wheel like a sitting duck, or she would have seen him.

Stay down, Daddy, please, she begged silently.

From her crouched position alongside the car, she could see, underneath, a dim streak of the cinder road where the miners' boots would have to pass. At least she would know if any of them veered over across the road to look inside the car.

As she heard the crunching boots almost even with the car, her chest seemed to squeeze in on itself.

"Hey, yal ... look yonder, Henry Whitfield's done wrapped his car in the ditch, looks like. Dog-drunk again, I reckon," came a deep, gravelly voice that seemed to fall out like smoke and drift in a thick screen under the car.

63

She knew she was going to choke—to cough—to sneeze. She was bound to give herself away.

"Whatever it is, ain't none of your nevermind, James Ely," came back the higher pitched, crackly voice of the old man walking all hunched over, leading the way.

"But oughtn' we take a look case somebody's hurt?"

Honor's heart raced as she kept her eyes on the big pair of boots that were dragging back, one toe pointed straight at her.

"Ain't nobody hurt, or his old dog here wouldn't be out like he always is wagging his tail and sniffing at my lunch bucket looking for that biscuit I give him sometimes. Go on, old dog, scoot on!" Honor knew the gruff command in the old man's voice was not a mean one. Everybody who knew anything about bird dogs in Margate had a respect for Lucifer, the only registered bird dog in town, and for the way he had proved himself over and over out in the field flushing coveys and retrieving. Lucifer was way past his prime now, but he was still the king of dogs in Margate.

"Come on James Ely and Clyde Junior. The Whitfields got their business and we got our'n. There's a'tuther mile to walk, and the mine foreman ain't going to keep nobody hired on the job can't clock in on time."

Their voices, in the quiet of beginning daylight, drifted back as they marched on toward Dr. Clark's hill. Honor listened for any hint that James Ely or Clyde Junior might have craned his long skinny neck and taken a good look inside the car and seen her father.

"I didn't see no blood or nothing. . . ."

"Wouldn't be none of your busines if'n you did. Your business is to tend to keeping hired on the job when word's done out there ain't going to be no more mines working past September. They shutting down the whole operation. You boys might think digging coal ain't the best living. You'll find out it pays better 'an chopping wood. Chopping wood don't pay diddly shit."

"They can't just shut down a whole big coal mine!" Honor strained to hear. "Somebody's full of bullshit."

After they were completely out of sight and hearing distance, Honor sat back on the edge of the ditch and let out a big relieved sigh. There was one thing about the Northcutt tribe, they might blow anybody's head off with their dead aims on their double-barreled shotguns if anybody happened to step foot, uninvited, on their land, but they respected the private business of other people more than anybody else in Margate—at least as long as Clyde Senior was around. "If Clyde Senior gives you his word, it's bullet proof," she had heard her father once say, taking up for him after her mother had been on a rampage about how the whole Northcutt pack was nothing but white trash and ought to be quarantined on their land. "They're dirt poor. They're like the very grain of these mountains. But they've got their own kind of dignity. You've got no right to wipe them off the face of the earth, Martha Jane, just because they don't behave—don't walk and talk and hold out their little finger like the Cunninghams used to do. The Northcutts are a proud bunch. That straggly patch of mountain-bluff land has been in their family from one generation to the next, since Indian days. They have a code they live by—don't forget it."

"They're still white trash in my book," her mother had insisted. "I still don't want my children around them."

Honor sat there another minute, letting her mind and chest settle back down. So far, nobody had seen her father in the Oakland, drunk again. There'd be nobody who could prove her wrong then, when she started the rumor around town that her father was on the wagon for good now. She had tested it that time with Lola, and Lola had seemed not much one way or the other about believing it. But then, she was going to help Lola run away, and people didn't listen to niggers anyway, even if Lola did stay on and tell somebody different.

If she set her mind to it, she could hang that rumor on the grapevine strong enough to get even Preacher Pullum convinced. People in Margate would believe most anything from the grapevine, though they seemed to like bad news best. Just look at the Northcutts picking up on a whopper like the Black Diamond Coal Company's shutting down the mines! That was a real lulu. How could anybody believe for a minute anything as dumb and crazy as that—with all those bulldozers out there to push around the cinder piles, all those coal cars and machinery? Besides, the coal company owned the whole town of Margate. If they shut down the mines, they'd have to shut down the houses and the company store.

If they could spread something like that around, it was going to be duck soup to figure out something about her father's being reborn.

She stood up and stretched, feeling almost as stiff as old Lucifer looked, standing there in the middle of the road staring up at her with that asking look on his face, wagging his tail, waiting for something to happen.

Her eyes were burning from lack of sleep, but she still had work to do before she could go back to bed. She jumped across the ditch and ran around to the driver's side, stepped up, and looked in. Her father had shifted his position and had his head and one arm hanging over the edge of the seat.

She opened the door and knelt on the edge of the seat, keeping the door open with her heels. "Come on, Daddy—time to wake up and go inside! It's daylight almost. Come on—wake up, you hear, 'fore somebody sees you drunk again."

She shook his ankles, then waited, and beat on his legs with her fist. "Wake up now! You hear me?"

She sighed and shook her head. Then she climbed out of the car. "Lucifer, I guess we'll just have to do it." She ran as fast as she could back across the front yard and around the dining room side of the house. Her figuring mind was racing along with her feet. She couldn't run water out of the outside hydrant because it always made the pipes pop and splutter all through the house, particularly after the town pump had been out of whack for a few hours and even more air had gotten in the pipes. She'd have to dip a bucketful out of the rain barrel at the corner where the sewing-machine window in the dining room met with the kitchen wall. She'd just have to hope her mother wasn't standing at that particular window looking out for a ghost to appear.

The dipping bucket was drifting on its side in the barrel. Honor untied the rope from its handle, leaned over, and dipped the bucket deep under the water, filling it up. Then she half-ran, duck-waddling style, trying not to splash any of the water out.

By the time she reached the car, her pants leg was sopping wet on one side. It felt rough and gritty against her skin. She'd have to work from the back seat, she decided. Kneeling on the edge of the seat, with the bucket poised on the back edge of the front seat, she took a deep breath, squinted her eyes shut, and turned the bucket upside down.

"Goddam! . . . What? . . ."

"Come on, sit up, hurry, Daddy!" She reached over and grabbed him by his soaked shirt sleeve. "Daylight's coming, and we don't want you caught out here sleeping one off in front of God and everybody!"

He sat up slowly, shaking his wet head and sending a smaller shower down in all directions. Honor sat blinking her own eyes in amazement at this strange sight of her father. His hair, soaking wet, looked as if it had been suddenly dipped in blackberry wine and had turned two shades darker than its usual brownish-red tones. And while he usually wore it waved back smoothly, held in place with Vitalis and those quick, fast strokes of his hairbrush, now it was plastered down across his broad, high forehead in scraggly patches. Little trickles of water ran down his face, dripping off his thick eyebrows and going on down the ridges by his long, straight nose. She watched him swipe one hand across the bottom of his strong stubby chin, missing the dent in the middle of it where one big glistening drop of water seemed to swim around in the deep, dimpled ridge.

"What the hell did you do that for? I'll be a son of a bitch. . . . Goddam, that's cold!"

"I couldn't sober you up any other way. I tried to shake you. Hurry though, you can dry off inside and get warm again. The living room is toasty warm, and I'll get you some dry clothes and you can sleep the rest of it off on the daybed."

"What's this damn thing?" he mumbled, starting to reach for the door handle and pulling at the drenched bathrobe which he had thrown off sometime during his twisting and turning around.

"That's just my old summer bathrobe. I tried to cover you up earlier—back in the night. I figured you looked cold."

He was still shaking his head. "That was thoughtful of you. Damn sight more thoughtful than pouring a bucket of water all over me. . . . Goddam . . ."

"That door's jammed in the ditch. You drove in the

67

ditch last night when Mama ran you off. Come on, this way."

"I must have thrown a big one, huh?"

"You don't remember?" Honor asked, pulling his sleeve to keep him encouraged. He looked as though he might slide back down in the seat any minute.

"My head's like a solid slab of rubber. I don't remember anything except I'm freezing my ass off dripping wet!"

"If you don't come on, you're going to get caught!"

"Nobody's after me. Who's going to catch me?"

"Well, J. T. Arnold would sure like to get some goods on you so he can get you fired and get your job landed for his brother. There's lots of people who'd like to catch you dog-drunk and get you fired."

"Let's get one thing straight, young lady! I'm not dog-drunk."

"You'd better move it anyway." She pulled harder.

He grabbed hold of the steering wheel and pulled himself up the tilted grade of the front seat. "Yeah, gotta haul ass."

"That's right, slide right on—this way, your feet over and down . . . a little more there," Honor guided his legs.

She turned him around and started pushing him by the arm toward the house. At the drainage ditch across from the front gate, Lucifer came to meet them. "Hi, old buddy," her father said, stumbling as he stepped down in the ditch.

"You kicked Lucifer last night," she said matter-of-factly. "You've got some making up to do with Lucifer."

"Did I do that to you, old buddy—to the best dog in the whole world? I wouldn't kick somebody as loyal and good a friend as you."

Lucifer was wagging his tail down low between his legs and licking her father's hand cautiously. "Come on, Daddy, hep-two-three-four. Upsy daisy."

"I'm sorry as hell, old buddy. I didn't think I'd ever stoop to kicking my dog."

"There ain't time for you to get on a crying jag now. You've already thrown your binge—your mad drunk. You can't have a mad one and a crying one all rolled into one."

"You sound like your mother."

"I don't, and I don't ever aim to sound like her. I won't

go through life, nag-nag-nag." She gave him a push at the bottom of the front steps. "Steady there . . . up you go."

"Your mother's a good woman. A good Christian woman. You ought to respect your mother."

"She don't—doesn't," she corrected herself, in case her mother had heard the racket and was standing in the doorway. "She doesn't always say the same about you."

He held on to the doorjamb for a moment to steady himself. "I never would make a good Christian . . . just a good-for-nothing—that's what I am."

"Just when you're on a binge," Honor said, giving him another matter-of-fact tug on the arm. "Most of the time you're—well . . ." She looked about and listened into the depths of the house but did not hear anything stirring. "Shhhh, come on. Maybe we can get by without waking everybody up."

After she guided him through the door, she turned him and gave him a push on both arms. "There, sit down and wait a minute. I'm going to dig out some dry clothes for you. Don't move!" She left him slumped in the armchair and noticed he had crossed his arms and was shivering.

In the dining room, she went quickly to the sewing-machine corner and lifted the top of the mending hamper. She tossed the odds and ends about until she came up with an old shirt put there for the collar to be turned and a pair of work pants that needed buttons and a snag in the knee repaired.

After some elbow tugging and coaxing, she finally managed to get him to take off his wet pants and shirt and get into the dry ones. Then, as though he had given out the last of his energy, he fell into a heap across the daybed. She tugged off his socks and shoes, gathered up all the wet things, and ran out the door, around the side of the house to the back porch. There, she tossed his rumpled clothing into the dirty-clothes basket and hung her own wet bathrobe on the line next to the dish towels.

Daylight was all around her now, the pink and orange just beginning to show above the tops of the trees in the woods across the road. As she passed through the living room, on her way back to her own bed, she took one last look at her father. He had thrown one arm over the side

69

of the daybed and was sleeping with his mouth open, making short, snoring sounds.

Without bothering to get out of her overalls, she crawled back into bed and dropped off to sleep before she reached the count of thirty.

6

There was one thing that had always confused Honor
about the day after one of her father's binges: regardless
of how bad it had been the night before—even when it
was one of those "mean" drunks, as her mother called
them—both her mother and father would go through the
next day being, if anything, extra polite and nice to each
other, pretending that nothing at all unusual had happened. On this particular day-after, though, Honor noticed
that her mother was holding her mouth in at the corners
with a little extra tuck, and she seemed to be looking in
every direction except straight at her father.

Honor was particularly polite herself, remembering at
the breakfast table to say "excuse me" and "thank you,
Ma'am." She kept her left hand under the table the entire
time, sitting with her back ramrod straight for good pos-
ture, and remembered not to tilt her bowl to get the last
of the milk from her cornflakes. There was no mention of
the soapsuds mouth-washing.

After Stuart and Buford were excused from the table
and received permission to take their guns and go off in
the open fields behind Dr. Clark's house to practice hitting
tin cans on fence posts, Honor quickly asked to be excused.

"What are your plans for the day, Miss Honor Jane?"
her father asked over his fourth cup of black coffee.

"I thought I'd—" she tried to think quickly of something
that would please her mother. "Well, I have some Bible
verses to memorize for my next Sunday school class." It
wasn't entirely a lie; she did have some verses to memorize
so that she could get a few gold stars in her slot on the
chart and not look as if she were a dumbbell, but she had
no intention of spending the day memorizing.

"It's high time," her mother said, stirring sugar in her coffee. "Miss Ada said you were behind the rest of the class. That's embarrassing to me, you know, to have Miss Ada make a point of it in front of the whole Missionary Society. You shouldn't embarrass your mother like that."

She was just ready to retort that it was Miss Ada who liked to do the embarrassing, but thought better of it. "Well, I'm going to shock her on Sunday," Honor said, heading toward the bedroom. "I'm going to recite a whole chapter and end up in one whack with more gold stars than anybody else."

Her father laughed. "That's a smart girl for you."

"She's getting entirely too big for her britches, if you ask me. I dread the day when she hits that boy-crazy stage. She's going to be a wild one to control."

Honor didn't stay around to listen. She went her usual way to the dining room table and crawled under. If her parents said anything interesting, she could hear without straining very hard. But mostly she wanted to get back to work on Lola's escape map.

She took out the notebook paper and pencil and thought a minute, chewing on the pencil. There was no doubt about it: the railroad would be the easiest way out. If she only knew whether Lola was willing to hop a coal car. . . . Just in case Lola refused, she had better figure out which were the safest back roads leading out to the main highway. Once Lola hit the paved road, she ought to be able to hitch a ride. Lots of times cars filled with black people went up and down the main highway. Or she might flag down the Greyhound. They'd let her ride on the back seat.

She drew a long wiggling line off the main cinder road that branched off just a little way down the road. She marked it "Stinnet Rd.," and then wrote down in the corner of the page, "This road leads to Ruthie Stinnet's aunt's house and ends up about two miles off the main highway." She put the pencil back in her mouth. She was going to have to figure out a sure-fire road from behind the Stinnets', leading out to the main highway. She had never gone beyond Ruthie's Aunt Maggie's house. But Buford had. Buford knew every wagon road and hunting path in that stretch of the woods. She could never let

Buford in on her secret plan to help Lola run away, but maybe she could pick his brains some other way.

Pretend, she told herself, that Lola makes it to the main highway and hitches down to Olympia. She wondered if Lola knew any of Suzie Daniels' kinfolks down that way. She'd need some place to rest up and get some hot food before striking out for Nashville or wherever she might want to hide out from the law. It ought to be easy to hide out with her own people. Her mother had told her once that all Negroes looked alike, that you couldn't tell one from the other. Lola was a purebred, though, and not like Suzie Daniels with her blue-speckled eye. And you could tell Suzie Daniels apart from Lola, even if you saw them from the back and didn't know about Suzie's eye—Lola's big bottom would give her away.

"I've hit a snag," she finally admitted, studying the finished parts of the map. She decided that she could at least add some touches of color to it. She got out her crayons and colored in green for woods, brown for empty fields, black for the cinder road, blue for the sky, and red for any danger zones. It was beginning to look like a picture, she thought.

After she had finished coloring, she was tired of it, and folded it carefully. Maybe she'd better keep it on her, with this much finished on it. Her mother might snoop around under the table and start asking questions, she decided.

At the thought of her mother, she lifted the corner of the tablecloth and listened. She heard her mother's voice climbing the scale in tone.

"Henry, I wish you would just quit harping on and on about being sorry and how no-good you are . . . and will I ever forgive you. Haven't I always forgiven you? Haven't I always taken you back? That is not the point I was making."

"Then why don't you kiss and make up?"

"It is simply not that easy! You just don't wipe away a hurt—hurts like those you gave me last night—with something as simple as a kiss. You might, but I don't forget that easy."

"I'm truly sorry I hurt you. All right, I won't say it again. But I am, Martha Jane, believe me! I promise that I will never do it again. Never!"

73

"Promises, promises! You promised me yesterday morning that you wouldn't touch a drop."

"But, honey, that was before I heard the news about the mines shutting down in September. When I heard that, it seemed that everything closed in on me. I was sitting there on that bank with an empty line. Every time I cast out and reeled in, empty ... empty. It was just like all those applications, casting them out and nothing coming back in. Do you realize this is August, Martha Jane, and not one single reply yet? And all I have for assurance on this job in Margate is their word. It's not in writing."

"Getting drunk doesn't solve one blessed thing. It only makes matters worse."

"You're right. I know that. But Clifty Randolph kept passing that bottle of Four Roses, which his cousin brought him from Kentucky, under my nose, and I hadn't tasted a good whiskey in a long time."

"I just can't believe the Black Diamond Coal Company would close down this entire operation. It seems impossible," her mother said. "They just can't do that!"

"Can't? They're going to. I got it straight from Buddy Matthews, and Max Fulmer confirmed what Buddy said. If the mine foreman and the bookkeeper tell you the same thing, there's something besides rumor to it. It's not just a tale hanging on the grapevine."

"It still sounds so farfetched to me, closing down a whole town. The company owns everything in it—lock, stock, and barrel. What will they do with all the houses?"

"Max Fulmer said they would sell them to anybody could afford to buy. They'll phase out in stages, according to him. They expect to be completely through by no later than spring."

"That means the school term will most likely have to finish out. There'll be those who can't relocate all that fast. What's going to happen to some of the poor souls up here, Henry?"

"Some will get jobs in other places operated by Black Diamond. Jobs are pretty scarce everywhere. I guess a lot will just end up in the bread line ... on relief."

"I didn't know—I had no idea."

"That was how it hit me. I was sitting there thinking about it, but I couldn't talk about it intelligently with somebody like Clifty Randolph. Being a weakling, I just—"

"I understand, Henry—I know it's been hard on you not having men on your own educational level to talk to. And I even understand about your kicking poor old Lucifer."

"I hate myself for that. I never thought I'd lower myself to kick a fine old dog who's made me so proud."

"It's the whiskey does that to you, Henry. You wouldn't harm a flea when you're sober. We all know that. Lucifer knows that too. Dogs know a lot about people."

"You're a very understanding woman, Martha Jane."

"There is one thing I will never understand though ... never!"

Honor thought her mother sounded choked up and ready to start in on a crying jag. She cupped her hand over her ear.

"How could you be unfaithful? Even under the influence? How could you touch somebody like that—that slut! I don't care if she is a niece of Buddy Matthews. She's still a common whore, and everybody knows it!"

"Martha Jane, I didn't! Believe me."

"But you had lipstick on your shirt. I saw it."

"That was from a kiss of gratitude that Clifty's wife gave me for bringing him home safe before he passed out and picked a fight with somebody. You know how Clifty picks fights when he's drunk."

Honor wasn't sure about the tone in her father's voice. It sounded a little too fast and high to be all the way truthful. Her mother, she noticed, must not have believed him all the way either.

"Well, I know Mildred is big up front. Men like that. And I never have been very well-rounded up there. I'm kind of flat-chested."

"You are just fine the way you are. You know how excited I get just touching—"

"Don't do that, Henry! You know how those children are always behind a door when you least expect it. Honor has got the biggest nose in town."

"Honor's out playing."

"You can never be sure—not here, Henry! It's not right. And I'm not over last night yet ... not by a long shot."

"Let me make it up to you. Come on—see . . . let me . . ."

"Somebody's bound to see."

75

"Come on—we'll pull down the window shades and lock the bedroom door."

Honor felt a hot, sticky taste in the back of her mouth. Then a fierce anger took hold of her. They had a lot of nerve—going off doing it. She knew what they were going to do in there with the doors locked and the window shades pulled down. Ruthie Stinnet had told her all about how married men like to play dirty—do it all the time, and women just have to bear the cross. But there wasn't time for that when the whole town of Margate was caving in on itself!

She clutched the map in her hand and ran out of the house, purposely slamming the front screen door as loud as she could.

For a moment, she sat on the front steps wondering what she should do next. Bible verses were out—all the way. Miss Ada and her own backsliding mother in there could take that package of gold stars and go jump in Doe Creek Lake with them. And they could take the whole Intermediate Junior Sunday school class with them.

She put her chin in her hands and thought. She could go track down Stuart and Buford. But at the thought of the loud popping-off sounds of the rifles—of the way they would get tired of shooting at tin cans after a while and start in picking off sparrows for no other reason than that they were sparrows and not good for anything—she turned that idea down flat.

There wouldn't be much use wasting time hatching up her story for the town grapevine about her father's being on the wagon for good, when there wasn't going to be a Margate after next spring. The thought of the whole town being wiped out was too much for her to grasp. She'd think about that again later on, piece by piece.

There was still the problem of Lola. She looked up in the direction of the Clarks' house. She had seen Mamie drive off in her big Packard earlier. She could maybe just meander—not slip up, but meander up and ask Lola . . . well, she could ask her if she had seen her brothers.

She stood up and inspected herself. Actually, she looked her best. Outside of the pink-flowered Sunday school dress, this blue and white striped seersucker with the sailor collar was her favorite. She had tried to look her neatest at the breakfast table and had even dug out her last year's tennis shoes and put on her Sunday school anklets. The tennis shoes were too short by a size now, and her big toes had long ago pushed through the canvas tops. Her white socks stared up through the frayed holes like fuzzy white eyeballs trying to see. In fast-running shoes, she could march up there; if Lola gave her a real cold shoulder, she could hightail it out in a hurry.

In a short time, she was standing by the shed where Dr. Clark kept his Ford V-8 parked. She tapped the ground with the stick she had picked up on the way, three times for good luck, and spit over her right shoulder for good measure. Then she held her head up as high as she could, straightened her shoulder blades, and marched straight on up to Lola's little porch and knocked at the door.

She tried to appear unconcerned and let out a little whistle, imitating Stuart, between her front teeth.

When there was no answer, she tried a light-hearted skip and went up to Dr. Clark's kitchen door, and, for the first time in her life, gave it a big, loud knock, three times.

Lola came to the screen door wiping her hands on her apron. "What you knocking on that door for?"

Honor closed her hands around the stick and braced herself against Lola's bearing-down look that asked for nothing short of the truth.

"I was looking for my brothers. Did you see my two brothers?"

"No, I ain't seen 'em." She did not move, but kept bearing down harder. "What is it you really knocked on that door about?"

Honor could not believe how, all of a sudden, out of nowhere, an earthquake of tears grabbed hold of her. She had never done that in her life, that she could remember. There she was, standing under Lola's gaze, tears splashing out like an April rain, and she couldn't seem to stop herself. She wanted Lola to open up the door and pull her into those big satin-brown arms and let her cry it out—whatever it was. "I just wanted—I didn't have nobody, with Buford and Stuart off killing sparrows just because they're sparrows and Mama and Daddy locked in their room with the shades pulled down playing dirty and with the whole town of Margate caving in on itself!" she blurted out.

"Well, I declare, that's a whole mess of things to go knocking on somebody's door about, I reckon." Lola pushed open the door. "Don't just stand there bawling—letting all the flies in. Sit down there at the table while I get this cake in the oven."

Honor sat down and wiped her face dry with the inside hem of her dress. She watched, fascinated, while Lola opened the oven door to the huge, modern electric stove with its shiny green enamel and fancy chrome trim. She noticed, too, that the Clarks' kitchen had a different smell from theirs. It wasn't just the smell of the cake batter either. It was a mixture of something like the Lysol smell from Dr. Clark's office all mixed in with good food odors.

"I'm sorry I bawled like a baby," she offered to Lola's back.

Lola didn't seem to pay any attention. "Here, you any good at whipping up cake icing?" She placed a big yellow bowl in her lap and handed her a wire-ended spoon. "Give that a few licks while I check out this jello—how far it's congealed." She opened the door of the biggest refrigerator Honor had ever seen. "Mrs. Clark wants the bananas added at just the right time. She don't like bananas floated to the top of her jello molds."

Honor was beating the egg whites and sugar as hard as she could, but after a few strokes her arm felt as if it would break. She stood up and put the bowl on the table and tried it that way. Still, the egg whites stayed at a frothy stage and wouldn't whip up in peaks the way she knew cake icing was supposed to. For some reason, she felt that she would burst out bawling again. "I can't seem to do it right," she mumbled.

"You doin' just fine." Lola came over and looked into the bowl. "That's just the right number of licks I wanted. If you get it stiff too fast, it might not hold up till the cake comes out of the oven." Lola sat down, pulled out her can of snuff, and put a dip in her mouth.

"How old are you?" she suddenly asked out of nowhere.

"Eleven—going on twelve. Why?"

"I was just wondering—some girls start in about your age, but you don't look filled out enough yet."

"For what?"

"For the monthly miseries. Girls get awfully teary sometimes before it sets in." She dabbed at her mouth. "Maybe you just needs a good dose of worm medicine."

"I don't have worms. Mama de-worms us every spring with Dr. Clark's medicine." She looked at Lola and tried to give her own face a bearing-down look. "What's the monthly miseries?"

"Lordie, Lordie! It ain't for Lola to be telling you the facts of life. 'Sides, you don't need to worry none about it yet. It's too early. I figured you might've found out about 'em by now. You seem to know a whole lot."

"I never heard of monthly miseries."

"It's somethin' happens to all girls once they reach a certain stage in life. It's one of the crosses women have to bear."

"Is it the same kind of cross as having to go in and let the husbands play dirty whenever they want to?"

Lola put her head back and laughed. "It's not exactly that. Look, it ain't nothing for you to fret over yet. Let me check out this cake." She got up, went over to the stove, and opened the oven door. Honor watched every move as Lola took a toothpick and stuck it into the cake. "Needs a little more time." She stuck the toothpick between her teeth.

When Lola sat back down, Honor asked, "Lola, did you hear anything said from Dr. Clark or Mrs. Clark about Margate being shut down?" She knew Lola would tell her the whole truth.

"Yeah, somethin'. Last night he broke the news to her at the dinner table. What a fit that woman throwed. She carried on like nothin' I ever seen before." Lola shook her head and laughed to herself. "I've seen lots of carrying ons about all kinds of things. I've heard hollerings and shoutings from about any cause you could name. But ain't nothin' match that fit she threw and fell back in. She said she wasn't moving to no other dinky coal-mining town no matter how much they raised his salary or let him charge on his house calls. She said she was taking her baby out of Bell Buckle and going home to Nashville, and he could just come and join her there if'n and when he decided he could make a living practicing his doctoring in a decent place. I mean to tells you she throwed some other kind of fit. She got herself such a whopping migraine headache she had to drive off down the mountain to Olympia to the clinic for treatment. Said she wasn't letting no doctor with as little sense as he had treat her headaches!"

"Mama threw a conniption fit last night too, but it was because Daddy slipped off the wagon again and came home drunk and kicked Lucifer. They had a big fight last night." It seemed so natural telling Lola all about it. It was nice, too, not having to worry about her broadcasting it on the grapevine.

"Yeah?" Lola nodded, encouraging her to go on.

"Yeah, he hit her some—didn't black her eye this time though. Then Mama came in squalling to me about it—how she had run Daddy off for good, and then she went off in the kitchen and made coffee and tried to stay up all night."

"That's what the light was doing on then," Lola said more to herself.

"You mean you saw it?" Honor asked, surprised.

"Some nights I gets my own kinds of inside fits. I gets restless and can't seem to fall off to sleep no matter which way I turn. Nights like that, sometimes I wander out in the backyard and stand under that big sycamore tree and look up at the sky. I gets company looking up at the sky." She seemed to be talking off into the space above the kitchen table. "I finds me the Big Dipper hanging up there, and I tells myself that that same Big Dipper is hanging the same way over everybody I know out on the old Franklin Turnpike, over every place I ever heard of. I thinks about that a whole lot. How some things in life don't change—they the same for everybody. That's the same Big Dipper hanging over that town down in Mississippi you was talking about last time. Same the world over. It's people under it who make everything all mixed up and different. Jesus s'posed to love all his children the same. We all s'posed to be equal—we all God's children."

Lola went back to the oven, took out the cake pan, and turned the cake out on a wire rack to cool. Then she picked up the bowl of icing and the wire spoon and started a beating of the icing such as Honor had never seen before. She watched, amazed, as Lola's big arms whipped round and round, without stopping or showing the slightest sign of getting tired. "That's about right," she said, putting the bowl down on the counter and placing the cake on a fancy round plate. "We'll let it cool a speck more before we put the icing on." She sat back down. "I'll let you lick the spoon."

Honor was still thinking of what Lola had said about God's children. "Lola, I don't believe in God," she finally said, confessing it out loud for the first time.

"I thought everybody s'posed to believe in God."

"I don't ... not the way Preacher Pullum is always hollering about God this and the Devil that. It don't always add up right. He twists it all around to the Baptist rendering and makes it all lean toward just the Baptists. I believe in something else." She was twisting the hem of her dress. She had never told anyone about the magic bluebird before.

"Yeah?" Lola was giving her a studying kind of look.

"I believe in the magic bluebird who lives up—oh, way up above the Big Dipper, and can fly anywhere he wants to and see everything with his magic eye. And the Devil is everywhere wrapped up in jaybird feathers."

"Is that a fact?" Lola dabbed at the corner of her mouth.

"It was this way," Honor explained. "Did you ever hear that part in the Bible where the angels got kicked out to hell? It's the same. The bluebird had this big palace built out of silver up there above the sky. The blue jay was all part of it. But he started messing around—getting in other birds' nests, you know how jaybirds do? Always picking at other birds—stealing their eggs and crapping in nests?"

"Yeah, jaybirds do cut up."

"Well, the bluebird got tired of that one day and he kicked the blue jay right out down to earth. The blue jay's still squawking about it. That's all it ever does. Squawk, squawk, squawk. He can't sing like other birds. Name me a time you heard a blue jay warble out its special song like say—well, a cardinal—most any bird you can name has its special song for you to know it by. The blue jay just squawks."

"Where'd you hear 'bout that?" Lola asked as she got up and went over to ice the cake. "I reckon I ain't heard that before."

"Nobody has. I made it up," Honor said.

"I figured maybe you did."

Honor watched Lola take a knife and start icing the cake in the prettiest way she had ever seen—and with such fast, easy strokes. Maybe that was how she learned how to use the razor.

"I just made up the part about the bluebird being magic and the jaybird being kicked out and sent to earth to put the evil eye on people. Everybody in Margate knows the bluebird song."

"I can't say I ever heard that one," Lola said, standing back and viewing her handiwork. "Looks right pretty, don't it?"

"That's the prettiest cake I ever saw," Honor said.

"Here—you can lick the spoon." Lola handed her the tablespoon and started washing out the bowl and the dirty pans at the sink.

Honor sat back down at the table and licked as slowly as she could, to make it last longer. "You want me to sing it for you, Lola?" she asked, between licks. She had never sung in front of anyone before, but with Lola she didn't feel embarrassed.

"I'd like to hear it." Lola was wiping the bowl dry.

"Listen to the words, and you'll see how I made up the rest of it."

> *Way up yonder above the sky,*
> *A jaybird built in a bluebird's eye.*
> > *Go limber Jim, you can't go,*
> > *Go weave and spin, you can't go Buckeye Jim.*

She stopped and scraped her feet back and forth.

"That ain't all of it, is it?" Lola asked, putting away the bowl and the clean pans. "Let me hear all of it."

> *Way up yonder above the moon,*
> *A jaybird lived in a silver spoon.*
> > *Go limber Jim, you can't go,*
> > *Go weave and spin, you can't go Buckeye Jim.*
>
> *Way down yonder in a sycamore trough,*
> *An old lady died of the whooping cough.*
> > *Go limber Jim, you can't go,*
> > *Go weave and spin, you can't go Buckeye Jim.*
>
> *Wake up snakes and come to taw,*
> *We won't have anymore of your link and law.*

Go limber Jim, you can't go,
Go weave and spin, you can't go Buckeye Jim.

"You ought to hear Tootie Farber sing it with his guitar," Honor said. "Tootie can really sing it right."

"Oh, you sang it the right way too, sounds to me. Ain't nothing wrong with the way you sing." She sat back down at the table and smiled, and Honor decided she would get to stay a little longer by that contented look on Lola's face. It would give her time maybe to talk over the map.

"Lola, if Dr. Clark and Mamie do move off, either to another coal-mining town or down to the big city, will they take you along or send you back to the penitentiary?"

Lola tapped her foot hard against the floor. "There ain't nobody alive gonna send me back to the penitentiary! I'd cut my own throat first."

Honor thought this was as good a time as any. She reached in her pocket and pulled out the map and started unfolding it. "Look, Lola, I'm working on an escape map for you. It's not finished yet—I've got some back roads to fill in."

"Who said anything about me wanting to escape?" Lola's eyes had narrowed down and were looking at her with a suspicious glint. "I never said nothing about running away."

"Nobody said nothing," Honor said, a little taken aback by the look in Lola's eyes. "I just figured it out that if you ever did maybe need to, you'd want to know the layout of the safest back roads to take to hightail it out of here."

Lola shook her head back and forth and dabbed at her mouth again. "I might at that—that is, if'n I had running away in my mind, which I ain't."

But Honor saw Lola looking hard at the map. "Did you do all that fancy coloring?"

"I love to color and draw pictures," Honor said. "It's my favorite pastime. Someday maybe I'll be a famous artist and make lots of money and build my whole family a big white house like that one Mama grew up in down in Maddoxville."

"Yeah, maybe you will. You color good. What's that Stinnet Road s'posed to mean? I ain't never heard of no Stinnet Road."

"That's what I call it, because it leads to Ruthie Stinnet's Aunt Maggie's house—though she was married to a Monroe Freeman. Most people call it the Freeman Road. It winds up there."

"You don't want to send me down no dead ends, do you?"

"That's just my trouble right now," Honor sat up excited. "Buford knows every wagon road, every back road there is. I'm going to get Buford to show me how to find a good sure-fire road that'll bring you out on the main highway—one that picks up where the Stinnet Road leaves off."

"Margate's dead end enough. Lola don't wants to get stuck back any deeper in these woods."

"The best way, the very best way, would be for you to catch a coal car on the freight train and get a free ride all the way down the mountain. Could you catch a coal car, Lola—I mean swing yourself up one of those ladders while it's moving slow, just picking up steam?"

Lola was shaking her head. "You sure have some funny ideas in your head. You are the strangest little girl. No, Lola can't catch her no coal car, 'less'un that is I wants a free ride all the way back to the penitentiary! Now what you think they'd do with a black woman paroled from the penitentiary—let out on certain conditions—riding in a coal car? Talk about railroading somebody to the pen!"

Honor was disappointed. She had been so sure that would be the easiest, most foolproof way. "Tell me this, then. If you come out on the main highway safe, could you hitch a ride on down the mountain to Olympia or flag down a Greyhound bus maybe?"

"I could flag me down that magic bluebird if I could find him," Lola laughed. "He could fly me up there to that silver moon you was talking about. Me and Buckeye Jim. Who's Buckeye Jim anyways?"

"Buckeye Jim? Oh, I guess that's the name of all smart-alecks. I figure maybe that's the bluebird's way of telling smart-alecks to go jump in the lake."

"You got an answer for everything, don't you?"

"Well, Preacher Pullum stretches the Bible to suit him. I guess I got as much right to stretch out the bluebird song. Anyway, I believe it!"

"You want me to keep this map?" Lola asked, already folding it into a shape that would fit inside her snuffbox.

"Oh, sure. I drew it for you. But it's not complete yet. I've got to fill in the rest of it."

"You ain't gonna ask Buford—is that the biggest boy? That'un carries the shotgun instead of the twenty-two?"

"Yeah, that's Buford. He's the oldest."

"Don't tell him nothin'."

"I wouldn't tell nobody!" Honor said. "But I aim to pick his brains about the best wagon roads."

Lola stood up and stretched, and looked at the kitchen clock. "I s'pect it's time for you to be running on now. Lola's got the bathroom to scrub and a whole lots more to do before Mrs. Clark comes back from the clinic. She's fit to be tied 'bout everything today."

Honor was admiring the cake on the counter.

"I'd cut you a piece, but she'd think I stole a piece off it. She'd accuse me . . . I'll try to save you some to taste. It tastes better'n it looks." Lola held the screen door open for her. "Don't you go fretting around no more now about them jaybirds gonna put the evil eye on you. Lola's got a way to stop that from happening."

"Is that with your voodoo power Suzie Daniels said you had?"

"Is that what Suzie Daniels says? Well, Lola'll have to tend to that." She looked down at her. "My Mama did come from New Orleans, and she had special powers she got handed down from her people, who got 'em in the land they was stole from—stole and sold. You might call it voodoo if you want to. Don't matter what you call it—it works. Lola's gonna see to it that you and your whole family gets a nice place to move off to. So don't you go stewing around 'bout your daddy not landing a job yet."

"Do you *really* have power?" She was checking out Lola's face carefully to see if there was any trace of her playing a joking kind of game. Lola was looking down with no expression at all that she could read.

"Why do you think Margate's being shut down? Lola put the hex on Margate the day she got here."

"Maybe that's why we've had so much bad luck lately," Honor said.

"No, that ain't why. Lola wouldn't put no hex on somebody as nice as you."

"Thank you—thank you kindly."

"Here's one more scrap of advice." Lola was looking

happier now. "If'n I was you, when I get home, I'd run around to the other side of the house and check on the window shades. If'n they pulled down, go chase a rainbow for a while. If they pulled up, it'll be okay for you to go inside."

Honor laughed back over her shoulder, already skipping toward home. It was good to know she had somebody else's hexing power lined up on her side of the fence. It looked as if they were going to need all the help they could get.

7

Honor was sitting on the steps of the front porch, busy counting the June bugs she had caught. She would pick one out of the lot, tie a string to its leg, and let it fly ahead of her, pretending it was one of Hera's secret messengers leading her to a special meeting place where she could find her magic prince, Ronald. She usually met him in her pretend castle in the middle of the woods across the road from their house. But the last time, Stuart and one of his friends had sneaked up on her and listened to her talking out loud and had mocked her for days afterward. It was hard finding a place secret enough, where she could make believe the way she wanted to that Prince Roland was galloping up on his white horse.

"Honor. Honor Jane, I need you a minute," she heard her mother call. "Come as quick as you can—it's urgent."

She put the lid back on the jar, tested the air holes, and walked slowly around the side of the house toward the back door.

"Yes, Ma'am," she said, hiding the June bugs behind the dirty-clothes basket on the back porch.

"I want you to run as fast as you can with these letters here," her mother said, licking a stamp and pressing it onto an envelope. "You can't dillydally even a minute. These have to get off on the ten o'clock mail truck, and it's going on ten already."

"What's so urgent?" Honor asked, irritated at losing her chance to search for Roland. "Why do I always have to be the one? Why can't Buford and Stuart do some of the running?"

"This is not the time for you to start getting stubborn on me, Honor Jane, when lately you've seemed so good and willing to help." She checked the three letters to be sure the stamps were staying in place. "These are important letters going to the school boards."

"When did Daddy write them? I thought Daddy was still staying in bed because he's groggy-headed—still hung over."

" 'Incapacitated' is the word, Honor—and in a way, he is. He's mostly worried sick over the mines shutting down in September and us with no word back yet. I wrote these letters yesterday afternoon when I went over to Miss Lacey's. Bless her soul, she's been so faithful to your father. In all these years, and with all the troubled times your father has put her through, heaping the entire teaching load on her back, there was never a complaint. And she was a wonderful help composing these reminder letters to the school boards. Her grammar is so perfect, you know."

"How long you think Daddy will stay—incarcerated?"

"That's not the word—*incapacitated*. There's a big difference."

"Sometimes big words all sound the same to me."

"Your father should be feeling better soon—well, actually, just as soon as we find out something. Any news is better, I sometimes think, than no news. It leaves you too suspended—dangling in thin air." She inspected Honor. "You could look better. Wash your hands, just in case. I don't want anything sticky on these letters."

Honor was soon out the front door. She stopped on the bottom step to decide what she'd try for good luck. She wanted something special to send the letters off. She took five giant steps, spit over her right shoulder, and gave a secret wink up toward where she imagined the bluebird was hovering above the clouds.

From habit, as she passed by Mrs. Clark's house, she checked out the front porch. But the wicker rocking chair was tilted with its seat toward the wall and the cretonne cushion was across the porch railing, being aired out. There was no sign of Lola.

She skipped fast down the hill, glad to be wearing her tennis shoes on such an important errand. She gripped the letters with just the right amount of tightness to keep from wrinkling them.

At the foot of the hill, she got ready to run past the

Hardees and the boy she thought they called Skipper who was swinging back and forth on the rusty iron gate.

"Hi, pukey duke," he said, jumping down from the gate and slamming it hard, sticking his tongue out at her. "Hi, you ole stuck-up pukey duke."

"I don't stop to talk to little boys who say ugly things," she called back over her shoulder.

"Shut up, pukey."

"Go blow your snotty nose," she yelled back, in spite of knowing she wasn't supposed to talk back to the Hardee children, who were so poor they had to be on relief.

"I'm going to tell my big sister what you called me, and Bertie Pate will whip the shit outa you!"

Honor walked on faster, not looking back. When she reached Mrs. Floyd's house, she couldn't resist dragging her heels a little to watch a hummingbird digging its long beak into the honeysuckles and flapping its wings so fast you couldn't see them move.

She was glad to see Mrs. Ewing's window shades pulled down. That usually meant she had caught a ride to Cookville to visit her boy in the C.C.C. camp.

She ran down Mrs. Ewing's steep hill and stopped at the footbridge. It would be bad luck not to stop and say hello to Moses. But as she leaned over the rail, she had a horrible feeling that she might drop one of the letters down into the tumbling water below. She couldn't run the risk of doing something that might leave the Whitfield family stranded in Margate when the whole town was going to be moving away—except for the Hardees and people like them who didn't have any place else to go.

She ran all the way up to the post office, stopping at the steps to get her breath. Then she pushed her way in past the line of people already waiting for the ten o'clock mail.

"Don't shove ahead in line, you!" Maude Gates yelled in her loud, booming voice as she leaned with one elbow on the writing shelf beneath the Ten-Most-Wanted poster, holding her place in line with one foot stuck out.

"I'm not getting in line. I'm mailing these letters in the slot so they'll get off on the mail truck. Miss Ada!" She rapped at the bars across the window. "Be sure you get those letters in the mail sack."

"Well, you don't have to yell it all the way down to

89

Doe Creek Lake," said Miss Ada, rising up from directly beneath the window where she was already pulling the ropes on the mail sack. "Besides, there's another whole ten minutes before the mail truck is due. I can't see for my life why the whole town has to flock in here ahead of time and camp out."

"We just want to make sure you do everything right, Miss Ada," Uncle Dave called out, nudging Tootie Farber in the ribs. "Ain't that right, Tootie?"

"You'd think you could trust me after twenty years of checking me out."

Honor watched the little brown knot of hair ride the jerking movements of Miss Ada's funny-shaped head. She wanted to see with her own eyes that the letters got in the mail sack. But Miss Ada wasn't through with her scolding.

"And I don't want anybody spitting on the floor or scribbling pictures and words on the writing shelf or the posters or the walls. Just because there's a lot of talk about Margate going to be closed down, this is U.S. Government property and there's laws to see that it's protected!"

She tapped her fingers across the narrow shelf behind the barred window to emphasize her remarks. "And how is your sweet mother?" she asked suddenly, leaning over and peering down at Honor. "How's she holding up during this strain she was telling me about—this waiting period?"

"Tolerable," Honor said, not trusting the look in Miss Ada's eye, and still intent on seeing the letters dropped in the sack.

"To the school boards again, eh?" She looked at each address, pretending she was checking for postage. Honor saw her shoot a meaningful look to Maude Gates. When she saw the letters go sliding down in the canvas sack and Miss Ada knot the rope and snap on the lock, Honor couldn't hold her tongue back any longer. As she turned away from the window to go to the back of the line, she said more to Tootie Farber than anyone, but loud enough for Miss Ada to hear, "I guess it's a good thing my Mama didn't write out what she had to say on postcards—else everybody here would know her business."

Tootie was the first to laugh, and then, as if they all wanted a chance to answer Miss Ada's scolding, the whole line joined in—except Maude Gates, Honor noticed. As Honor stepped in behind Tootie, Miss Ada's head popped up behind the bars. "You've got a lot of nerve, little Miss smart-aleck! Accusing me of reading postcards in front of the whole town practically. I could answer you back plenty—you and your father. Imagine, the daughter of the town drunk sassing me!" She yanked down the dark green window shade behind the iron bars.

Honor tried not to see the smug, grinning look on Maude Gates' face. She swallowed hard. No matter how much she needed to cry, this bunch of post office loafers wouldn't catch her crying.

"Don't pay no 'tention to that loudmouth," Tootie Farber said, turning around and patting her on the shoulder. "Hey, did ya'l know this here's the best little checker player in Margate?" he called out.

"Yeah, she shorely is," chimed in Uncle Dave. "Come up here, sugar, and I'll give you that buffalo nickel you wouldn't take from me the other day. Here." He shoved it at her. "And don't you worry about Ada getting so hot under the collar. She did that 'cause she does read postcards." He raised his voice so Miss Ada would have to hear. "I'd like to see her pick on somebody her size. But she's too chicken, back there hiding behind her window shade. Somebody ought to write Franklin D. a letter and tell him how his postmistress up here in Margate spends her time picking on little girls instead of tending to the business of running a post office."

Honor took the nickel, to show her appreciation of Uncle Dave's taking up for her. "Thank you—I guess I'll buy the Hardee kids some bubble gum with it," she said, thinking her mother would approve of her taking money for that.

Maude Gates seemed to think it was her turn to tune in, Honor noticed, as Maude heaved her big shoulders around and squared her feet. "You ought'n to take off on Ada Bly, Dave Blaylock—or you neither, Tootie. She's upset along with everybody else over the news. Even if the post office is U.S. property, they won't keep no big post office open when there won't be nobody left to get no mail. Besides, young smart-alecks shouldn't ought to ever sass grown-ups."

"And grown-ups shouldn't say 'shouldn't ought,' " Honor

called back, holding the nickel with one hand and Tootie Farber's hand with the other. "It's bad grammar."

"I don't need no little smart ass telling me how to talk. In my book, what Ada said about your father was right."

"It's not! My Daddy is on the wagon now for good. He's never setting foot in Bohunk Town again. I'm glad Margate's shutting down and you're going to be left high and dry in your boardinghouse without any boarders."

"Don't get Maude riled up," Tootie whispered. "You are being a bit sassy."

"Yonder comes the mail truck," called out Uncle Dave, pretending to step out in front of Maude to get a good look at it, but Honor saw his elbow push Maude back to her place in line.

After the mail had been sorted out, Miss Ada sent the window shade rolling up with a noisy snap and passed out the mail to those in line lucky enough to get anything. Honor took the letter Miss Ada shoved at her through the iron bars of the window. She looked at it curiously, wondering who the Cunninghams from Route #1 in Barnesville, Georgia, were. She had never heard her mother mention anything about any Barnesville, Georgia.

As she left the post office, she stopped and watched Tootie and Uncle Dave getting their checkerboard put back in place again. "I thank you both kindly," she said, smiling down at them. "I didn't mean to cause you no trouble."

"Wasn't nothing. You're much obliged," said Tootie, slowly lining up his orange crush tops.

Honor held up the buffalo nickel. "I'm going to buy some bubble gum or maybe some candy with this. I am to give it to the Hardee kids, them never having spare change to buy extras with." She didn't want Uncle Dave getting any big ideas.

She ran on toward the company store and hurried up the steps. In front of the glass top that held the boxes of candy and the jar of jawbreakers and bubble gum, Honor's mouth watered. She tried to decide what would last the longest and be the biggest treat for the Hardees. "What's the most candy I can buy with this nickel?" she asked Mr. Arnold.

"Well, 'es see here, I reckon it'ud be jelly beans—jelly beans or gumdrops. 'Bout the same. Which'un you want?"

"Could I have some of both, please? In two different sacks?"

"Both mixed up in two sacks or gumdrops in one and jelly beans in the other? I swear, nobody ever gives me their order right." Honor was surprised to hear Mr. Arnold sounding grouchy. He was usually cheerful, no matter what was on his mind. Maybe he was worried about not getting transferred, she thought, or maybe having to step down a notch or two if he did land a job in another town operated by the Black Diamond people.

"Whichever pleases you," she said, smiling. "Either way is fine with me." She handed him the nickel.

He looked at her with a cross shrug and mixed the gumdrops and jelly beans together, pouring one scoop in one sack and a thicker scoop in another. Honor neatly folded the tops of the sacks down for easy carrying, and hurried out.

With the letters safely locked in the mail sacks and now on the truck, Honor didn't feel the need to rush. At the footbridge, she grabbed hold of the rough splintery railing and leaned over as far as she could. "Hey, Moses, come out from under your rock over there." But it wasn't a good day for crawdads to be out looking around, she decided. She stared hard at the patterns of the water twisting and whirling around the rocks, sliding down in miniature rivers and joining up again, disappearing in one long running ribbon of water around the bend of Mrs. Ewing's hill.

Before she left the footbridge, she took a last look back up at the post office and felt Maude Gates' hateful voice ringing in her head and Miss Ada's bird-eyes glaring down at her. It seemed to her that the post office was leaning to the left.

They'd better close down the post office, she told herself with satisfaction, before it *falls* down.

She hurried along up the Ewing hill and skipped down the cinder sidewalk, past Mrs. Floyd's. As she came up to the Hardees' house, she saw Bertie Pate and Skipper sitting side by side on their door stoop, as if they were waiting for her. But before Bertie Pate could loosen her tongue and say whatever was on her mind, Honor called out in as cheerful and natural-sounding a voice as she could, "Uncle Dave and Tootie Farber asked me to give you this on my

93

way home." She held out the heaviest sack of candy. "They gave me one and sent one to you."

Bertie Pate came to the gate slowly with Skipper hanging behind her. Honor noticed that Skipper had sores again. Somebody had painted him in big dots with the purple medicine the county health nurse brought up once a year and left at the schoolhouse, to be passed out free of charge.

"What's in it?" she asked, glaring at Honor. "Did you call my brother snotty nose?"

"Just after he called me pukey duke. He kept calling me that, and it finally made me mad. I know I shouldn't've answered him back." Honor opened up the sack of candy for Bertie Pate to take a look. "It's jelly beans and gumdrops, almost a nickel's worth."

"That's funny, them sending us a sack of candy." She still didn't take it.

"Oh, it's all right. They gave me one too. I guess they wanted to do something nice since the mines is going to shut down and there won't be no more Margate after next spring."

Honor Jane Whitfield, you might be the school principal's girl and live in a big fancy house with a toilet 'at flushes, but you just full of white lies. . . . You always telling white lies." She reached out and took the candy. "Skipper, did you call her pukey duke?"

Skipper was trying to reach inside the paper sack. "I didn't mean nothing by it. Gimme some, Bertie Pate! Gimme a jelly bean!"

"Not 'til after Mama divides 'em," said Bertie Pate, holding on to the candy. "She might want to take Daddy some next time she visits the TB hospital."

For a moment, Honor almost handed Skipper the second bag, but she had a secret plan for it. She was going to have to find some way to keep the candy fresh because she would need it later on. But jelly beans and gumdrops ought to last for months, she told herself.

When she slammed the screen door to announce her arrival home, her mother came into the living room, wiping her hands on her apron. "Shhh, your daddy's napping. What's that letter?"

"Something from Barnesville, Georgia. Who lives in

Barnesville?" She watched curiously as her mother sat down in the armchair and ripped open the letter.

"Your great-aunt, Martha Sue. I was named after her in part. I wrote to her for a reason."

"What reason?"

"You run on now and let me read this in peace. I'll talk to you about it later on. Did you get those letters there in time?"

"Yes, Ma'am." Honor hoped she wouldn't ask her any more questions.

"What's in that paper sack?"

"Oh, it's just an empty I found. It's got some smooth pebbles in it I fished out of the water by the footbridge."

Her mother was too busy with the letter to try reading her face, to see if she was telling the truth or not. It wasn't that she meant to tell white lies; there were just times when she had to, Honor thought, hurrying out to find a hiding place for her sack of candy.

8

Honor wanted desperately to get back to the living room and find out more about the letter from Barnesville, Georgia. There had been something about the look on her mother's face, something about that letter she didn't exactly trust. . . .

It didn't take her but an instant to remember the round tin container painted with red Christmas holly berries in which she kept her favorite keepsakes hidden beneath a rumpled pile of winter underwear in the bottom drawer of her dresser. It would be the perfect place for hiding the candy, she thought, sitting back on her heels in front of the dresser drawer and working hard to free the stuck lid on the container. She was in such a frenzy to open it that she was twisting her mouth back and forth in unison with her struggle; and when the lid did come off, it did so with such force that her right hand flew up and hit her bottom lip.

She hurriedly checked out each keepsake, against the chance that one of her brothers might have been snooping around in her dresser drawers. But they were all there: her best good-luck pieces, the shiny buckeye and the sky-blue streaked marble taw; the lace handkerchief she had won from Miss Ada when she had taken the whole Sunday school class by surprise at the last minute and recited two whole chapters of memorized Bible verses out of St. Luke; the tobacco papers and the sack of Old North State tobacco she sometimes sneaked into the woods for a secret smoke; and the broken piece of green shiny glass that she liked simply because it was pretty to look through, and made the world look different.

She made room for the sack of candy, jammed the lid

back on, and shoved the container under the pile of underwear. She slammed the drawer shut so hard the whole dresser wobbled on its flimsy legs. Then she darted back into the living room, stopping in the doorway to try and put a just-happened-to-walk-in look on her face.

Her mother was sitting in the armchair holding the yellow pages of the handwritten letter spread open in one hand and a crisp ten dollar bill in the other. She looked furious.

Honor sat down primly on the daybed and straightened out the hem of her dress. She even remembered to cross her feet at the ankles, the way her mother had told her was polite.

"You mean that whole ten dollar bill was folded up inside that letter?" she asked, a little shocked at the thought, since it would have been awfully easy to have dropped the letter into the water at the footbridge when she was leaning over looking for Moses. Ten dollars was a lot of money to be carrying around, not even knowing about it.

"Ten—yes, a measly ten dollars is what it is, all right." Her mother's voice seemed to slice the air with bitterness.

"Ten dollars will buy a whole lot at the company store."

"One hundred would buy ten times more. One hundred is what I asked for and what she can afford. She's got money to burn. She knew I wouldn't have asked if I hadn't needed it."

Honor looked puzzled. She hadn't heard much about anybody in the family, on any side—even far-off cousins-removed—who had money to burn. She decided to sit back and wait for her mother to do the talking, though she felt an impatience rising inside of her.

Her mother took the pages of the letter and hit at her leg with them, as if she were trying to knock away some pestering fly. "It's the way she said it that burns me up the most—spreading on that old Southern molasses, trying to cover up the fact that it's really vinegar she's giving me to drink. Oh, I know that Southern way they have down in Georgia and Mississippi. After all, I grew up on it—the way they say things in that sugary-sweet tone when they don't mean it in the slightest."

"Can I read it?" Honor's fingers were itching to reach out for the yellow pages.

"*May* I. Honor Jane, when are you ever going to learn?"
She took off her glasses, blew on them, and wiped them
clean with the corner of her apron. "Here, I'll read it out
loud to you. But you've got to promise me you'll sit still
and quit that squirming around like a worm in hot ashes
making me so nervous I could die. I guess you ought to
hear it anyway, since it does concern you."

Honor opened her eyes wider. That look was coming
back on her mother's face—a guilty kind of look. But before she could think up a question to ask, her mother had
started in on the letter.

"'Monday morning,' it starts out. No date a'tall. You'd
think if that Cora Mae she talks about in here is so dern
smart she'd have sense enough to include the date. Honor
Jane, when the time comes for you to start writing letters,
always remember to put the address and the date in the
upper right-hand corner. It's a sign of good upbringing.
This Cora Mae girl has to be ignorant."

Honor scraped her feet back and forth along with the
rising waves of her impatience. Her mother was looking at
her, she thought, in an awfully strange way.

"Now, Honor Jane, I want you to understand, when I
get to certain parts in this letter—I don't want you
jumping to conclusions. But I think you will understand.
Well, anyway, here's what my beloved Aunt Martha Sue
wrote."

She started to read with a voice that sounded dry and
crackly, like kindling catching fire; and as she read on, it
caught on full blaze, roaring hot.

"Dear Martha Jane,
    "If you don't recognize this handwriting, it is be-
cause my eyesight has failed me so bad lately that I
have to hire me somebody to stop by and read my
mail to me and answer letters for me. I have the
nicest girl, Cora Mae, who lives on the place next to
mine, who is not only nice, but so smart she won the
county spelling bee last year. I made her promise to
write down every word I say, and I know she's so
bashful and modest she would rather leave that part
out."

Honor heard her mother take in a deep breath. "I just
98

bet she's bashful! She's probably buttering Aunt Martha Sue right up a mile a minute—draining her of every dime she can get." She adjusted her glasses and went on:

"It was, I must say, awfully nice to receive your letter after so long a time. I was surely sorry to hear such bad news though, particularly the part that says Henry's still drinking up every nickel in sight. It seems to me like, in that last letter you wrote so long ago I can't remember when, you said he had stopped drinking for good. But my memory is getting bad on me too. I can't trust everything I think I remember, when it's that far back.

"It was mighty sweet of you, offering to send down your daughter, Honor Jane, to live with me for a couple of years or so to help me out with the housework and keep me company in my old age, as you put it, while you and Henry try to get yourselves relocated. Well, the truth is—"

Honor sat straight up. "What do you mean—send me off down to somebody I don't even know—to help out with the—"

"Do not interrupt while I'm reading, Honor Jane. That is not polite. Just listen. Wait until you've heard it all."

"But I—"

"Do you want me to finish reading this letter to you or don't you? Kindly sit there and don't interrupt."

Honor sat back, glaring hard at her mother and fighting back a terrible urge to burst out crying. Her thoughts were racing in a kind of blind panic. Of all the things she had imagined or pretended—even when she pretended she was dead and the whole family was standing over her casket crying, or when she got mad at Stuart or Buford and wished that the bluebird would turn her into a magic bird herself so she could fly away—somehow it was always of her own doing. The family would always welcome her back. It had never crossed her mind that her own mother would want to get rid of her—ship her off to some dirt farm in Georgia with a stingy old woman blind as a bat.

Her mother's voice seemed to be snapping at the words she was reading.

"—the truth is, I have Lottie Lee, this colored woman who's as loyal as the day is long, who's been working on my place since before your Uncle Walter died, and stays right here, in the back of the house, of course. Plus that, ever since I hired Frank Thompson to be my sharecropper, it was signed in our agreement that he'd tend to feeding the fieldhands, and without those men tromping into the kitchen with all that mud and dirt from the fields, there's hardly enough housework left to keep Lottie Lee from sitting around with her hands folded in her lap all day. We barely mess up anything, just the two of us.

"And as far as company goes, well, just last month when I went to Dr. Reynolds for my regular checkup, he told me I ought to cut back on so much company. I have already quit my sewing circle, due to my bad eyesight. There's my church work, naturally, that no doctor will ever make me quit as long as I've got health enough to do some little something for my blessed Lord.

"Which reminds me, I was pleased to hear Cora Mae read that you are keeping up with your Missionary Society work. This old world, in the shape it's in today, needs every little ray of help it can get from us dedicated Christians. It still bothers me that we can't somehow bust up all these split-off denominations and join up as one big Baptist church. It would cut out a lot of backbiting over the right way to interpret the Bible, if you ask me. Well, at least we are good Southern Baptists, right?

"I want you to know that I have asked our pastor to lead the entire congregation at our next Wednesday night prayer meeting in a prayer to ask God's help to put an end to Henry's drinking problem. I'm sure you will do your fair share of praying about that too."

Honor had held back as long as she could. "Daddy will hit the roof if he hears about that!" she cried out, clenching her fists. "If anything will drive him in a beeline back to Bohunk Town, it'll be finding out a whole flock of Baptists are praying over him!"

"Honor, I warned you. I said I would not tolerate this

100

rude interrupting you are bound and determined to keep on doing. I was just getting to the part about the money, where she really spreads on the molasses. Listen. 'I am enclosing a ten dollar bill. I wish I was rich so I could send you a whole lot more.'"

Honor wanted to stop up her ears. She didn't care about the ten dollars. She only knew that her mother had been willing to send her off—to get rid of her. She could barely see her mother as the yellow pages blurred, swam away from her.

"I'm sorry to have to tell you this, Martha Jane, but this year our cotton crop wasn't worth a hill of beans at the market, prices being what they have been since the Depression hit. Even our peaches this year didn't bring in what they used to. We have our problems down here in Georgia too.

"Now, don't you worry about me anymore though. Just remember that I have Lottie Lee, a good honest Negro, and this nice young girl, Cora Mae. Plus, I have Cora Mae's mama, who is a good Baptist too, who gives me rides back and forth to church and any other place I need to get to.

"Promise me you'll try to write sooner next time. I'd surely appreciate a snapshot of you and the family. Why, it's been so long since I've seen you, I probably wouldn't even know you. Is Honor Jane as pretty as you were when you were a little girl? I hope so.

"Give my love to all.

Your loving aunt,
Martha Sue"

Honor tried to focus on her mother's face as she put the letter back in her lap. Through the fuzziness of her tears, her mother's mouth looked puckered up, as though she had a green persimmon stuck in it.

"Don't that letter beat all?" she asked, shaking her head as she carefully folded the letter.

"*Doesn't*," Honor corrected, wiping her cheeks with the back of her hand.

"One thing I don't need right now is any correcting of my English from you, young lady! I know how to talk. It's just that I slip into bad habits when I get upset and excited."

"I'm pretty upset and excited myself," Honor said, a fresh run of tears spilling out in spite of her efforts to hold it back.

But her mother didn't seem to notice. She was caught up in her own thoughts, her eyes glued to the yellow pages and the ten dollar bill in her lap. She seemed to be talking back to the letter. "When I think how that aunt of mine—my only living blood aunt on my mother's side—has neglected me all these years, really. And me her only namesake. I've never asked her for a red cent before. Oh, I might have hinted for a helping hand now and then, but I've never come right out and asked anybody in this wide world for a direct handout before. It's humiliating enough to even have to ask, much less to be put in my place."

Honor popped her knuckles, trying to push back the flood of tears swelling bigger and bigger.

"Don't pop your knuckles. Don't you know you're going to end up looking like a man? You weren't born the prettiest girl to start with. You don't have to add to your troubles. It's going to take a lot of know-how to help you overcome what nature dealt out."

"It's not my fault I was born ugly, that I'm so gawky you want to ship me out and get rid of me and take me away from my brothers and my Daddy." She had tried to hold back her tongue, but once the first part was out, she raced on. "What other big ideas you got cooking up? Now that they won't take me down in Georgia, where else've you got in mind to send me off to?"

"You just cut out that kind of sass to your mother, Honor Jane Whitfield! And quit that bellering like a young calf. All I was trying to do was to hold this family together in some kind of way. I was trying to find something to help tide us over since there's not one blessed thing, absolutely nothing in sight in the way of a new job for your father." She dabbed at her own eyes with the corner of her apron. "A lot you know! A lot of right you've got to be jumping up so high and mighty sassing your mother."

"What the hell is going on in here?" Honor looked up to see her father coming into the room, running his long, big-knuckled fingers through his tousled, thick dark hair. He tied the belt of his old flannel bathrobe and sat down

102

on the daybed beside her. "What's all the fuss about—the tears?"

"She's sassing me again, as usual. Lately, every time she opens her mouth, out comes some new brand of sass."

"I wasn't sassing!" Honor cried out, encouraged by her father's arm around her. "Mama's trying to slip behind my back and send me off to a dirt farm in Georgia where I'd have to can green beans and tomatoes and sweep floors for the rest of my life, with some old crazy aunt who's blind as a bat and hates everybody except Baptists!"

"See what I mean? If that isn't sass, what do you call it?"

"Maybe something bordering on fear—on heartbreak, Martha Jane, or is that concept too much for you?" He was looking at the letter and the ten dollar bill, trying to piece it all together. "Just what have you been up to, behind her back? Behind my back, if you please?"

"It's a strange thing to me, that every time I try to pitch in and save this family from disaster, I have to defend myself. I have to explain. Oh, it's easy enough for you to come charging in here, jumping out from under the covers and acting like Mr. Supreme Court himself! Well, I'll tell you—"

"You don't have to shout."

"I am not shouting. I am merely telling you that I simply wrote to my Aunt Martha Sue, the one on my mother's side with that nice place down in Barnesville, Georgia. We stopped by there once, right after we were married. Way back then, when I was still full of romantic notions and pretty and believed in life and—" She buried her head in her hands, her shoulders shaking with a fit of crying.

"Crying won't solve anything, Martha Jane. Go on, tell me." His voice was softer. "I was full of romantic notions then too."

"You bet your life you were! Stuffed full of silly poems and powder-puff ideas that poof—look where it got us. Faced with the poorhouse, that's where."

"We're not going to any poorhouse, Martha Jane. I've been writing a letter or two myself on the side." He took his arm away from Honor's shoulders and started popping his knuckles.

"Henry, would you please not pop your knuckles. That is one habit I simply cannot stand. It sends shivers all through me." She dabbed at her wet chin and cheeks with her apron. "Before you tell me about your letters, I would like to finish explaining about my intentions. They were not, as Honor's bawling would have made you think, of a criminal nature."

"Why won't you let me read the letter?"

"Because I'd rather not."

"Because she doesn't want you to see the part about all those Baptists praying for you to quit drinking up every nickel in sight." Honor was still furious with her mother.

Her father reached out with one swift grasp and took the yellow pages, along with the ten dollar bill that was mixed up in the middle of the letter.

"You've got no right. It's my letter, my ten dollars!"

"It's my daughter—and about me, obviously. So you're broadcasting it all the way to Georgia now? You're not happy to chitter-chat behind my back with your cronies from the Missionary Society, with Preacher Pullum, with anybody who'll support your martydom. That big heavy cross you have to bear, huh, Martha Jane?"

"That's right. Turn against me. Hate me! I told you, I merely suggested that she take Honor Jane for a year or two while we get relocated. I asked for some money too. Not ten dollars, but one hundred. Yes, I was rock-bottom desperate. But I was just trying to help." She sent out a loud, piercing wail. "I wonder sometimes why I was born, why God puts me to the test every day of my life!"

"Martha Jane, for once, couldn't you think beyond the Baptist context? Couldn't you try to think without propping yourself up with those flea-bitten, worn-out clichés? Try."

"Go ahead and knock my church. The only thing I've got left. Not that going to services in a schoolhouse is my idea of going to church, but I have tried to be faithful to what I was taught was right. I have tried to give the children something substantial, something that lasts and can be depended on, something strong that won't go down the drain with a bottle of whiskey!"

"I'm not interested in this goddam letter. Here." He shoved it back at her.

"What about my ten dollars?"

"If you don't mind, Martha Jane, I would like to use it for bus fare to get to a place called Hartman, Kentucky, where there's a good chance I can get a teaching job. I have an old college roommate who's settled there and is anxious to help me out in whatever way he can. He's been very successful in the farm-machinery business and he picked up some real estate for nothing during the crash. He says he can give me something, even if the teaching doesn't pan out."

There was a stunned silence in the room. "But you never told me, Henry. You never said a word."

"I was afraid to, until I heard back. I'm still afraid."

"But why? Why, when it sounds like it could be the big chance you've been waiting for?"

Honor felt the pink roses and green leaves in the pattern of the cretonne slipcover begin to swim around in her head. It was going too fast for her.

"I am afraid because, because Nathan Dobbs used to look up to me. He used to think I was the best thing to happen to the University of Tennessee because I could quote poetry and write his essays for him and bring in the good grades. He doesn't know about—well, he doesn't know."

"He doesn't have to know anythng. The only reason, Henry, that I told Aunt Martha Sue anything was to get her melted down a little, hoping she would send me that one hundred dollars I asked for. You know how sometimes you have to say things."

"But what can I say to somebody like Nathan? Somebody that successful. He probably lives in some big colonial home and looks like a million dollars. I don't have a decent suit even."

"Is that what's bothering you? Now, Henry, your blue serge just needs a little repair, a good brushing, and a spot or two taken off. I've been saving that white shirt you got for your birthday. It's brand new. I can fix you up to beat the band." Honor watched amazed as her mother jumped up, flinging off her apron. "It's like a dream. It's what I've been dreaming of!"

"Where's Hartman, Kentucky?" Honor asked, squinting her eyes doubtfully. "What size place is it?"

"Hartman is down in the corner of the state bordering on Tennessee. It's right on the Mississippi River, the county seat. Near Parnell Point, Kentucky. I could take the train, but the Greyhound is cheaper."

"It's not that much cheaper, Henry. And this time you're going in style. I've got a little cash hidden away, some I've saved up for emergencies. I think there's enough for you to stop off in Olympia and buy yourself a new pair of shoes. There's nothing more telltale than a run-over pair of shoes on a man and a frayed shirt collar. And I'll borrow a suitcase. Mamie Clark told me once if you ever needed to you could borrow one of the doctor's alligator bags, one of those expensive ones she bought down in Nashville. Oh, Henry, you'll go in style all right. And you're still a very handsome man. You are. You've held up through these rough times a lot better than I have. I'm—I've lost my looks."

"No, no you haven't." Honor saw her father struggling. It was hard for him to tell a lie and not have it jump out in his eyes and in the way his mouth crinkled to one side. "You hardly have a wrinkle."

"I'm downright mousy. I am. I looked in the mirror at myself the other day and thought to myself, it's no wonder Henry looks at people like that Mildred Matthews. I'm sallow-looking and don't have a decent dress."

"If I do get a good job, we'll see to that. I'll send you to the beauty parlor in Parnell Point, and you'll go into Hartman in style too. A new permanent wave, a new dress, a pair of high heels, whatever you need."

"Oh." She flung herself around. "I never dreamed. Here I was worrying my head off, writing all those letters off in every direction I could think of. And all this time you were Mr. Foxy, sneaking one in on me. Did you have it sent in care of the school? Did that Beatrice Lacey know about it all this time?"

"Not what the letter said. She knew I got one."

"She's the most loyal friend to you and me both, Henry. When you think how she's stuck by you through thick and thin, covered up for you, and taken on most of the teaching load when she had to. Never a complaint."

"Sometimes she can be a pain in the ass."

"She does talk through her nose—those adenoids."

"She's been a good person."

"She loves to hear you recite poems. She told me. She thinks you missed your calling, that you should have been on the radio or something." Honor heard a strange, crackling laugh come out of her mother's throat. She could not remember when she had ever heard her mother really laugh before. "My goodness, listen to us carrying on about Beatrice Lacey when we've got so much to do to get you ready. When can you leave, Henry? What day? Just think, a county seat. County seats are always good towns. Can you imagine, after all these years up here on top of this mountain, we'll have real churches, concrete sidewalks! A real town, Henry."

"Let's hope it works out."

"It will. Oh, it will, Henry. You'll do fine. You'll have somebody who understands you again, somebody to share your ideas and like your poems. It'll all change again, back to how it used to be. Oh, I know it. I can just tell!"

9

It was decided at the supper table that night that the soonest, the very best day for Henry Jason Whitfield to catch the L & N train to Parnell Point would be the next Tuesday. The sooner the better, since there might still be a chance for him to fill a vacancy in one of the schools somewhere around Hartman for the fall term. He wouldn't be choosy. Any school, elementary or high school, located in or near the county seat, would be a step up from being the school principal in a four-room schoolhouse in Margate, Tennessee.

On Saturday, after a morning full of her mother's frantic efforts to get everything done for his big trip—washing and starching shirts, darning socks, giving orders this way and that to anyone in sight—Honor was relieved when her mother made a hurried trip to the kitchen sink, sudsed up the bar of Lux in the washpan, washed under her arms, threw on her pink-flowered dimity dress, pinned on her straw hat with the wobbly artificial pink rose on the side, dabbed Evening-in-Paris cologne behind her ears, and dashed out the front door and up to the garage in front of Dr. Clark's house. She was just in time to get a ride with Mamie in the big Packard to go to the regular bimonthly meeting of the Missionary Society.

She had shot out one last command as she was half-running toward the Packard: "Let your father rest quietly in bed this morning, Honor Jane. Stay outside and play."

But the day seemed to be buzzing round and round, like flies in endless circles. Honor slipped quietly back into the house and crawled under the dining room table. It would be a good time to try to work out the rest of the map for Lola. She had pumped Buford hard about where

108

the back roads were and which would be the easiest and quickest to take from behind the Stinnet house on out to the main highway. Lola was going to have to be sure of her route. One bad turn could land her right back in the state penitentiary.

After taking out her paper and pencil, she leaned back against the pedestal for a moment and listened to the house. It seemed to let out its own sigh of relief now that things had settled back down. She waited for the familiar creak here and there, and listened to a big black-green fly buzzing against the window pane over the sewing machine—the one piece of furniture her mother couldn't live without. And then she heard the deep, crunchy sound of the sagging bedsprings as her father turned over in the big double bed in the bedroom directly behind the thin dining room wall. She cupped her hands to her ears to hear better, and pulled up the flap of the tablecloth. She heard the distinct thump of his feet hitting the floor and what sounded like the vanity stool being pulled out. Her father wouldn't be sitting at her mother's vanity, would he, looking at himself in the mirror?

On her hands and knees, Honor crept out from under the table, being careful not to bring the tablecloth along with her. She eased up to the wall separating her from her father and flattened herself against it as closely as she could, just in time to hear the unmistakable creak of the vanity mirrors being turned and adjusted. She knew that sound well because she liked better than almost anything to slip into her mother's bedroom and sit at the vanity and pretend she was powdering her face, putting on lipstick, primping up for a fancy party. She knew exactly how to adjust the little side mirrors so she could see every angle of her face and even the back of her hair where it was cut up on her neck in a way she hated. But she had never heard of a man sitting at a woman's vanity, primping. On top of that, she could hear him talking to himself in the mirror.

"Maybe you can pull it off, Henry, old man. Maybe you won't sag in on yourself when you come face to face with what success means, when you see old tub-of-lard himself, Nathan E. Dobbs."

The muffled tone of his voice coming through the wall

made it sound as if he were calling out through a hollow log. Honor followed every word.

"At least you'll look okay. You're not so bad a specimen for a man in his late thirties." There was a silence. Honor guessed that he was looking at himself up close in the mirror. "Yeah, you'll pass physical inspection. Maybe Hartman, Kentucky, is a good idea at that."

His voice suddenly deepened, booming out like the radio announcer on "One Man's Family."

" 'You are but an impression, and not at all what you seem to be. . . . Don't you know, don't you remember, sir, that ideas shoot up like sprouts, wither and rot away, change into forms and come up again? . . .' "

There was another squeak of the vanity mirrors and the sound of the stool scraping back across the floor. He still had the radio announcer tone in his voice.

" 'Remember that you are an actor in a play, and the playwright chooses the manner of it: if he wants it short, it is short; if long, it is long. . . .' "

There was a laugh next, a loud laugh that seemed to be answering someone else's laugh. It gave Honor an eerie feeling.

"Good to remember you again, old friend, Epictetus. Stay with me, old buddy. I'm going to need every quote I can conjure up from those old rah rah days. I've got to give my friend Nathan some kind of show, present some kind of impenetrable front to my successful benefactor. But I must be very, very subtle. Wouldn't you agree? I must argue my cause, my need, that is, with subtlety."

His voice rumbled deeper, grander.

" 'The subtlety of nature is greater many times over than the subtlety of argument. . . .' Then, I shouldn't argue my position a'tall with Nate, old tub-of-lard, Natey boy. I should instead—ah, Nate is a nature lover. I should lead him to nature, take him back to our Walt Whitman days. Come with me, my noble benefactor with your round belly and your Jewish nose, and let us wander into the world of nature and celebrate ourselves!"

He laughed again, and his voice was hitting the wall at a higher pitch. Honor thought he must be standing somewhere near the foot of the bed, maybe looking at himself from a distance.

"Come Nate old fellow . . . 'I lean and loafe at my ease

observing a spear of summer grass. . . .' You remember that, don't you, Nate, those long hikes we used to take up the Gatlinburg trails in the Smokeys, when spring ran through summer into the browns of autumn, into the dark of winter grass? 'Darker than the colorless beards of old men . . .' But you and I, we aren't old men yet, Nathan. Look at me, still handsome, my wife tells me, wearing the years well, I still have cause to celebrate myself."

Honor had spread her hands flat against the wall, and her ears seemed to be throbbing from some deeper pulse in the back of her mind that was trying to understand what her father was saying, why he was spouting off poetry to himself. His voice seemed to be taking on a kind of deep moaning, a sad sound that reminded her for some reason of the time she heard Tootie Farber moan out loud over his only son's closed casket after he was killed in one of the cave-ins at the mines.

"'The smallest sprout shows there is really no death . . . And if ever there was it led forward life, and does not wait'—*does not wait*—how does it go after that? *Does not wait!* . . . I can't remember. Goddammit, I can't remember it all. Nate, remember when I used to stand at the foot of your bed while you were spread out like a beached blubber whale on your back looking up at me as if I were the poet saint giving you the nourishment for your soul? *Does not wait*—"

Honor heard a loud, crackling laugh, and then his voice rose higher, like the revival preacher getting ready to give the altar call after a long, down-deep sermon.

"'All goes onward and outward, nothing collapses . . . And to die is different from what anyone supposed, and luckier . . .' But it's all a goddam lie, Natey old boy!" His voice had reached that top blasting pitch. "It does collapse. The collapsing does not wait. I'm alive, Nate, but I'm really dead. But I am not the luckier kind of dead. I'm not lucky enough to die completely!"

Honor felt her fingers turn to a numbing cold, which seemed awfully strange to her, when her face was burning hot and her heart seemed to be pumping out fire in her chest. There was a humming lack of noise on the other side of the wall. And then she heard a deep muffled sound of him crying, her own father in there bawling like a dy-

111

ing bull. Because he was alive instead of dead and the wrong things were collapsing.

She'd have to do something. He couldn't cave in on himself and die off when there was a job waiting for him in a county seat town on the Mississippi Rver.

She raced on tiptoe into the living room, eased open the front screen door, and then gave it a vigorous slam, to make him think she was just coming in from outside. She tried to whistle a tune, but even "Yankee Doodle Dandy," which was easy, got stuck in her mouth, which was as dry as cotton. She had to give him some warning, a chance to hide his face all the way under the covers if he was ashamed to be caught crying like somebody little being shipped off to Georgia because they were born ugly, instead of acting like a man who was still handsome enough to beat the band and could quote enough memorized poetry verses to get his family moved off the mountain all the way to a big county seat town in Kentucky. Finally, she managed to sing with a kind of squawking sound:

> Way up yonder above the sky,
> A jaybird built in a bluebird's eye.

She tried to force a skip to her feet as she entered the bedroom where her father lay in a crumpled heap across the bed.

"Why, goodness gracious, Daddy," she said in as surprised sounding a voice as she could manage, "I didn't know you had turned sick, that you had caught a fit of chills and fever. Have you caught the typhoid fever?"

He reached up, fumbling with the covers, and pulled a pillow down over his head. "Go on back outside and play. I'm—"

"Don't you worry about a thing. I'll fix you up. I'm good at treating chills and fevers. I'm a real expert with migraine headaches. I'll have to get something from the kitchen."

That should give him time to straighten himself up a little, she thought, as she went to the kitchen, wondering what exactly to do next. Her mother always liked a cold washrag over her eyes when she had a nervous conniption fit or was getting over a crying spell.

She poured fresh water in the washpan, got two big

chunks of ice out of the icebox and dumped them in, took a pink washrag that didn't smell as sour as the blue one the boys were supposed to use, and went back into the bedroom, walking slowly so that she wouldn't slosh the water out of the pan.

When she came into the room, she saw that he had tossed aside the pillow and was lying on his back with one arm thrown across his face to hide his eyes.

"I've got some ice water here."

"You're not planning to dump it over my head again are you?" His voice sounded as if it came from far, far away.

"Oh, no. This is my special treatment for chills and fever." She put the washpan down on the vanity and twisted the ice cold water out of the washrag as best she could. "Here, I'll fold this up neat like a bandage and over your eyes it goes." She did it so fast that he wouldn't have time to worry about whether or not she had seen his wet eyes. "Ice-cold washrags are the best things in the world for fevers."

"They're not so hot for chills though."

She reached down and pulled the edge of the chenille bedspread up and covered him. "That'll help the shivers." She sat down on the edge of the bed next to him.

"What other remedies have you got?" His voice sounded a little closer, louder.

"Well, if I knew anything about how to use a razor, I'd help shave off some of those hair sprouts showing on your chin. You can't ride on the L & N to Kentucky looking like one of the Northcutt boys."

"I'll shave before Tuesday."

"Daddy, what's this Hartman town? Hartman, that's not a very fancy-sounding place. Is it really a big county seat town?"

"It's a nice town. County seat of Hartman County."

"Hartman is so ugly-sounding. Why, even our whistle stops in Bragg County 've got better names. Lookit— DuCasse, Bon Air, even Margate sounds better, and not one of 'em is as big as a wart on your finger compared to what a county seat ought to be."

"You can't judge everything by its name." He laughed one of those funny-sounding laughs again. Honor's eyes widened a little. "Words, words made up out of the alphabet—sounds—impressions. Oh, God."

"Here, I'd better give you a fresh treatment." She grabbed the washrag, wheeled around before he could stop her, and redipped it in the washpan so hurriedly that the rag was still dripping from the corners as she all but splashed it down across his eyes again. Then she took the bedspread and dabbed at the sides of his face. "There, that's better. Feeling better, huh?" She sat down on the edge of the bed again. "Won't be long now till the fever'll go, poof, just like that." She snapped her fingers. "Tuesday—why, on Tuesday you'll be all right again and ready to go catch the train. I just know you'll land a good job, Daddy. It won't make any difference if it won't make you rich. You'll be the best teacher they ever had. You can—maybe you can teach them poems they never dreamed of."

"Poems. People don't have much use for poems these days. Poets—God should have made a big cave for poets to hover in like bats."

"Not bats—bluebirds. Bluebirds are better for poets than bats." She looked with alarm at the way her father's mouth was twitching as if he was tuning up to cry again. She'd have to think of something to get his mind off poems.

In a moment she had decided what to ask him. "Daddy, do you really believe in God? I mean, really God, not the Baptist rendering."

There was a thickness in the air that seemed to hang above the folded washrag. Finally his voice came out, slowly, far-off again. "Why—why did you ask me that?"

"I was just wondering. I mean, well, I don't, exactly. I believe in—promise you won't tell Mama on me."

"I promise."

"I believe in the magic bluebird, and something on behind the blue sky where the bluebird lives. Something bigger and more magic than the bluebird—though it's pretty magic—something that doesn't have a shape like God or Jesus that Preacher Pullum's always hollering about. Not like those pictures in the *Bible Stories* book. It's kind of floaty and one of the prettiest streaked kind of light blues in the whole world. And it won't let anything or anybody backbite at it or look hateful looks when they're trying to smile a sugary-sweet smile, or go around with any kind of killing whatsoever in their souls, like all the Baptists do."

Her father suddenly reached up and pulled the washrag

114

off his eyes, dropped it to the floor, and propped himself up on one elbow. He looked at her hard. "Not all Baptists have killing in their souls. Don't make the same mistake they do and generalize—lump everybody into the same shoebox with a size six on it."

She looked puzzled.

"Size six. I wrote a poem a long time ago. I called it "Six is a Shoebox." But it was a lousy poem. It's just that I tried to say something about clichés, generalizations. Maybe you'd better get that wet washrag off the floor. Your mother won't want any spots on her floor."

Honor bent over and picked it up and then looked at her father closely. She didn't think anybody would guess he had been crying. "You look like you could use a smoke. You want me to load up your pipe with some Old North State—I mean, with your tobacco—some Prince Albert?"

"You've been snitching some Old North State again? Your mother told me the other night she thought she'd been smelling tobacco on your breath. Your mother's pretty handy with the hairbrush. Better watch your step. She hits hard."

"It's just the Baptist in her, that's all."

"You mean, it's her way of killing?"

"It's—well, one of 'em. I don't mean to sound sassy. I don't mean not to honor my mother according to the Commandments." She didn't want her father to pick up something she said now, pull it out of his hat some night if he ever got on a mean drunk again, and use it against her to really bring on a whipping.

"I didn't think you sounded sassy," he said. "Honor, there's something I'd like to say to you—try to say." He rubbed the stubble of his beard. "Sometimes people can't help being the way they are, can't help the causes that made them." He started over again. "Let's say a baby is born. Life tugs at it, this way and that, molding it and shaping it, most often, I think, against its born nature. Sometimes a pestilence, a kind of sickness of the soul, sets in along with the other molding and shaping. Maybe it's nobody's fault in particular but the gathered faults of a lot of people, a long history of people. It runs, this sickness, through the makeup of a person until they don't even

115

know it's there. You call it 'killing in the soul.' But maybe it's a killing in the soul to keep from being killed."

"You mean like Lola's slicing that white man's throat when he tried to make her do certain things?"

"That's—that's a drastic example. But, yes—well, yes."

"How do people ever get rid of it, the sickness of the soul?" She picked up the washpan and turned in the direction of the kitchen, lingering for his answer.

"They don't. At least, most of them don't. Sometimes they might though, if they could just hold on to their own beliefs, their dreams, their ideas, long enough, tough enough and not bend to the ways of the horde." He sat straight up in bed. "Wait a minute. Don't go."

She had already reached the doorway. She stopped a moment, uncertain. He had a kind of wild, anxious look on his face, as if perhaps he had just seen a black panther in a nightmare, or maybe Lola standing at the window with a razor dripping blood. "Honor, listen to me. You keep believing in that bluebird of yours, you hear me? Don't trade it in for anybody else's beliefs, in God, in anything. Don't listen to any loud, fist-pounding revivalist, to any voice of any kind that tries to persuade you."

Honor looked at him as firmly as she could. "You'd better get back under that cover. You're catching the fever again."

"Hear me. Listen to me. Don't let anybody tell you, you are wrong. They'll destroy you. They'll kill you and your bluebird. They'll scald it and pluck out every feather, one by one, and then roast it and eat it before your very eyes. They will. They did it to me, to my poems. To me! Honor Jane!"

Honor ran into the kitchen, the water sloshing out of both sides of the pan. She threw it into the sink. In the hallway, she could hear her father's voice coming closer. "Don't let them, Honor!" she heard him screaming.

Her heart was pounding in her chest, setting it on fire. "Daddy, oh, poor dead Daddy!" she cried as she ran out the back door into the blinding hot, white August sun.

10

Honor ran across the backyard, behind the coal shed; she was just ready to climb up the wooden fence onto the roof of the shed when Lola's voice caught her in the middle of her spine.

"You running away from a ghost or something?"

Honor whirled around, still holding the fence post with one hand. Lola was standing in the lower corner of Dr. Clark's acre-wide side yard where he kept his chickens and two tom turkeys. Honor was so startled by the unexpected sight of Lola there that she didn't answer.

"If you ain't really got anything special to do up there on that roof, maybe you'll climb over the fence here and help me round up this scrawny rooster I'm s'posed to get on the stove for supper. I never saw no kind of chicken scatter and skitter 'bout fast as this old dude."

Honor climbed over the fence slowly, keeping one eye out for the biggest tom turkey, the one Buford had told her was so mean it would chase you and peck your eyes out if it got half a chance.

"What's you so scared of? Chickens ain't going to bite you." Lola was pulling her apron up like a net. "You told me once you wasn't scared of nothing or nobody."

"That big tom turkey, he'll peck my eyes out."

"That big tom ain't budging off his roost 'less'un that is somebody shoots it full of BB's. Somebody pelt me with a BB gun and I'm going to try to peck his eyes out too. Now you head him off over thataway. I'll close in from this direction." She flung the apron out in front of her like a white flag and started throwing her arms around like a windmill. "Shoo ... shooeee ... shooo ... head him off. There. Ah got him!" She closed in with one enormous

117

sweep of arms and apron flying in all directions and tucked the rooster into the trap of the apron.

Honor was watching Lola, who was breathing hard. She wondered how Lola was going to walk five miles down a rough wagon road to escape if she didn't have wind enough to chase a rooster into a corner. But suddenly she was transfixed by what Lola was doing.

She had yanked the old rooster out from her apron and had it by the neck. She was flinging her arm around and around, the chicken feathers flying. Before Honor could catch up with the fast-flying arm, the rooster's body was on the ground, flopping about wildly, this way and that; and Lola was tossing its head, the eyes fluttered shut and the red crown like melted rubber, into a clump of bushes over near the fence. She knew all chickens had their heads wrung off, but she had never seen it done before. She felt sick to her stomach at the sight of the flip-flops of the rooster slowing down and finally stopping altogether. It reminded her of the time Buford had chopped off the head of a snake, and they had stood watching the rest of the snake's long body twist and curl about for what seemed like a long, long time before it stretched out still, like a piece of rope. She wondered if people would flop their arms and legs around still trying to run if somebody chopped off their heads.

She swallowed hard against the throwing-up feeling rising steadily in her throat. Lola bent over and picked up the rooster by its feet.

"You want to help me pick it clean?" she asked, heading toward the house. "You ever pick a chicken before?"

"No," she said, swallowing again. "I don't know how."

"I'll show you. Come on," Lola said, matter-of-factly.

Honor followed obediently. One part of her was curious, curious to see and curious also to talk more with Lola about the escape map and the new back roads she had asked Buford about; but another part of her wanted nothing more to do with killing chickens or eating them either, for that matter. She followed along silently.

"I got my water boiled up ready," Lola said, stopping at the big iron pot where two crossed logs were burning, licking out flames, and sending the smell of burning oak into the hot August sun. She plopped the rooster, feathers and all, into the iron pot. "Mrs. Clark, she don't like no chicken feathers inside her kitchen," Lola said. "We got to do the picking outside." She fished out the scalded rooster with two sticks and carried it over to the porch of her house, where she had an old bent-up dishpan waiting. She sat down in her chair, putting the dishpan in her lap. "See, first you got to scald it good, then 'at makes them feathers come out nice and easy. Then you jes' starts in, one by one."

Honor had never seen anyone's fingers go so fast, even Miss Lacey's playing "Under the Double Eagle" on the upright piano in the schoolhouse.

"You want to try your hand at it?" Lola held up the rooster that was already half-cleaned of its feathers. Honor wanted to draw back from the sight of the pimply skin with the little holes that were turning a bluish color where the feathers had already been picked. The skin of the rooster looked shivering cold. "I'd rather watch you," she said, looking off at the top of the sycamore tree.

Lola finished quickly, dumped feathers and innards inside some folded *Nashville Banners*, and dropped the package into the rusty barrel beside the kitchen steps. "You never seen no chicken picked before?" But she didn't seem to want an answer. She walked over to the iron pot, holding the picked rooster by its feet, and dropped it back into the boiling water. "I'll let that old bird soak a minute whilst I clean out this pan here." She went over to the hydrant and rinsed out the dishpan, propping it up against the house to dry in the sun. "You sit there on the porch a minute while I get this ole Buckeye Jim of a rooster out of the flies." She opened the back screen door. "Good thing ain't but two 'specting to eat off this scrawny thing."

Honor looked up, surprised that Lola had remembered the name of Buckeye Jim. Somehow, hearing her call the poor plucked rooster that made it easier on her stomach. She sat back down on the edge of Lola's porch to wait.

Lola was gone longer than she had expected. She could hear the pots banging, the cabinet doors in the kitchen closing, the big refrigerator door banging shut. Then Lola started humming, above all the other sounds she was making, running her voice up and down like a fiddle bow, only deeper and nicer sounding. It made Honor's arms feel as if they had just been feather-picked.

119

"You sing nice," she said when Lola finally came back out and sat down in her chair and leaned back against the wall. She took out her snuffbox, got a dip ready, and looked down at Honor.

"I used to sing a whole lots. Sometimes I feel like it. Most of the time though, since it happened, shut off in the pen and stuck off up here, mostly I don't let out and sing no more. Humming ain't the same as singing."

"Do you feel like singing now?"

"Naw. I feels like catching my breath and sucking on this snuff here. All that chasing, running ole Buckeye Jim to yonder and back's done wore me out. Lola's getting old, rusty in the joints."

Honor looked at her, studying Lola from head to toe. "Do you think you'll be able to make it all the way on foot from here to the highway?" she asked.

"I ain't going no place. What's I got to be worrying about that for? Lola ain't got no business on the main highway till I got me someplace else to head on out for from there."

"But you are going to. I mean, you won't be staying on in Margate with everybody planning to pack up and leave with the mines closing down."

Lola was leaning back, her eyes half-closed, as if she was studying a cloud floating by in the sky. "Ain't no big rush. The time to go has to be the right time to go."

"Well, when it does get to be the right time, that is, if you need it, well, Buford told me about this old sawmill road that hooks up to the main highway on down past DuCasse. You pick it up just behind Ruthie's aunt's house, on that road I drew on the map for you." Lola didn't seem to be paying much attention. "That's a good sawmill road, easy to walk on, Buford says. It runs alongside the Northcutt property. 'Course, it don't run on it. The Northcutts'll blow anybody's head off steps foot on their property." Lola might as well get every warning she could.

"Now, don't you go fretting around 'bout Lola and them back roads. Lola's got a few plans on her own, and they don't have to get no nice little girl like you mixed up in 'em. You the type allus going to end up getting caught. You ain't bad enough inside to get by with anything. You ain't evil. When you's good, you gets caught."

"Is that why you got caught when you killed that white man?"

"I reckon, maybe." Lola closed her eyes all the way. "How you and your family getting along these days?"

Honor looked at Lola closely, to see if she could find any signs on Lola's face that she might have heard her father yelling out in that crazy-sounding way.

"Tolerable," she said, not being sure.

"Your daddy found him a new job yet?"

Honor changed her position, leaned back against the post that seemed to barely support the tin roof of the porch. She took a small twig and traced a crack in the floor, up and down, up and down. "He's got a good chance. Fact is, he's leaving on the L & N passenger train from Olympia next Tuesday, riding all the way to Parnell Point, Kentucky; and once he gets off the train, one of his old friends, a real rich man who used to be Daddy's college roommate, is going to meet him and ride him in to Hartman. Hartman's a big county seat town, and Daddy's going to try and get him a school to teach in. He might have to start out low on the ladder, but he 'spects to work his way back up to school principal. Only it won't be the same. Being school principal in a big county seat town is more important than being one in a place like Margate's dinky little ole schoolhouse."

"That sounds mighty fine, it do."

"Mama was so excited when she heard about it she 'bout wet her teddies. Ever since, she's been running around like a chicken with its head cut off—" Suddenly she stopped short. For as long as she could remember, she had been saying that expression, but now that she had actually seen a rooster flopping around like that, it didn't sound right. Her mother's running around was in a kind of mixed-up, happy way—not like the rooster fighting up to the last ruffle of its feathers.

Lola suddenly laughed, a cheerful, light-sounding laugh. "You so funny-looking when you get all serious like that. You too little a girl to go 'round being serious all the time. You got to quit taking everything to heart so much. Now, you take that scrawny old rooster. That old dude done had his day out there struttin' his stuff with all them big sassy dominicker hens. He's one of the tiredest old roosters you'll ever see, else he ought to be. Why, he's led

121

him a dandy life being king of the coop so long, but he ain't good enough for them feisty hens no more. See that big dude sitting over there on the fence post?" She pointed at the rooster perched by the gate. "Look who's Mr. Shit-on-the-Stick over there now. Loudest cock-a-doodle-do you'll ever get outa a rooster. Now, you take poor ole Buckeye Jim. Considerin' how good a job he did all that long time, don't you think it's fittin' for him to go out in style, smelling up with all that good sage and sitting there so dandy in a big fluffy pile of Lola's dumplings and gravy? He never knew what got holt of him when I wrung off his neck. I'm good at that, don't make 'em suffer a'tall. Lola just hopes when her time comes, it'll be as easy on her as ole Buckeye."

Honor didn't say anything for quite a while. She kept tracing idly with the twig. Lola leaned over and spit onto the ground.

"Lola, what would you think if you—of a man who bawls like a baby?"

Lola thought a minute. "Depends on what he's bawling 'bout."

"What about if he looks in vanity mirrors at himself and starts making speeches out loud?"

"Well, that'ud depend too, I reckon. If he thought he was all by hisself and there wasn't no big ears listening, maybe he'd just be needin' to test out somethin' on his mind to see how it'ud sound. Sometimes things sound different when you're just saying 'em inside your own head and when you say 'em out loud. They sound all cockeyed sometimes, out loud, not what you had in mind. It's smart sometimes, testin' things out loud before you say somethin' cockeyed you can't take back, once somebody's heard it."

"But what if it's something like—just poems mostly?"

"I'd say, well, I'd say just let him be. Let him say whatever he needs to say out loud to hisself. And I'd turn my little ass around and back off and let him be." She waited a moment. "Spying's not so bad sometimes, but if'n it's spying in on a man's soul, it's wrong. See, sometimes a man gets a lot of his own kind of grief built up. He gets turned upside down backward inside hisself and don't know whichaway to turn next. This world can be hard on its men. 'Specting everything outa them. Always got to

122

show how strong they be. Got to be the biggest rooster with the biggest, biggest cock-a-doodle-do."

She laughed to herself, rocked down so the chair was no longer tilted on its back legs. "Yep, mens is always s'posed to prove something. Some is stronger, some is like the runt in a litter. Some likes one thing, some likes anuther. Only one thing I guess they all likes." She stood up and stretched, putting her hands in the small of her back. "That Missionary Society bunch, what time you s'pose they let out today?"

Honor shrugged her shoulders. "I guess they'll have a lot to talk about and vote on, everybody getting ready to try and relocate."

"Maybe it'll work the other way 'round," Lola said, taking one last look at the sky and the top of the sycamore tree. "You ain't noticed something. Ain't been no blue jays in that sycamore tree since, well, since Lola tended to a little business."

Honor looked up, amazed at the sudden thought that she hadn't heard a blue jay squawking all day long.

"Well, I 'spect I'd better get ole Buckeye fixed the rest of the way up. Got to make him look his best." She opened the screen door and turned back for a moment. "I been a'thinking and a'thinking 'bout what you told me the other day 'bout that magic bluebird of yours. I'd like to see that nice bird sometime. I'd be obliged if you'd point him out to me."

Honor looked at her curiously and saw that Lola's face was serious.

"He might fly over one of these days," she said, and took the same way, through the side yard, home.

11

On Sunday, it was decided in the open discussion period, before Preacher Pullum lit into his regular weekly sermon, that since Black Diamond Coal Company was indeed closing down its entire Margate operation the revival should be pushed up ahead of schedule to the first week in September. The layoffs had already begun and the official word had been issued through the mine's foreman. Everyone, in the year ahead, was most likely going to be scattered to the four winds, relocating, so the revival would be before school started and before bad weather set in, and not held off for the usual weekly run in spring, the week before Easter.

"We'll make this the best revival to ever hit Margate," Preacher Pullum yelled out to the congregation that to Honor seemed much larger than usual. Not only were all the desks and regular chairs filled in the main seventh- and eighth-grade room of the schoolhouse where town meetings and church services were held, but extra folding chairs had even been lined up in front of the stage. Miss Lacey sat with her fingers resting on the keyboard of the upright piano, waiting for the cue to start the last hymn before the sermon. "We'll make this mountain top ring with God's word!"

Revival week, next to Christmas week, was Honor's favorite time of year. Not only did the whole town of Margate turn out, Baptists and Methodists, and even those who normally wouldn't set foot in any church door, but they came from far back in the mountains. Holy Rollers traipsed in, in droves, all of them seeming to want to outshout the next one, or else steal the whole show away from the Baptists.

The schoolhouse wasn't big enough for revivals, so volunteer men got together with axes and saws and hammers and hacked out a selected spot in the woods next to Charlie Blaylock's filling station, where they could run electricity off his wiring and borrow his RC and Coca-Cola iceboxes. Sawdust from the log cutting was spread out on the ground to make a soft floor. Rough benches were made out of planks milled on the spot and hammered together. The roof was made from the leaves and the branches of the cut-down trees. These were all heaped and laced in a tight network overhead, forming the "brush arbor" where only the church-going regulars and converts were allowed to have a privileged seat on the benches. At the far end, an altar was built, leaving plenty of elbow room for the traveling evangelist's musicians to play their guitars and fiddles and bang their tambourines. Sometimes they brought along a portable organ, and last year, Honor remembered, the tambourine player had a big bass drum on the side that he beat every time somebody got caught in the beginning throes of seeing the light.

Even the Bohunk men came to the edge of the revival, driving their teams of horses, pulling wagons loaded down with fruit jars and RC bottles that were tightly corked and filled with ruby-red wine. Their fierce German police dogs were chained to the wagon seats, barking and growling low at anyone who came near the wagons. Honor liked to watch the olive-skinned Bohunks with their shiny black eyes. They moved in and out like shadows among the clumps of men standing far away from the brush arbor lights. The foreign accents of the Bohunk men fell softly, invitingly, among the other men, who would slip out, one by one, and head for the wagons, their hands already dipping into their pockets for their billfolds and loose change.

More than once at past revivals, Honor had seen Mildred Matthews swinging her hips and tossing her curly hair around, being followed farther on down the road than the Bohunk wagons, until she and whoever trailed her would be swallowed up by the night. Then she would come back just toward the end of the revival meeting and sit on the front fender of a car pulled in close, swinging her legs back and forth and looking as innocent as you please, as if she'd been perched there all along, and not just for the final altar call, which nobody wanted to miss.

Honor always tried to get standing room just outside the last string of electric light bulbs, so that she wouldn't have mosquitoes and moths diving at her, but could still be seen and at the same time watch what went on in the shadows out beyond the ring of big-eyed gawkers waiting for a good shouting fit to take place. She usually stood along with Ruthie Stinnet, so they could whisper and point out different things to each other.

As the open discussion droned on, with one question after the next being asked about the coming surprise revival, Honor tried to find Ruthie. Ever since the time when Honor had refused to play doctor and pretend she was going to have a baby and let Billy Cummings look up her dress, Ruthie hadn't spoken to her. She spotted her over by the window, sitting behind Billy Cummings' regular desk, sitting in a way that made the points of her new brassiere stick out for the whole world to see. Honor sank her own chest in, aware of the miserable flatness there, wondering if she'd ever fill out like Ruthie.

She turned her attention back to the open discussion. Ruthie could take her new lace brassiere and her games of doctor and go jump in Doe Creek Lake.

Miss Ada had the floor. She had worked herself up into such a stew that the vein on the side of her neck reminded Honor of a trapped wiggleworm as it bulged this way and that. Miss Ada was speaking her mind about who should take charge of the regular box suppers the Missionary Society always sold to help raise money to pay the Evangelists—not to mention who ought to bake cakes for the cakewalks and whose cakes weren't fit to eat. She was also presenting her idea of selling chances on a surprise box and was furious because someone from the back row had asked what kind of surprise box.

"We're a smart enough bunch to figure out a surprise that's nice enough to be worth spending a nickel on. It ain't what's in it that's the question here, it's the necessity of hurrying up and having somebody with a nice printing hand write up the chances and getting a committee appointed to go out and sell 'em. It takes a lot of time to get ready for a revival. And seems to me like—with everybody in this town knowing that our Missionary Society has always played the biggest part in raising money to pay those high-falutin' traveling revival preachers with those honky-tonk musicians that, in my opinion, do not exactly get across God's word in the way I think it is fitting—that somebody could've slipped us a good solid hint about the revival coming up so's we could have voted and appointed committees and got a head start. Why only yesterday we had our meeting."

"Set down, Ada Bly," came the low, unmistakable voice of Tootie Farber from the back of the room.

Then, somehow, Preacher Pullum had the reins again and Miss Lacey was playing the piano and everybody was standing up singing "Love Lifted Me." Even Preacher Pullum seemed to be tired out from all the extended open discussion and cut his own sermon far shorter than usual, and mercifully, the last "Amen" was sifting its way out over the heads of the restless congregation who had started waving their paper fans back and forth to beat sixty.

When the Whitfield family got home, Honor's father, in a good mood, took the boys out for target practice while Sunday dinner was being prepared. Honor sat on the edge of her mother's bed, watching her take off her straw hat, unsnap her dimity dress, and yank at the strings of her corset.

"I thought there for a minute we were going to be stuck with Preacher Pullum for the last revival," Honor said, looking with fascination at the deep crease between her mother's breasts where her brassiere pushed them in against each other. Honor wondered if she'd take after her mother in the chest, even if everybody said she was the spitting image of her father.

"Well, when you figure how little actual cash we've got left in the church's annual budget, he really ought to, by rights, preach it on his own regular pay," her mother said, carefully pulling off her hose. "Besides, I agree with Ada Bly. Those traveling musicians might as well bring along a ferris wheel. I swear that bunch last year stepped right out of a carnival sideshow."

"Will Daddy be back from Hartman in time to go?" Honor asked, remembering how last year her father had taken one too many trips to the Bohunk wagons and the whole family had had to sneak him into the back seat of the Oakland and drive off even before the altar call on the last big shouting night. Her mother had made excuses to

Miss Ada and to any bigmouth apt to talk that she had a migraine headache from all the sawdust being kicked around.

"I'm sure he'll be back in plenty of time. It won't take him but a few days, I suspect, to get the lay of the land." She jammed a hairpin in the back of her head and stopped to fan herself with a folded newspaper. "I'm so hot and sticky today I could die. And I feel like I picked up every smell from those Blaylocks stinking up the whole place. That Sadie, did you ever smell anything like that in your life? Wouldn't you know she'd plunk herself down right next to me. I thought I'd suffocate before church finally let out. It went on and on today."

Honor was looking at the opened alligator suitcase with the shirts carefully folded in one side, and the socks rolled up in little balls. For some reason, she was thinking about Lola, how she'd pack up when the time came for her to run off. She'd have to carry her things in a paper sack. A suitcase would be a dead giveaway.

Suddenly an idea came to her. She studied her mother's movements and expressions carefully by keeping her eyes on the vanity mirrors, as her mother went about hanging up her dimity dress and slipping into a housedress. "Do you think they'll let Lola go watch the revival?" she asked, as casual-sounding as she could.

"I can't imagine why she'd even want to go. She'd be— well, she'd certainly stick out like a sore thumb. Where would she even sit or stand? They aren't supposed to mingle, you know."

"Suzie Daniels always comes and sits as big as you please up on the car hood of Charlie Blaylock's wrecker, which is one of the best looking-spots around."

"But Suzie's different. I mean, well she's been among us so long, living out there on the Whitakker place and helping raise those poor little motherless children. Besides, she's half-white and all. Nobody has to worry about Suzie keeping her place."

"But why can't—I mean, if Lola wanted to be saved from her sin of killing that white man, couldn't she come up for the altar call?"

"They have their revivals; we have ours."

"I still don't see why she couldn't ride in the back seat of old Mamie's Packard like she does when she rides along

128

to buy groceries sometimes, just sit in the back seat and watch."

"I never want to hear you call that lovely lady, Mrs. Clark, 'old Mamie' again. That is not the proper respect." She dabbed under her arms with a handkerchief sprinkled with Cashmere Bouquet talcum powder. "Honor Jane, I've got enough on my mind, tending to the last-minute details to get your father off on that train on time on Tuesday, as well as fixing Sunday dinner. I certainly don't have time to stop and worry over the social life of some nigger killer let out of the state penitentiary, which I am not sure I approve of at all. And I never want to hear that you've been trying to hang around her doorstep either. Remember, curiosity killed the cat."

"I don't hang around her doorstep," Honor said.

"I should hope not. Unless you entertain the idea of maybe getting your throat cut open someday when she goes off in some blind nigger rage. They say they do that, they revert."

"To what?"

"To the jungles where they came from, that's what. And don't ever forget it."

12

Honor hadn't intended it, but for some reason she couldn't look her father straight in the eye. She kept hearing his voice yelling out in that awful way, chasing after her, and seeing him with her mind's eye standing before the vanity mirrors making poetry speeches to himself. She carefully kept a close watch on him though, when she was sure he wasn't looking. He seemed to have wound up some kind of toy machine inside himself that made his eyes dart around this way and that and made his hands kind of jerk at things, rather than move in that easy, calm way they usually did.

On Tuesday morning the whole family got up at sunrise, dressed, and gathered in the kitchen.

"Don't cook a big breakfast for me, Martha Jane," her father mumbled through the shaving soap lather from in front of the kitchen sink. "Some raw eggs in milk with a little sugar is all my stomach can take this morning. It's jumping around on me."

"Now you just quit worrying so much, Henry. Everything is going to be just fine. You're going to win over that whole town. And you don't have one thing to explain, to let on you're ashamed of." Honor tried to eat the egg that was too runny and keep an eye out on everything at once. Her mother was giving one last vigorous, stiff-haired brushing to the blue serge suit coat. "You look so handsome. I'm so proud of you, Henry. I just don't have the slightest doubt about your landing some kind of job. It won't have to be the top job, you know that. Just something that will get one foot in the door and give us that brand new start."

It had been agreed that, considering the questionable

state of the brakes on the old Oakland, and with only their father having experience driving around the curves going down the main highway all the way to Olympia, it would be best for the family to drive him only as far as the main highway in DuCasse and let him flag down the Greyhound. It would get him into Olympia in plenty of time to catch the afternoon L & N train into Parnell Point.

By half-past seven, the entire family had piled into the Oakland, and the last-minute flurries of checking on every little detail had been tended to. Buford and Stuart, for once, hadn't fought over who would get to sit by a window. They sat knee to knee, balancing the alligator suitcase between them.

"Don't streak it up with your greasy thumbprints, boys," their mother called over her shoulder from the front seat. "People are going to think your father is a very rich man, carrying such a fine piece of luggage. Wasn't that nice of Mamie, honey, lending it without a moment's hesitation? Dr. Clark, I declare, that man has a closet full of suitcases. And suits of clothes. I never saw so many suits, and all he ever wears is that same old baggy pair of gray-striped trousers hiked up with those suspenders." She lowered her voice, and Honor leaned over closer to hear. "From what I gather, he doesn't tend to things on the home front either. Hasn't for years, Henry. Which explains a whole lot, if you know what I mean, about Mamie's nervousness and all those migraines. She says he couldn't care one hoot and holler about anything in this world other than treating his sick people. And half of them hardly worth the saving. Some of those pitiful little ole white-trash kids would be better off dead than alive anyway. And with the mines shutting down, what's to become of some of these poor people up here, Henry?"

He didn't seem to be listening. He had let the motor chug and sputter itself into a warmed-up, smoother state. "Where's old Lucifer? I kind of wanted to tell him good-bye."

Honor thought he looked a little teary-eyed again.

"Goodness gracious, that poor old dog is probably still curled up asleep under the front porch. He'll be there when you get back, Henry. It's not as though you'll be gone till Kingdom Come and back. It's just a few days."

He let the emergency brake off and the Oakland coasted a moment down the sloping grade of the alley. At the turn into the main cinder road, he put the car in gear and spurted out over the little rise of cinders heaped in an edge where the road grader had passed since the Oakland had last been driven.

"Honor Jane, don't lean hard against that door," her mother flung back at her. "I don't want to have you falling out."

Honor sat up straight and stared for a moment at the back and angled profile of her father, who sat grimly behind the wheel, his knuckles tight as he turned the wheel this way and that, his eyes glued to the road ahead.

Before she realized it, they had picked up speed and were heading down the hill, across the hollow where the road turned off to Ruthie's aunt's house, the road she was definitely going to have Lola take. She pressed her nose against the window and watched the trees fly by in zips of shapes and colors.

"This hasn't been such a bad place to live," her father's voice came out with a lonesome kind of sound. "The boys have had plenty of roaming space. Boys need to learn to hunt and fish to grow strong. The air's such good mountain air."

"It's got its good points, that's true," her mother agreed, bobbing her head up and down. Honor wanted to reach over and push up a long hairpin that was slipping out from the wad of hair her mother had bunched up barely off her neck in her rush to get everybody out of the house on schedule. "It's time for a change though. It's time we moved on to bigger and better things. And we are. We will, Henry. Isn't it just wonderful that you have something reliable like a teacher's certificate and don't have to depend on something like digging coal for a living. Oh, we are lucky."

"I haven't got a job yet." His words seemed to move out one by one, like a turtle picking up one foot, setting it down, then the next.

"But that nice friend of yours, he'll give you a temporary fill-in job. He said he would. That was an awfully nice letter he wrote to you, Henry. And to think you never mentioned a word to me about it. Mr. Fox, you were. Oh, I'm just so proud of you."

132

The boys were getting fidgety, poking at each other and whispering.

"Settle down, boys. My stomach is kind of jumpy itself," their mother said, pointing her finger in a wagging warning. "Henry, it's going to seem awfully funny not having you around in the house. Sleeping all by myself." She let out a dry, nervous laugh. "Don't you go letting any pretty girls get your eye now. Don't get yourself sidetracked over anything."

Honor looked across out the opposite window at the clearing in front of Uncle Dave's house where the men gathered on Sundays to pitch horseshoes. It was full of speckled guinea hens pecking at the ground. And then the car was headed down the hill again, past the town pumphouse on the right side of the road, and on past the graded-off hill, the railroad bank, and Doe Creek Lake hidden behind that.

Buford pointed his finger at the railroad bed. "Yonder goes one of the Northcutt boys with his fishing pole. I bet he don't have a fishing license."

"I bet there ain't a game warden in the state of Tennessee who'd argue with a Northcutt over it," said Stuart.

"Just listen to you boys, *he don't, there ain't,*" said their mother, clucking her tongue. "When we do move to Hartman, or somewhere in the surrounding territory, you children are going to have to remember what you've been taught. You'll simply have to cut out all this mountain grammar, or lack of it. We've got to make a good impression, every single Whitfield included."

"I wish you'd wait until I have it all sealed up, Martha Jane." Her father braked the car at the stop sign by the highway, looked right and left, then sped across the highway and onto the dirt road that led up the hill to the rag store that was owned by a rich man down in Olympia and operated by Dorabell Hembree.

"Henry, where in the world are you going?" her mother called out in alarm.

"You are jumpy today," he said, biting his lip. "Just turning around and heading you back in the right direction. I don't want to risk your stripping the gears backing up. You aren't the best driver, you know."

"Thanks a lot. Thanks for building me up in front of the children."

"They know you're not a good driver. They've ridden with you before."

"Let's not start an argument now, Henry, before you get on the bus. I want you to leave on a happy note."

Honor wondered why her father had turned suddenly cross as an old bear. He was glaring ahead as he crossed back to the Margate side of the highway and pulled the Oakland over to the side of the cinder road.

All four doors seemed to fly open at once. "Be careful, children. Stay off that highway, boys. You'll get run over."

Buford and Stuart were running up and down in their bare feet across the pavement, waving their arms around like cartwheels. "I wish we had a pair of roller skates," Buford yelled.

"You can skate all you please when we move to Hartman. They'll have plenty of concrete sidewalks there for you to skate on. Now get off that highway."

"There's not a car in sight. Ain't nothing out this early."

Honor walked up to the stop sign and leaned against it, looking down the road in the direction from which the bus would come. The highway stretched out like a long gray ribbon, narrowed down, and came together with the white line down the middle in one final point that disappeared into the trees. Up the dirt road by the rag store, a big-eared hound dog stood barking down at them, disturbed by the unusual presence of people at the crossroads.

Her father had picked up the alligator bag and put it down next to the stop sign. He was just turning to say something to her, a smile on his lips, when her mother came from behind and tapped him on the shoulder. "Henry," she was trying to whisper, "I know I promised I wasn't going to bring it up again, but will you promise me once more, you won't, whatever happens, take a drink until you get back home."

"You're giving me a condition," he said, a strange smile hovering at the corner of his mouth.

"I wouldn't object, I really wouldn't, when you get back, to bring home a little Bohunk wine maybe to celebrate, if you'll just not touch a drop in all those hard-liquor stores. It's going to be an awful temptation for you, Henry, having extra money and all, and being so worried."

"I'm not worried." He looked down the highway.

"I think you've got plenty of money to do you, don't you think, Henry?" she said, twisting her wedding rings back and forth. "It's eighty-eight dollars altogether. That's a lot, Henry, but I don't want you to be caught in need. That friend of yours, what if he don't—he doesn't show up in Parnell Point to meet your train?"

"He will."

"But he might not. He might get it all mixed up. Maybe your letter didn't get there on time."

"I'll check into some hotel—boardinghouse—for a night. Get my bearings and then go on my own into Hartman. It's not that difficult, Martha Jane. I did grow up in Chattanooga. I have been around some."

"Oh, I don't doubt your ability. Don't pay any attention to me. It's just—I am nervous. I want everything to work out and—"

"It's here. It's coming down the road," shouted Buford, as both he and Stuart ran to the edge of the highway and started waving their arms back and forth like the railroad flagmen directing coal cars being hooked up to the steam engine.

Her father reached over calmly, picked up the alligator suitcase, and stepped up to the bus. The door made a swishing noise as it opened. Honor looked up at the grinning, round-faced bus driver.

"You going to bring along that nice little girl?" he said, booming out a laugh. "Where to, Mister?"

There was a flurry of motion as her mother flopped her arms around and the boys crowded in for one last look at the size of the tires on the bus and the big exhaust pipe.

Inside the bus, their father took a seat by the window and smiled down at them, waving his hand in one single gesture, like a salute. Her mother dabbed at her eyes under her glasses. And then the bus's wheels ground into the cinders, edged back onto the smooth pavement of the highway, and with one enormous groaning sound, rolled away.

Her mother seemed to gather herself up in one determined motion. "Come on, children, get in the car. And before we do, I want one thing understood. I don't want one single fight, one nervous action to distract me from my driving. I most certainly do not want you, Honor Jane, to

135

start in giving me instruction on how to drive. I won't need one bit of help from you on telling me when to mash in on the clutch and when to shift into second. You understand? Buford, you're the oldest. You may ride up front with me."

13

It was Stuart's turn to call for the ten o'clock mail that Thursday morning, over a week later, when the first letter from their father finally arrived. Since, for the first time in the Whitfield family, the children had all wanted to call for the mail, their mother had put it on a rotating basis, starting with the oldest. With the prize in hand, Stuart had run all the way home at top speed.

Their mother immediately called the three of them into the living room, where she directed them to sit, in order of age, in a row on the daybed. She sat across from them in the big armchair, her hands trembling as she ripped open the long, fat envelope.

Honor scooted as far away as she could from Stuart, who was breathing hard and smelling strongly of sweat and the Vitalis hair oil he had started slicking his cowlick down with. Buford was nervously cracking his knuckles back and forth.

"Do you children realize this letter is the first occasion your father has had to write me a letter since our courting days," their mother said, cleaning her glasses and adjusting them in a maddeningly slow way that made Honor start jiggling her feet up and down. "He used to love to write letters. And he had such a fine hand, a way with words. I wonder—Buford, will you please stop cracking your knuckles? And Stuart Lee, what is that clicking noise you're making with that sack of marbles? You've simply got to sit still, all three of you, so we'll all be able to think, to listen. It's—oh, this letter, whatever it says— it's so important. Honor Jane, if you're squirming around because you need to go to the bathroom, I wish you'd run this instant and get it over with."

"No Ma'am," she lied, holding her legs tightly crossed and trying to sit as still as possible.

"I just don't want anything making me any more nervous than I already am. I declare, I'm so stopped up, choked up, for some reason."

She opened the pages up full and for a long silent moment scanned the first page. "It's happy sounding. Oh, it is. It has a tone I recognize. And since it is addressed to all of us—"

She began to read, her voice dry and somehow distant-sounding.

> "415 Alton Avenue
> Hartman, Kentucky
> August 26, 1938

"Dearest Martha Jane and children,

"These past days (I cannot believe that almost a week has gone by already since I left you in Margate) have been so full of events, of one exciting discovery after another, each one happening in such rapid sequence and being of such significance that I hardly know where to begin. I feel as if some strange metamophosis is taking place. It is around me, inside of me; I am a part of it, it is me, and yet I have not caught up with myself. In one way, it is as if a part of me that has been stored away in mothballs in some old attic trunk is looking at me, while another new me is trying to look back."

Their mother paused, coughed to clear her throat. "Your father always did like to test everything out in writing, to explain. In case you all didn't get the meaning of that big word he used, it means change." She look at Stuart. "I would appreciate it if you'd put away that sack of marbles."

"When I got on that bus the other day, I was so full of self-doubt and a complete certainty that I would fail us. Maybe that isn't the right thing for a father to confess to his children. But I want you to know. I was sure that I could not help my family find a new way. I, personally, didn't, to be completely honest with

138

you. Had it not been for Nathan Dobbs, I fear that my life would still be a dismal mess right now.

"To set your mind free, Martha Jane, because I do know you tend to put a lot of stress on details, Nathan was there with bells on waiting to meet me at the train station. All five-feet-five of him, with that big grin spread from ear to ear and squinting up at me through those thick glasses of his. In some ways, he looked exactly the same as he always did. Of course, he is older, fatter, uglier, I guess. But behind all that is a giant of a man with a heart bigger than I could ever tell you. Martha Jane, I know your feeling runs deep against Jews, but you must promise me that you never apply one of those feelings to our friend, Nathan Dobbs. You must promise that on the very kind of oath that you took when you married me. It is that important to me."

All three children had a different question in the same breath. It was Buford's deeper voice that got the floor. "What's a Jew anyway?"

"It's a race, a religion. But I'll discuss that at another time. Not that I have any deep feelings, as Henry—your father—is implying. Being a Christian I naturally find—I'm not sure that I agree with your father on this subject, but right now, please, children, no more interruptions."

"I will tell you that Nathan has become a very well-to-do man around these parts. Perhaps there is a certain native, merchant shrewdness that comes with being Jewish. Regardless, he has done the right thing at the right time. He had his money stashed away in his own private vault, for instance, before the banks closed down. He had cash on hand to go around and pick up choice pieces of property for a song. This house where I am this moment, for instance, is his now. It used to be Captain Abercrombie's place, a man who made his fortune on the river, and who had lost a great deal of it before the crash hit. That wiped him out all the way, and when he died, his widow just couldn't hold on.

"Right now, I am sitting at an antique desk in front of a big window on the second floor in the guest bedroom. I am looking down, far below, at the Mississippi River sweeping around the bend. I'm also looking down over jagged rooftops. Some are blue, others are red, black, and green. They seem to be in layers, as the streets wind down the hill to the business district at the very foot. I see a huge merchant marine ship pulling in behind the seawall to dock. When we move here, as we are going to do, our house will not have so grand a view, nor will it be so grand a house, but we will be able to see a glimpse of the river from certain windows, and you will know then what I am trying to share with you now."

Stuart could not contain himself. "Will we get to ride on a riverboat, on a ship?"

"Will you let me finish? Sometimes I wish Henry wouldn't drift around so. Oh, it's nice reading, but I'm so nervous."

"But more to the point. I am not even applying for a teaching job, Martha Jane. Nathan feels there is no real future for me there. He thinks I have a good personality for selling, and he wants me to try my hand with his farm machinery. With the experience I have had dealing with the mountain people, he feels it will help me communicate with the regular, everyday, dirt farmer. Apparently, they don't trust him too well. There aren't many Jewish people in this area, and they seem to bear grudges against success.

"I will get paid a base salary and commissions on what I sell. Too, he wants me to help out collecting his rents, and learning, in general, about real estate. I never dreamed I could be as excited about a job. I feel a new hope for us all, a new life ahead.

"My specific plans are these: Nathan wants me to stay on here a little while longer, to get the feel of the business and to learn the ropes a little. I get the feeling that he wants company badly too. He has never married, and in spite of having so much, he seems lonely.

"However, he does understand that I'm a family man. He has already given notice to the family who is renting the house he owns where he wants us to live. We should be able to move in by January the first. In the meantime, I am going to drive up to Margate in one of the company cars and pick up some things I'll need, tend to loose ends, and make sure that you all will be settled there until Christmas.

"I know this will be a hardship on you, Martha Jane, but I will have money to send to you, and it will give you time to get packed and ready to move. We will spend one last Christmas in Margate.

"We won't move all the junk we have. Nathan has acquired a lot of extra furnishings along with some of the property he has bought up these past few years. He says he can practically furnish the whole house for us, if we don't mind second-hand things.

"I must stop writing now. Nathan will be by to take me out into the farm country soon. I will try to be home in another two weeks or so. I have written in my resignation to the school board. I am enclosing some money for you, Martha Jane.

"Boys, take care of your mother and your sister. You are the men of the house while I'm away.

Your loving husband and father,
Henry"

There was an awkward moment when no one spoke or quite knew what to do. The letter had excited each child in his own way. Honor was on the very edge of the day-bed, fighting the urgency to make a dash for the bathroom. And then, as if some violent storm had hit inside their mother, she bent over in one groaning explosion of sobbing that seemed to tear at her ribs and pull the very weight of her shoulders sagging toward her lap.

The three of them moved in a kind of huddle around the armchair. Buford put his arm around her shoulders, fighting back his own embarrassment over the newness of the gesture. Stuart looked as if, at any second, he would burst out into his own fit of crying. Honor found herself standing with her fists clenched, getting madder by the minute. Somebody ought to take charge.

"Stuart, go to the kitchen and fix Mama up a big whopping dose of salts in warm water," she ordered. "Buford, put some ice in the washpan, and bring me the pink washrag. She's going to need it, the migraine this'll bring on."

"I don't know how to fix up salts," Stuart wailed.

"Then I will. You stay with her, you hear?" Honor darted through the dining room, the kitchen, and into the bathroom, where she hurriedly relieved herself. In no time, she had dumped a tablespoon of salts in a glass that didn't look all that clean but, she decided, would have to do. She motioned for Buford to place the washpan on top of the Philco radio.

"Stop squalling and drink this down," she ordered her mother, whose entire body was still shaking with her sobbing.

Her mother gradually raised her head, swiped at her face with her apron, and took the glass with a hand shaking so badly that she could barely hold it. "Drink," Honor commanded again.

The room was silent. "That's an awful big dose," she said like a child, and drank it down, frowning disagreeably as she gulped swallow by swallow.

As she dabbed at her mouth with the apron and dried her eyes further, Honor stood with one hand on her hip. "Why're you bawling when everything is turning out so hunky-dory? Better than anybody ever dreamed?"

"I'm sorry to break down like that in front of you children," she finally managed. "It's just that I haven't, ever since he's been gone, I've hardly slept a wink, worrying so over whether or not he was safe, or somewhere wallering drunk. I didn't know. And I had so little faith in him." She started crying again, the tears sliding down her cheeks and her shoulders perfectly still now. "I'm ashamed, that's what I am. Ashamed of how I've been acting. I'm ashamed of—oh, how I look. What kind of impression will I make when I hit town. Look at me, I'm a mess. I'm a worn-out, dreary mess. A man, all he has to do is get slicked up in a suit with a nice haircut and shave and polished shoes and he looks fine. Me, I'll not measure up. Henry'll see me with his new set of eyes. Men get funny ideas when they start getting close to middle age. Oh, I shouldn't be saying this in front of you children. I don't know what's come over me."

Honor squeezed out the washrag and gave her mother a little push back in the chair. "Well, it's a good thing he

142

can't see you now." She placed the cold cloth over her mother's eyes. "You look like something on the wrong side of a mud fence."

Her mother smiled and dabbed at her cheeks, at the dampness from both the crying and the dripping wash-cloth. "Sometimes you sound exactly like your father, Honor Jane. Thank you, that feels good."

"Okay, boys, out!" Honor ordered her brothers. "Let's let her get a little peace and quiet. Maybe she can ward off a migraine."

14

After the letter came there was a shift in mood, a new feeling in the Whitfield household. It was as if the rubber band of nerves inside Martha Jane, which had been stretched out to that last fine line before snapping, had suddenly been released and had curled back in on itself. Honor watched the way her mother seemed to be smiling to herself, humming little songs off key, and sometimes looking as if her long skinny feet would break out into a Maypole dance.

The late August sun blazed as hot and humid as ever. But Honor had a feeling, for some reason, that the thermometer on the wall out by the back screen door had dropped way down.

Due to the lack of rain in the past eight weeks, Doe Creek Lake had dropped its level seven and a half feet, Uncle Dave had told those waiting in line for the ten o'clock mail that Friday. Honor noticed on the way home from the post office that even the branch water running under the footbridge had slowed down to a trickle. There was no sign at all anymore of the crawdad Moses, who, she decided, must have crawled back into his secret damp hole under the rock to wait out the dry spell.

Then, the next day, while their mother was at the Missionary Society's emergency meeting for the last-minute preparations for opening night of the revival, Buford found old Lucifer dead.

Lucifer had crawled away on his own; without one whimper to anyone he had found a quiet, secluded place in the far corner of the yard, out of everybody's way, behind a bush that had sprouted up beneath the rotted-out apple tree.

Buford took charge of the burial. They decided not to wait for their mother, whose good mood none of them wanted to destroy. The boys took turns digging the grave, and all three of them wrapped Lucifer carefully in an old tow sack Honor had found in the coal shed. After they had covered the grave and Buford had stomped the dirt in firmly, Stuart planted a cross of sticks bound together with a new sailor knot that wouldn't come untied. Honor placed the last straggly bunch of roses in a limp bouquet beneath the cross.

"You say the prayer, Honor," Buford directed.

"I don't know any dog prayers."

"We ought to think up something," said Stuart. "Lucifer wasn't just any old bird dog."

"Yeah, a registered bird dog like Lucifer ought to have some kind of special speech." Buford cracked his knuckles.

Honor wished suddenly that their father were there. He'd know just the right words. And he loved Lucifer better than anyone. She felt hot tears sliding down her cheeks, but she didn't know whether they were there because her father was going to be so sad over Lucifer—not having been able to tell him good-bye—or because of her own deep feeling of loss. "It was time for him to die," she finally said matter-of-factly, licking at her tears with her tongue. "He lived to an old age for a dog. Besides, he was the best bird dog to ever hit Bragg County. Everybody knows that."

"Yeah, he was." Buford had ducked his head and was popping his knuckles one after the other, first the right hand, then the left. "He would've had a hard time getting used to a fancy county seat town anyway—no fields to roam in."

Stuart swiped at his eyes with his shirt sleeve. "Yeah, a place like that ain't no place for a good bird dog like Lucifer."

"*Isn't any* place," Honor corrected, and turned away. They could think up their own prayers. She had her own low-sunk, buried feelings and sadness to sort out. Not just about Lucifer dying, but about everything that would no longer be a part of their lives once they moved off the mountain. Lately, the funniest little things had become very dear and precious to her, things she couldn't lock up in a round tin can: the smell of a honeysuckle vine, the

145

footbridge, even the same old bunch standing in line every day calling for the ten o'clock mail.

She could not stop crying. The tears seemed to slide out from some hidden well and ease out in trickling rivers down her face, even when she tried to hum a song, muster up a whistle, and wipe them away.

One thing she could not stand was for somebody to see her bawling, even if she wasn't making any crying noises. In a kind of frantic run, she headed around the side of the house and in through the front door, in a beeline for her favorite hiding place.

For a long time, she stayed under the dining room table, crying softly to herself.

The following afternoon, Honor waited impatiently for her mother to show some sign that they were going to opening night of the revival.

"I can't see any sense in hanging around that awful brush arbor meeting with every Tom, Dick, and Harry craning his neck just to see what's going on and not one bit interested in the preaching, not when—well, we simply don't have to worry any longer about pleasing anybody in this town, about doing what is expected of us." She threw her arms out in a wide-sweeping turn, as if she might break into a dance. "What a wonderful, wonderful feeling that is for me, Honor Jane, after all these years. Oh, I'm coming out of some of my mothballs too. You just wait and see."

"But aren't we going, even to the big shouting night?" Honor asked, keenly disappointed.

"I explained to the sponsoring committee at the meeting yesterday that I'd be perfectly happy to donate a caramel cake and one of my brown bread loaves everybody likes so much. I said I'd even pitch in a whole five dollar bill, not that I ought to, but it being the last time and all." She put her hands on her hips and laughed to herself. "I can't be expected to attend every night without my husband along to properly escort me, I told them. I guess I shouldn't have, but I did lay it on a little thick about Henry's new job. I wish you could've seen Ada Bly's and Maude Gates' faces. To think I'll never have to put up with the likes of them after Christmas!"

"But even if Daddy doesn't make it home by Saturday night, can't we go to revival?" Honor insisted.

"Oh, I'll take you children the last night, just as one last time for a brush-arbor meeting. They won't have those in a place like Hartman, you know. They'll have only dignified services with dignified ministers. Real churches with pews and an organ, and with a spire."

"Special church houses?"

"Just churches, not church houses."

"They won't be the same, you mean, as Margate Baptists?"

"Well, no, I mean, religion has the Bible as its pillar of truth, of course, but the ways of people do make a difference, a huge difference in how a worship service is conducted."

"It'll be the same, I bet," Honor said.

"No, silly, it won't. Oh, you'll see, you'll see. Now run on and find something to do. I want to get started on culling out all this junk we've called necessities all this time."

"Don't cull out anything of mine," Honor said. "I'm taking everything I own with me."

"Don't be so bossy, Miss Priss. We've got a long time to Christmas. Oh, I can't wait. I want to know what the house is like, the furniture he's giving us. I bet secondhand for him will be elegant, fine pieces of furniture." Her mother crossed her arms over her chest, hugging herself. "I really can't wait."

Then, finally, Saturday came, and by six o'clock that evening, they were dressed and ready to leave for the closing night of the revival meeting, with plenty of time for their mother to get a good bench and for the children to find their friends and stake out their standing-room places.

Honor sat rigidly in the unwanted middle place on the back seat of the Oakland, determinedly setting her mind to keep from breaking the long silence their mother would insist on during the drive. She didn't know which she dreaded the most, the silence or the fitful, jerking way her mother drove.

She tried not to listen to the uncertain chugging, clattering noise as the engine almost flooded. She concentrated instead on the artificial white rose bobbing on her mother's hat, showing how, starting under the rubbery

147

blue veins on the backs of her shaking hands, the trembling was running in nervous little ripples all the way through her and coming out through the droopy petals of the white rose.

For a moment, she tried to force Buford, with her stare, to look up from fingering his necktie and scraping his feet back and forth as if he were the one pushing in on the clutch and shifting the gears and applying the brake. When he wouldn't give her even a glance, she turned toward Stuart, who was staring out the side window looking as if he might be waiting for the county health nurse to give him a typhoid shot, clicking his teeth on his thumbnail like a squirrel chewing on a black walnut. She didn't like the way her mother drove, but at least she wasn't a fraidycat like Stuart.

They drove down Mrs. Ewing's hill and took the fork of the cinder road that led out the back side of Margate. As they bumped across the railroad tracks, Honor suddenly remembered they would have to go up Randolph Hill. No wonder Stuart was scared. She sat back in the seat herself at the fearful sight of the steep hill looming ahead. She wanted desperately to tell her mother to put the car in low right then, not to take a chance of stalling midway up the hill and maybe falling all to pieces and forgetting where the emergency brake was and having her long foot feeling around all over the floorboard instead of finding the place it ought to be. If the old Oakland started flying down the hill backward, out of control, they'd be goners. They'd be like a big-bottomed buzzard with its wings chopped off, plunging down and down and down through the big empty hole of air.

She squinted her eyes tightly together, just as the grinding noise of the gears did shift and the cinders flew out behind the wheels as her mother gunned it.

"Whew!" her mother said, arriving at the top and jerking the car back out of low. "I despise that hill."

Everyone seemed to let out a sigh of relief. And soon they were turning the last curve before the site of the brush arbor came into view.

"Lookit all the cars already lined up in the good places," said Buford. "Can we park up close so we can watch from the car fenders?"

"I'm turning around while it's still daylight and heading us back in the right direction. It'll depend on where I can find enough room to park."

"Then you'll need a ten-acre field," grumbled Buford.

"I won't need any of your smart-aleck lip. Be quiet and let me decide where to do the parking. And another thing, I don't want to be pestered by being nickeled and dimed to death tonight. I'm giving each one of you a quarter for spending money, and once that's used up, you'll just have to want."

She drove past the people already milling around the cut-out place in the woods, standing in clumps around the filling station. On up past there, she turned into the road that went into Pete Thompson's place, backed out slowly, and crept along the edge of the cinder road. "Over here there's nobody lined up yet. I'll take this side."

The car doors flew open. "Remember where we're parked, children. I want you back here as soon as the last 'Amen' is said. I don't want to get caught in the crowd leaving. Honor, are you going to sit with me?"

"No ma'am, I promised Ruthie I'd stand with her."

"You behave yourself, you hear me? Don't get any funny ideas, and don't go straying outside of the arbor. I don't trust everybody, even if it is a religious gathering." She was already waving her hand at Miss Lacey and hurrying toward the benches to get a seat near the middle.

Honor wandered over to the filling station and bought a Baby Ruth and a big orange drink and put her change in her pocket. Then she strolled around, keeping an eye out on the crowd and trying to get a glimpse of Ruthie Stinnet.

A long bright-blue van, which was really an old hearse painted up to look more like a rainbow, pulled into the reserved space by the side of the filling station. "BROTHER LIGHT AND HIS TRAVELING GOSPEL SINGERS" was written across the sides. Honor stood sucking on the edge of her big orange, but not actually drinking, to make it last longer, and watched the musicians unload.

There was a bustle of guitar cases, drums, men moving in and out, straightening their fancy shirt collars and brushing off their striped, shiny pants. Honor had slipped

149

around out of sight, but within easy hearing distance, where she could see from an angle.

"This is one son of a bitchin' place I'll be glad to get out of," said the skinny one with the big Adam's apple, yanking at his guitar. "Ain't it the shits?"

"Well, it'll buy the gas on down to Nashville, hep us make our way and try out for the Grand Ole Opry. Playing a brush arbor ain't the worst thing."

"Not for somebody's done had his back broke and can't cut the mustard no more." A huge, fat, grinning man who reminded Honor of the bus driver on the Greyhound slapped the one complaining on the back. "Ain't that right, Shorty Farnsworth?"

"Yeah, he wouldn't know a piece if he saw one."

"Yal better shut up and start acting like we s'posed to act. Get that holy look wiped on your ugly face, Pee Wee."

"Goddam. Least this is the last night. Maybe we'll get a hot-kicking holy roller stirred up. See us some good shouting."

After they had moved on across the side turn-in to the filling station and made their way over to the brush arbor, Honor sidled on through the gathering crowd, looking for Ruthie.

"Where you been? I been looking everywhere and then I just give up and came over here to hold us a place," Ruthie called out from over by the big wrecker truck.

Honor didn't hurry her step. She could play as hard to get as Ruthie had lately. She noticed Ruthie had the three top buttons of her blouse undone so you could see the lace trim on her brassiere. She had tangerine-colored lipstick smeared across her mouth. "Where'd you get the lipstick? Your mother know you're wearing lipstick?" Honor asked, coming up and climbing onto the hood of the wrecker. "How long you think we'll get to stay up here before Mildred Matthews comes and runs us off?"

"She's got her a new place. I've been every night and I know where she slips off to do it too." She looked at Honor smugly. "And who goes off with her and how much they pay."

"I don't care," Honor said, trying not to look curious.

"You want some lipstick?" Ruthie asked, taking out a

150

tube from a small pocketbook. "I slipped it off my big sister."

Honor thought about it a moment. "I don't reckon. Do you want some of my candy bar?"

"Peanuts stick in my tooth that's rotted. Listen, Honor, when everything gets going and they start whooping and hollering it up, I'll take you where we can watch Mildred Matthews. It's a lot better'n playing doctor."

"Won't we miss the shouting?" Honor wasn't sure about the taste coming up in the back of her mouth. "I don't want to miss out on the last altar call."

"We won't." Ruthie laughed, kicking her feet and grinning down at Billy Cummings who was sauntering past the wrecker. "Mildred starts in as soon as it's dark. She knows nobody'll give her any business while it's altar call. Other night, she took two on and still got back in time."

"I don't care," Honor said, taking the last bite of her Baby Ruth. "You're making it up anyway. I told Mama I wouldn't stray off away from the arbor."

"Mama's little baby. Shit." She jumped down from the fender of the wrecker. "If you're such a mama's baby, I'll find somebody else to go with me. It's not every day you get a free sideshow of Mildred Matthews on her back."

Honor jumped down and joined her. "If it's dark, then how do you see?" she asked. "You just talk about it because you've got playing dirty on your mind all the time. You're boy crazy, Ruthie."

"Look, if you don't want to see somebody do it, I ain't begging you to come along. It's easy to get somebody else."

"We'll get to watch part of the revival, won't we? I mean, first we'll get to hear some of the singing, the music?"

Ruthie laughed. "Sure, that'un plays the electric guitar is one of Mildred's regulars. He pretends he's going to get him a cold drink, but he's really slipping off with her. He goes off the minute the sermon starts, and he comes huffing and puffing back just in time to pick up his electric guitar."

"You're just making that up," Honor said stubbornly.

"Want to bet a dime?"

"Yeah, I'll bet a dime."

As they turned to wind their way around the edge of

the crowd to find a good standing place, Honor fell a little behind Ruthie, who was elbowing her way ahead without the slightest "excuse me, please." Then she was out of sight completely.

Honor turned this way and that, momentarily bewildered by the heaviness of so many people clustered together. In one way she wished Ruthie would just stay lost. There was something she didn't like at all about slipping off in the dark spying on somebody, whatever it was they were doing. Besides, dimes didn't grow on bushes.

At that moment, she felt a strange unseen pressure on her back, as if some magnet were pulling at a hard metal ball lodged between her shoulder blades. She wheeled around to the left, where three cars had pulled into a rutted-out place not fit for parking but where the viewing from the front car fenders would be excellent. Perched on the Whitakkers' old Ford jalopy was Suzie Daniels, no more than ten feet away, with those funny eyes of hers boring a hole straight at—at *me*, Honor thought, turning her head quickly to see if possibly Suzie was looking at somebody else just over her shoulder.

She stood in a stunned, fixed way, unable to move away from that robin's-egg blue eye doing a kind of speckled dance with the other light brown eye.

"You're the Whitfield girl, ain't you? Honor Jane Whitfield?"

Honor had never heard Suzie Daniels' voice before. It came out softly, reaching out through the little empty place between the Ford and the edge of the crowd. For some reason it reminded Honor of cold Karo syrup slow to pour out of the pitcher. Her own voice had turned to glue, and there was something about the way Suzie was looking at her, as if she knew some secret thing and was trying to send some silent message to her, that sent cold ripples up and down her arms and made her feet feel as if they had turned to sawdust.

When Ruthie's shrill, irritated voice raked against her back, "If you're going with me, Honor Jane Whitfield, then keep it moving," she fairly fell over her own feet in gratitude. But even as she stumbled along after Ruthie, bumping into Ada Bly's big leather pocketbook hanging off the crook of her arm in everybody's way, she could feel Suzie's eyes following her like the steady beam of a carbide light. Suzie wanted to tell her something—something about Lola. She'd bet her last dime on that.

15

<hr>

"Fans. Anybody want to buy a pretty paper fan here? Knock off the gnats and hep pay the preacher at the same time. Nickel'll buy you two." It was Uncle Dave, doing his part.

Honor reached in her pocket and pulled out the nickel and dime she had left. "I'll take two," she said, handing him the nickel.

He reached over and patted her on top of the head. "If'n they was mine, I'd give 'em to you 'cause you're my special little sweetheart." He picked out two of the cardboard fans. "I got one here with Kimmel's Funeral Home on the back and peacock feathers on the front, and one's different. One's put out by the printing house for the church and 'es got a pretty angel on it."

"I'll take two peacock feather ones," Honor said.

"I hear your daddy landed him a fine job. I hear you're going to be leaving us."

"Next Christmas," Honor said, examining the fans. "Right after Christmas we're moving into a big white house with lots of new furniture." She said it more for Ruthie's benefit than for his.

"I'm mighty pleased to hear it. Fans, anybody want a fan?"

"You're just making that up," Ruthie said, taking the fan Honor offered her and hitting the side of her leg where a mosquito had landed.

"Want to bet a dime?"

"Wait till I win yours first."

At seven o'clock sharp, the traveling revivalist came to the pulpit and pounded for silence. There was a last-minute hurrying and elbow pushing as people took their places. Honor and Ruthie pushed in directly behind one of the posts holding up the roof of leaves and branches. "We don't need to look out for Mildred till dark," Ruthie said.

"Brothers and sisters, I see we've got us quite a gathering here tonight, and I aim to find out how much the spirit of the Lord is here among you, all you sittin' here inside who are the regulars and all you who's dropped by the wayside standing out there looking in. It don't feel so good, standing on the outside looking in. You know, don't you, you missing out? You know the word is here and the way is here and Heaven is up there, and some of you seem bound and determined to find out the hard way where Hell's at." There was good-humored laughter among the crowd. "Well, I'm Brother Light. That's what they call me. My real name's George B. Skinner. Brother Light is a name I've earned because I've been blessed by God. Yes, ever since I saw the light myself and went off the pathways of sin, I've been leading others to God. I've led so many into the fold they nicknamed me that. I ain't bragging. I'm just thanking God right here in front of you fine people that I've got this one last chance to maybe say the right thing here tonight that will bring some of you standing out there looking in right down that sawdust aisle there to fall on your knees and give yourself to God. I hear the mines is a'shuttin' down and a lot of you people will be out looking for new jobs. You're going to need the Lord to lead you in the right path, brothers and sisters. You put your faith in God. You listen to Brother Light here and these fine musicians. These gospel singers came all the way from Knoxville from the thick of the Smoky Mountains to play their guitars and fiddles and show you how God means his gospel songs to be heard. Yep, we've got some fine music for you. I think I've got the feeling here in my breast tonight to show God, to show you, what you've been missing, standing out there looking in." Then he turned and looked down and pointed his finger across the wave of faces looking up from the benches. "Don't think I don't see backsliding written all over some of your faces too. You regulars ain't all that righteous. There's more'n one of you sitting there squirming right now, wondering if God'll forgive you for the evil inside

155

you. Sometimes I don't know if it's worse standing out there looking in and knowing you're a bare-faced sinner or being a hypocrite sitting inside here on a bench. I'm not accusing any one of you. I'm just saying, if the shoe fits, God knows it. *You* know it. We're going to open tonight, our closing night, with some fine guitar and fiddle playing and gospel singing." He stepped aside and waved to the musicians.

Honor punched Ruthie. "Which one is Mildred's regular?"

Ruthie looked around to see if anyone was listening. "Shh, not so loud, dumbbell. It's that'un playing the electric guitar, that'un they call Pee Wee."

"Which one is Shorty?"

"It's Pee Wee you keep your eye on. When he ducks off to the left, it means he's going to be excused. When he goes to the right side and puts his guitar all the way down in the case, then he's going to find Mildred."

"I don't see Mildred," Honor said, looking around.

"She waits till they get going good. Then she saunters around. She don't sit perched up hiking her dress above her knees like she used to. She does different things now."

Honor turned to listen to the music.

He's the Lily of the Valley, the bright and morning
   star,
He's the fairest of ten thousand to my soul.

The preacher stood up and waved his arms in the air. "Everybody join in! Raise your voices to the Lord!"

He'll never, never leave me, nor yet forsake me here,
While I live by faith and do his blessed will,
A wall of fire about me, I've nothing now to fear,
With his manna he my hungry soul shall fill.
When sweeping up to glory, to see his blessed face,
Where rivers of delight shall ever roll,
He's the Lily of the Valley, the bright and morning
   star,
He's the fairest of ten thousand to my soul.

Then the electric guitar took the lead, and the one called Shorty picked up the drumsticks. "They're better than the ones last year," Honor said, whispering.

156

"They're all so old and ugly though. Last year they had that cute one with red hair."

"You're just boy crazy, Ruthie. How they look don't mean how they play."

"Here she comes." Ruthie poked her hard in the side. "Look, she's made her so much extra she's bought her a new polka dotted dress."

Honor didn't see her at first, because there was a shifting in the crowd as different ones turned this way and that, getting ready for the next number from the gospel singers who were tuning up again. Ruthie jabbed her harder and motioned over her shoulder.

She had never seen Mildred up so close before. As the red and white polka dots swayed nearer, a strong drift of perfume seemed to hang in the air. Honor found herself waving the peacock feather fan back and forth, then turning it around so it said Kimmel's Funeral Home. She didn't want Mildred to see her staring, but she couldn't help taking in the bright red lipstick to match the red polka dots and the way Mildred was chewing her gum, kind of rolling it out on her tongue and at the same time grinning up at Lucian Arnold, who was already turning his back to the singing.

"She's been after Lucian all week. I bet Lucian got paid yesterday. He's got him some money, wanna bet. Come on, Honor." Ruthie pulled at her.

Honor hesitated, then, fanning herself, tried to pretend she was hot and was moving out for some cooler air. "Hurry," Ruthie ordered her, and darted around behind the crowd.

"But Mildred went thataway."

"I know she did, silly, but I know where she ends up. She uses the back of Tootie Farber's car 'cause she knows Tootie and Uncle Dave are the last to leave and won't catch her. And they don't take time out for a nip off the bottle either." Hurrying along behind Ruthie wasn't easy. Honor felt her feet climbing one on top of the other, getting in her way every other step. "Don't go so fast. I can't see," she called after Ruthie, who was out in the road running.

"Come on, we've got to get up on the bank before they get down there."

"How do you know where they go?" Honor asked, when

157

they had scrambled up the bank. "I can't see for nothing, Ruthie. What if there's a snake up here or poison oak?"

"There ain't neither. Shhh. Billy Cummings showed me."

"You and Billy—you've been playing dirty too?"

"Nothing that's any of your business. I don't like him anymore. Now be quiet and listen."

"I dropped my fan."

"You can have this one back. I don't need no fan."

They had spread out, on their stomachs, behind a bush. "We can't see diddly squat from up here," Honor fretted. "Besides, there's not anybody coming down here. Listen, all you can hear is the music playing. He's not even preaching yet. We're missing out on the music."

"She has to make her pitch, silly. She's got a crush on Lucian anyway. She likes him for real, but he knows she puts out, and he won't give her the time of day."

"You said he was going to. You said he got paid."

"Listen. See, I told you. I hear her high heels on the cinders. Hear her giggling? Don't breathe out loud. Don't make one move, Honor Jane Whitfield, or we'll get skinned alive."

"I know you had the wrong idea about me," Mildred was saying, giggling low. "What people make up and say behind your back is just downright awful. Just because I'm of my own mind and know I'm better looking than most girls around these parts, they've got to say things about me and call me—I know they call me a whore."

"I don't call you that. I don't call you names," a deep husky voice was saying. "I just thought you—I mean they said you liked money and all."

"I like pretty things. I should say 'most any girl in her right mind would. I like handsome men too. Lucian, you'd never look my way once. All I've ever tried to do was get your attention, make you jealous and get you to go after me."

"Where can we go?" He had stopped in the middle of the road. Honor could see them standing close together. "Let's cut out all this talk."

"I just wanted you to know how I felt. I do have a heart, Lucian. I have my pride, you know."

"Where'ud you say?" His voice was deeper than ever.

"We can sit awhile in Tootie Farber's car, I reckon. It's

the last one parked. He parks it so he can get an easy start rolling down the hill."

"How'd you know that?"

"Why," she giggled, "I've known Tootie all my life. I know his old car anyplace, and I saw it on my way to the arbor. I happened to notice it was the last one parked and—well, it don't matter to me. You sound like you doubt me."

"I don't believe in paying nobody."

"For what? For heaven's sake. I simply said I was tired of standing around listening to the same ole songs night after night and nobody shouting or nothing. I said my feet was hurting and I thought—you seemed to like me."

"Get in," he said, gruffly. "I like you. I been watching you switch that pretty ass around, flirting right and left. I've been planning on it a long time, and if I have to, I'll pay."

"I really don't like you saying that."

"How do you unbutton that thing?"

"Don't you rip my new dress, Lucian Arnold. There ain't no need you tearing at my clothes. If you're going to act like that, you'll have to pay me two dollars to fix up my dress."

"I'll give you two dollars."

"Wait a minute. I don't do nothing unles you put on a rubber. You so rough, you're going to owe me more'n any two dollars. Slow down, buster."

"You got me so riled up." There was a heaving, shoving kind of noise coming from the car. "At least let me get off my step-ins." There were more noises. Honor had a horrible fear that she would get a case of the giggles the way she and Ruthie had done once in Sunday school class.

"This goddam back seat. Scoot out this way. That's right, put 'em up around my waist."

"I hope Tootie put a rock under the wheel," Honor whispered to Ruthie as the old car seemed to go into a convulsion.

"Shhh . . ."

"They're making so much noise they couldn't hear it thunder."

"You should have heard that guitar player—snorted like a bull," Ruthie whispered back.

After a moment, the car was quiet. It was Mildred's voice that spoke first.

"You're something, Lucian Arnold. You are really something."

"You're something yourself. I was too fast. I didn't mean to be so fast."

"It was just right, Lucian."

"Hey, you crying? What you crying about?"

"I didn't think it would be like that. I mean—"

"Look, if it's two dollars you worried about, I'll give you five. I mean, if I tore your dress and everything."

"It's not the money."

"Don't cry. I don't like to see nobody cry. It's not like it was your first time. I mean, well, we ain't fooling nobody now, Mildred. Why're you all of a sudden bawling about a little—"

"But I like you. I've always liked you."

"We can do it again. I'm ready anytime you are."

"It's not just doing it. I mean . . ."

"We'd better be getting back to the arbor."

"I'm going to stay here a spell. You go on."

"You expecting somebody else? I heard you took on two the other night."

There was a loud slap, and a torrent of four-letter words. "You're just like all the rest. Give me my five dollars!"

"You said two."

"I said *five*. And next time, buster, it'll be ten!"

He got out of the car and hitched up his pants. After a moment, he mumbled something to himself and started up the cinder road alone.

Ruthie gave Honor a nudge. "Listen. She's sitting in there crying, bawling like a dying bull."

"Didn't he give her her money?"

"She's not crying about that, silly. She's crying because she wanted him to like her for his sweetheart. He's just like all the rest. He thinks she's nothing but the town whore."

Honor listened for a moment to the desperate-sounding gulps of crying that tore at the darkness. All of a sudden she was furious with Ruthie. It was all her fault! Spying on somebody doing it was one thing, but just like Lola had said, when it was spying on somebody's soul, it was different. Even if it was just a town whore.

"Can we go? Will she hear us slip away?"

But Ruthie didn't answer. She was cupping her hands up to both ears, trying to hear every sob. "Maybe she ought to go up for altar call," Ruthie said. "Maybe we ought to tell her to go talk to Brother Light."

"Maybe we ought to mind our own business," Honor said, her voice tight in her throat. She got up slowly, trying not to rattle the leaves or step on a sharp twig. She wished she could see a little better.

"We ought to tell her something," Ruthie insisted.

"Yeah, maybe to relocate. To move off from where people spy on her when they got no business spying." Honor made one last turn toward Ruthie who didn't seem anxious to go. "You're ugly, Ruthie. And I don't like you anymore."

Honor fairly slid down the embankment, the loose dirt flying. She hoped she never laid eyes on either one of them again.

She ran blindly up the cinder road, stretching out her whole body trying to reach the circle of light and the shadowy forms of the crowd standing outside the brush arbor. Just as she came within a few feet of the outer ring of light, an arm shot out and closed down on her shoulder blade with biting force. In the chocolate light of the shadows, Suzie Daniels' eyes beamed down on her with a fierceness she had never seen before. She felt pinned down by the look, even though she couldn't tell now which was the robin's-egg blue one and which the brown one. Somehow, she would feel safer, she thought wildly, if she could tell.

"Listen. You listen to what I have to say!" Suzie's voice had lost that Karo syrup tone. "Lola showed me that map and told me about your big idea of how she ought to run off." Her voice seemed to cut the air like a razor. "You don't know your little ass from a hole in the ground 'bout things like that. What you've done is get her all stirred up so she won't listen to nothing else, to nobody who makes good sense. We—her own people—is trying to work out a plan. Something safe. You mind your business from now on. Stay in your own backyard!"

"Turn me loose, Suzie Daniels." Honor jerked her shoulder free. "Else I'll tell everybody in Margate how you forgot to keep your place."

"I'll tell everybody in Margate how you forgot yours!"

Honor felt her heart fairly split her chest apart as she stumbled ahead, out of Suzie's reach and away from the sound of her voice.

She managed to push her way to the inside ring of the gawkers. They were standing in a restless, fidgety mass listening to the droning of Brother Light's voice, anxious for him to finish the preaching and for the shouting and talking-in-tongues to get under way, if enough Holy Rollers had showed up. She looked past the regulars sitting on benches and finally spotted her mother's white artificial rose bobbing to one side of her hat as she fanned herself in quick, nervous little moves. From down deep inside her, a wave of long-forgotten need spread through her: she wanted her mother's arms to close tightly, protectively, around her. She wanted her mother to soothe her, to push her hair off her forehead the way she had done once when she ran a high fever and Dr. Clark thought she might be coming down with pneumonia. She wanted to put her head on her mother's shoulder and fall off into a safe sleep and dream about the big county seat town and the Mississippi River. She wanted to be anywhere but at this hot, stinking, awful brush-arbor meeting with Suzie Daniels probably this minute hexing her with those funny eyes.

Lola could burn up the map for all she cared. She could take her razors and her snuff and run off any old way she wanted to.

In one quick, blind move she ducked her head and raced down the aisle to the bench where her mother was.

"'Scuse me—sorry, Ma'am. 'Scuse me, please," she mumbled, stepping over feet and dodging waving paper fans. Her mother looked up, obviously irritated. "Don't wrinkle my dress. Sit up." Her mother's arm felt as rigid as a poker.

Honor drew herself up stiffly, the watery feeling that had come to her knees as she ran down the aisle began to ooze out. She felt somehow drained. Even her eyes were dry, the way they felt sometimes after a stiff March wind had been whipping at them.

She tried to concentrate on Brother Light, and from this

162

close she saw the greasy spot on his black bow tie and the mole on his chin. His hands, waving out this way and that, looked more like hands made out of pale gray wax, that would belong to one of the undertakers at Kimmel's Funeral Home down in Olympia, or to one of the bodies they had just embalmed.

She studied the peacock feathers on the fan Ruthie had handed over to her and tried to straighten out the bent place where it had been folded under when they were lying on their stomachs behind the bushes, listening to Mildred.

Her mother had a songbook lying in her lap. Honor reached over, smiled up at her mother, and slipped the songbook into her own hands. She opened it up to page 71 and started reading the first verse of the hymn.

Have you read the story of the Cross,
Where Jesus bled and died;
Where your debt was paid by the precious blood
That gushed from his wounded side?
He died an atoning death for thee.
Oh, wondrous love!

She looked up at her mother, who was still waving her fan and staring respectfully up at the pulpit, but who seemed not to really be seeing anything in particular, as if her thoughts were somewhere else. "What's *atoning* mean?" Honor whispered.

"Shhh," her mother whispered anxiously. "He's ready to close."

Honor slammed the songbook shut. Her mother had certainly splashed on the Evening-in-Paris thick enough tonight, she thought, waving her own fan to try to brush the heavy, sweet smell on down the bench a little.

Brother Light stepped up in front of the pulpit, and the musicians bent over and started getting their instruments ready. Honor saw that Pee Wee was twisting the strings on his guitar and giving some kind of high sign to the one called Shorty. He had stepped off to the right during the sermon, but he hadn't been gone long enough to stay any time at all with Mildred.

"When you hear the music, brothers and sisters, when

163

our fine gospel singers start in on the altar-call hymn, I want each and ever' one of you to open up your hearts and be honest. If you're a backslider, it ain't nothing to be ashamed of. If you've always wanted to confess and open up your heart to God, you don't have to worry about what anybody thinks, what somebody is going to whisper behind your back about. God opens his arms to all sinners. Ain't no sin too big God can't forgive. He bestows his love, his everlasting love, on the lowest sinner. The very scum of this earth can become holy if they just open up their hearts and let God's love pour in. All you backsliders sitting on these benches, all you sinners trying to hide out in the dark out there, God sees every hair on your head. He's here right now pleading with you, using my voice to call you down that aisle. He's giving you a open road to the ways of the good, the righteous. You might think you're stuck on the road to hell, that you've done too much wrong and there ain't no way. I tell you, there's room in God's heart for everybody. Jesus died and shed his precious blood just to make you sinners white and pure again. No matter how dark and stained you are, you can be washed as white as the lamb of God." The guitars and fiddles were playing softly in the background, and his voice was rising in that last pleading, mournful call. "As these fine musicians start the first verse, I want you to forget all about anybody out there watching you—what they might be saying. I'm calling out to the worst sinner amongst you. I'm pleading to you. I'm telling you it ain't too late, brother . . . sister. Don't be ashamed. Come right on down this aisle here, this pathway to the Lord, and he'll receive you in his blessed open arms. You'll be reborn! You'll start over in life like a new-born babe, a little lamb of God, pure as snow."

> Just as I am without one plea,
> But that thy blood was shed for me.

There was a stirring of people looking around to see if anyone was coming down the aisle, a looking back at the singers, who had reached the chorus:

> O, Lamb of God, I come, I come.

Brother Light looked angry. He stepped back up and raised his arms high over his head. "I know there's sinners out there who ought to be thankful for this chance to come down this aisle. You ought to be glad to get to crawl down it for the blessing of the Lord, the forgiveness of your sins. What's the matter with you? You scared? You think somebody's going to laugh at you? You scared somebody's going to trip you on the way down? Ain't nothing but God's blessing and a release—a release of all your griefs and burdens."

He waved to the musicians. "Strum for a minute, boys. Let's hum this next verse softly so we give God's voice room to be heard. I want every sinner out there to hear!"

Honor felt a weariness engulf her. It came from the mixed-up heat gathered under the brush arbor, from trying to sort out why she was both mad at Ruthie and ashamed, and yet still glad she had spied on Mildred. And she felt mad at Lucian Arnold too, though she wasn't sure about why either. Under all those feelings, she wished there had been some way they could have said something to Mildred. No matter why she was crying like that, it was the kind of crying that was for real, that came out from the part inside that hurt the most. And she didn't like Brother Light either, up there acting so high and mighty, getting mad at everybody just because he hadn't made a good record of converts all week long. He ought to go off and sit awhile and hum to himself and see if he could maybe hear something that would give him a nicer look on his face than the hateful one plastered on it now.

Without realizing it, she leaned over against her mother's shoulder. She felt the warmth of her arm coming through the dimity dress and smelled the familiar odor of Evening-in-Paris cologne.

"Sit up," her mother whispered, irritated. "You're wrinkling my dress."

Honor sat up and waved the fan. One thing she'd never buy when she was old enough would be Evening-in-Paris cologne, she told herself firmly.

And suddenly Brother Light's whole face lit up, and he was stretching out his arms and walking down the aisle toward some sinner who must not be seeing all that well or listening all that hard, Honor thought.

There was a general stirring and turning around and a

165

buzzing among those seated on the benches. "I don't believe it!" her mother gasped, fanning as fast as she could.

As Honor turned around, she heard the same kind of sobbing noises she had heard coming out of Tootie Farber's car. Brother Light had grabbed Mildred by the arm and was half-pulling her along with him. As the red polka dots swam by in a blur of motion, there was a loud moaning, wailing cry coming out of Mildred that reminded Honor of a whipped dog. Honor had a fierce urge to reach out and grab her and yell, "Don't go!"

The musicians had struck up the last chords of "Just as I Am," and Brother Light was hollering "Praise the Lord!"

Then he waved his one free arm, while trying hard to hold up the swaying, hysterical Mildred. "Brothers and sisters, I want all you who feel the Lord's voice inside you to come down this aisle right now and pray with me over this poor creature here who wants God's mercy. Let his voice shout out if it wants to. Let it say what God wants it to say." He was trying to hold Mildred's sagging body up straight. "Sister, you've made the right choice. There's no forgiveness like the mercy of God."

Honor saw Pee Wee poke Shorty in the ribs and give one of the same kind of grins that Lucian Arnold had smeared on his face. She hated them all.

Brother Light yelled at the top of his voice, over the noise of those tuning up to shout and those just moaning low and hollering "Hallelujah." "Play us some joyous music, boys. Let's praise the Lord!" He looked back out at the crowd. "Anybody else want to come down here to the altar and help us pray?"

Honor felt her mother shift her weight, as if she might be getting ready to stand up. "Are *you* going?" she asked, aghast.

"I should say not! I'm just getting ready to slip out the minute they start in on the sideshow part." She fanned vigorously and smiled one of those polite, sweet smiles at Miss Lacey and Ada Bly, who were watching her. "The minute I tell you, get up and leave and head straight for the car."

Honor took one last look down at the altar, where so many people had ganged around and so much noise was going on at once she couldn't tell which was Mildred crying and which was the show-off shouters trying to work themselves up to their final sawdust rolling fit.

"Now." Her mother nudged her and gave her a push toward the aisle. "We're beating the crowd leaving," she whispered down to Miss Lacey, that Missionary Society smile on her face again.

Honor didn't look right or left as they hurried out from under the brush arbor. Her mother was waving frantically at Buford and Stuart, motioning them toward the car. "That's the last time for that," she said, opening the door and pulling off her hat with the white rose. "Is everybody in, the doors shut tight?"

Buford turned around from the front seat as the motor sputtered into being. "Even the Bohunks didn't show up this year," he complained to no one in particular.

"No, wasn't nothing worth a dime seeing," agreed Stuart.

Honor sank into the far corner of the back seat, on the side of the car next to the pitch-dark thick woods. She did not look into them. Suzie Daniels' eyes would be there, like panther eyes, glaring at her.

The headlights shot out and her mother spun the back wheels as she headed the Oakland onto the main road. "At least you'll have known what a brush-arbor meeting is all about," she said, sighing heavily. "They won't have them in a place such as Hartman."

And they won't have a Suzie Daniels or a Mildred Matthews or a Ruthie Stinnet or anybody else she wanted to forget. Honor's thoughts were spinning.

"Did you spend your whole quarter?" Stuart asked Honor from his side of the back seat.

She let her fingers close tightly around the sweaty dime. "I've got a dime left," she said, her voice squeezing down as tightly as her fingers. "You don't think dimes grow on trees do you?"

"That'll be enough, quite enough for one night, you two!" her mother fairly shrieked. "Hush up. I've got to keep my mind on my driving."

"I hate you. I hate everybody," Honor whispered to no one in particular, trying to loosen the burning grip of fear gathering darker than the night inside her.

16

The following weeks seemed to Honor to fall off the calendar, as quickly as the oak and maple and sycamore leaves were falling off the trees. The leaves had turned early that year due to the long dry spell, and when they fell to the ground, the trees looked skinny and cold and not at all ready for what everybody predicted would be a rough winter.

On schedule, as announced, the mines closed down, and every day it seemed that another house was standing empty, with the glass windows staring out like blind eyes and sometimes even the front doors left open to bang with the stiff winds that whipped cold rain turned into sleet across the mountains as early as November.

Honor moved, as if in a fog, along with the new pace, trying to adjust to the strangeness of it all: of the boxes packed and shoved into every corner in the house; the china cabinet emptied out; and even the Sunday tablecloth starched and ironed and packed away, leaving her old hiding place under the dining room table bare and exposed.

Miss Lacey, assisted by Ada Bly's sister, Cora, held down the teaching load of the ever-dwindling school roll, dividing her teaching time between groups of primer, first, second, third, and fourth grades in the morning and between fifth, sixth, seventh, and eighth grades in the afternoon.

As a rule, a letter arrived every week, usually on Wednesday, from their father. He had fallen into a new schedule of his own. On Sunday afternoon he would sit at the antique desk in front of the window of the guest bedroom in Nathan Dobbs' house, looking down over the rooftops at the Mississippi River. Here he would write to his family about what he saw: about the changing weather, his new job, his new life in Hartman. In his own way he was trying to boost his family's spirits as they waited out the time until he could come with the big moving truck and take them to their new home. Once a month he included money, and in November, he sent extra for their mother to send off to the Sears Roebuck Catalog and order Christmas presents for their last Christmas on the mountain.

Sometimes, after a letter came, Honor would hear her mother off crying to herself out of lonesomeness. There were still those days when the migraine headaches would grab hold of her, and nothing any of the children did could please her. But overall the house had a calmness, a kind of silent, empty waiting, like a ghost, lurking in it.

As often as she thought she could get by with it, Honor would complain of a stomach ache so she could stay home from school. She'd cover up under the heavy wool winter quilts, or curl up in the big armchair in front of the fireplace in the living room, two of the things that hadn't changed, that were safe. While watching the crackling flames leap up, she would see in her mind's eye the awful kind of big, open-eyed, blank look that was on the faces of so many who came, from time to time, to call for the mail, those who hadn't found a new job or another place to move to.

There were times when she thought about Lola and tried to figure out some solid excuse for paying her a visit. But it was hard, in the wintertime, with everyone staying inside huddled around the fires, to gauge where anybody would be, what they were doing, or when. It was the coldest spell anyone could remember ever having hit Margate. Even the Missionary Society meetings had been broken up for good, with Preacher Pullum already having moved on to a real little country church, up near Turnersville.

One night at the supper table, when the icicles were dripping down like long, jagged daggers at the kitchen window, their mother said, "Mrs. Clark told me today that they'll be moving around the last of January, or February at the latest. They've found a place on the outskirts of Nashville, where she can keep Jerome in Belle Buckle and

169

where Dr. Clark can still feel he's got 'country' patients."

"What's going to happen to Lola?" Honor asked, buttering a biscuit and trying to look unconcerned.

"Why, I haven't the faintest idea. I suppose, I reckon she'll go along."

"Won't they make her go back to the state pen? You said the only way they'd let her out was if she was stuck off in some far, way-out place where she wouldn't be a risk to people."

Her mother sipped her coffee. "I guess there were some conditions to her parole. But whatever they are, I'm sure it's something Mamie and Dr. Clark will take care of. It's none of your concern, Honor Jane. They're perfectly capable of handling their own affairs."

All that next week, Honor tried to find some way to get up to see Lola. But it was test week at school, and their mother kept them inside, reviewing them at every turn, making sure they would arrive in the Hartman schools with mostly A's on their grade cards.

And then it was time to get ready for Christmas—"for the last Christmas we'll spend in Margate, thank the Lord," their mother kept saying as she went about her usual pre-holiday routine of baking cookies and making divinity candy, dried-apple cake, brown bread, and boiled custard. Honor had already seen inside the packages that had arrived from the catalog and had been practicing looks of surprise for when the time came to open up the new sweater, the mittens, the pair of rubber boots, and the game of Chinese checkers.

Their father wrote that he would most probably arrive home late in the afternoon or early evening on Christmas Eve. "I'd like to get there earlier, but Nathan has started depending on me more and more. He wants me to stay until the very last minute. I think he hates to spend Christmas all alone too."

"It sounds to me," their mother fretted, when she read that part of the letter, "like this Mr. Dobbs is leaning just a little too hard on Henry lately. I hate to say 'I smell a rat,' but I swear he doesn't want Henry to come back for his family. He wants him all to himself, it sounds to me like."

But whatever her fears about Mr. Nathan Dobbs, she was grateful to him and excited over the fast-approaching day when Henry Whitfield was coming back to Margate to spend one last Christmas on the mountain and then move his family away forever.

Honor, in the meantime, had devised a way of paying a visit to Lola. If someone objected, she'd at least have a good excuse.

On the morning of Christmas Eve, when her mother was running around the house in a last-minute flurry of preparations for their father's arrival, Honor tended to the loose ends of her plan. Earlier she had gone into the woods and had found just the right size little cedar tree for Lola's house and had strung a special string of popcorn for it. She had taken her lace handkerchief out of the round tin box and also the sack of gumdrops she had been saving all these months; they were hard on the outside but still sugary and sweet to suck on. She wasn't entirely happy with the few things she had been able to sneak out of her mother's belongings and wrap up as presents for Lola. There was the black wool shawl in the trunk in the bathroom; this Honor had aired out to get rid of the mothball smell, ironed out smooth, and wrapped up. In the round tin can that she decided she would no longer need for her keepsakes, she put eight cookies, three pieces of divinity candy, two sticks of Wrigley's spearmint chewing gum, and six pecans. She longed to slip in a piece of the brown bread and the dried-apple cake, but since they weren't cut yet, she'd get into too much trouble.

The little cedar tree seemed awfully bare to her. She thought about borrowing some ornaments from their own tree, but her mother knew each ornament by heart. At the last minute, she took some shiny wrapping paper and tried making her own, wrapping it around sweet-gum balls that she had saved from one of her last hikes in the woods before winter hit.

It was almost two o'clock that afternoon before she found the right moment to slip unnoticed out the back door. Her hands were full. She carried a paper sack with the presents in her left hand, and in her right hand she held the decorated tree as straight up in the wind as possible. As she made her way up the back alley, the wind blew the branches against her cheek, and the popcorn tinsel trailed like a ribbon behind her.

Finally, she stood on Lola's porch, knocking self-consciously at the door.

It seemed a long time before Lola came to answer. The wind whipped her skirt about her bare knees, and her fingers were red with the cold. She had a hearty "Merry Christmas" ready in her throat. But it took longer than she had expected, and when Lola finally opened the door, nothing at all came out.

There was something about the look on Lola's face, a bearing-down, suspicious glare, as if she had forgotten all about the nice times they had spent together and the friendly way they used to talk. Nor did Lola open the door more than a couple of inches or so. She seemed to be peering through the crack, as though she might even be hiding a razor behind her back.

Honor fairly thrust the Christmas tree at her. "I—I thought maybe—well, since you didn't have your people, with everybody you know on the old Franklin turnpike outside Nashville and everybody moving off from Margate and Mama saying the Clarks are going too—" Lola's look was bearing down beyond her endurance. She hadn't dreamed bringing Lola a tree, even if it was a kind of puny one at that, would make her so mad. She was cold, and she needed to go to the bathroom, and in spite of herself, she started crying. "I just brought you some Christmas presents, a tree. I didn't mean to make you mad."

Lola seemed to come to some kind of decision. She opened the door a little wider. "You by yourself?" She still made no move to reach out and take the offerings.

"I slipped out while nobody was looking," Honor cried out, wishing desperately that she could throw everything down and run back home and warm up in front of the living room fire.

"Of all the times." Lola suddenly flung open the door, look about right and left. "Come on in, quick."

Honor stepped in awkwardly, half-stiff with fear and cold and confusion. The little room was mostly in shadow, but Honor saw in a flash that Lola had a lot of things piled up on the bed. Suddenly Lola had her hand on her arm, squeezing hard, out of some fear of her own.

"Aren't you even going to take 'em?" Honor asked, barely getting the words out, she was so frightened, all of a sudden.

Lola seemed to relax a little. "Look. Look, little girl . . ."

"Honor. Don't you remember my name even?"

"I'm sorry. Lola's sorry. I don't mean not to show my appreciation," she mumbled. And then she threw out her hands, as if she didn't know what to do next. "It's just, well, you took me by surprise while I was in the middle of—"

Honor had taken that moment to study the bed more closely. There on the lumpy-looking iron bed was the pink-flowered silk dress she had seen Mamie Clark wear dozens of times, and the maroon-colored winter coat with the brown fur on the collar. Lola herself looked different. She was wearing Mrs. Clark's navy blue crepe dress with those funny loops making a collar and with that puckered-up place on the skirt where she had spilled Coca-Cola on it one day.

"Mrs. Clark's dress fits you nice," she said, barely able to speak, her heart thumping fiercely. She was still holding the paper sack and the Christmas tree. "Did Mrs. Clark give you those when she was culling out to move, for Christmas presents or something?"

Lola reached out and took the tree and held it a moment, straightening out the loose string of popcorn tinsel almost tenderly. "That's a mighty nice thing for you to do, fix up Lola a Christmas tree."

Honor didn't take her eyes off Lola. "I brought you some presents too," she said, holding out the paper sack.

Lola laughed nervously. "I say there, if that ain't something now." She tried to make her laugh sound stronger.

Honor put her hands on her hips and looked Lola straight in the eye. "Why're you scared? Why're you scared, 'cause I took you by surprise? Are you running away?" Just in case Lola wouldn't like what she had said, she pulled herself up on her tiptoes, ready to bolt for the door.

But Lola suddenly let out a long sigh and slumped her shoulders in. "I declare if you ain't the funniest little ole girl, always buttin' in when you is least expected." She sat down on the bed. "Yeah, Lola's running off. But I reckon you won't be telling on me. You likes secrets too much for that. You won't tell nobody?" Lola looked at her hard.

"Did Suzie Daniels—your own people—did you work out a safe plan?"

"Suzie Daniels, if I waited for Suzie, grass would grow under my feet. I'd be looking out through bars again. Lola's got her own plan. Lola's going down that sawmill road."

"But, but what if it's not the same as Buford said it was? What if I didn't—didn't know my ass from a hole in the ground? Suzie Daniels said I didn't. Suzie'ud put a big hex on me."

"Suzie ain't putting no hex on nobody. Don't get that funny look, messing your face all up ugly like that when you look nice and pretty." Lola smiled at her. "Look, ain't nothing going to happen to Lola that ain't Lola's fault. But I 'spect I better be gettin' on. Time's passing."

"If you're going to really take that sawmill road, it's already past two o'clock," Honor said in alarm. "You can't lose any time a'tall." She looked about frantically. "Why're you—I guess I'm buttin' in wasting your time, messing you up."

Lola laughed. "Why'ud you think I acted so funny when you came knocking on my door scarin' shit outa me? I thought it was her done missed the clothes I took and come home early from her trip down the mountain."

"Look," Honor said, suddenly jumping up. "Come on. I'll take you down to behind Ruthie's aunt's house. I know a shortcut and that way I'll know you'll get headed out the right way. If somebody sees us, we'll say we're looking for a Christmas tree."

"We'll be Santa Claus's helpers." Lola quickly got up and put on the maroon coat with the fur collar. "I don't wants to get you caught up in it. I don't wants you getting in no trouble. I figured I won't get lost. Suzie studied the map, figured it out with me. She says it'll be okay."

"I'm going," Honor said. "My Mama's running around like a chicken with its head chopped off, she's so stewed up about Daddy coming home to get us. She won't miss me. And Stuart and Buford went up to Clifty's with Uncle Dave. They're trying to kill some quail to surprise Daddy with a quail breakfast Christmas morning. They won't be running around to see us."

Lola was gathering things up and putting them in a paper sack. "Look, Lola, there's a wool shawl in there that maybe you ought to take out now and wrap around your head. It's cold outside. You don't watch to catch pneumonia on your way running off."

"You a regular little Santa Claus, ain't you?" Lola reached in the sack and pulled out the Christmas presents.

"You don't have a lot of time, Lola," Honor warned. "You've got a whole lot of hiking ahead of you, and you're not used to it."

"What else you brought Lola?" she asked, unwrapping the black shawl and tying it around her head. "This is nice. This'll keep Lola mighty nice and warm like a big woolly bear."

"There's candy, cookies, lots of things. But not much either if you look at it one way. It was all I could slip out without anybody missing it."

"That'll make me a nice picnic now, won't it?"

"Come on, let's hurry," Honor urged.

They went out together, with Lola slamming the door a little extra hard behind her. Honor looked up at Lola. "Listen, you head on back thataway, behind our house through the field. I'm going to run in the house a minute and find us some gloves. Your hands—you'll get frostbite."

"God's going to bless you, honey," Lola said, shaking her head again and staring out toward the field.

Honor dashed into the house, threw aside coats and jackets hanging on hooks, and finally came up with her woolen leggings and her stocking cap with the adjustable earmuffs. She found her own mittens, but wasn't quite sure what to get for Lola. Then she remembered the new pair of leather gloves wrapped up for Buford. She hated to steal his Christmas present, but she couldn't stand to think of Lola's hands getting frostbitten.

She tiptoed into the living room and slipped the package out from under the tree. In the kitchen, she stopped to listen for sounds of her mother. She was in the bathroom, taking a bath and singing "Jingle Bells" at the top of her lungs without coming close to being on key.

She raced across the back pathway, ripping the Christmas paper off Buford's gloves. When she caught up with Lola, she held out the gloves and stopped to get her breath. "I think they'll fit."

Lola took the gloves and looked at them closely. "You sure nobody's gonna miss 'em? You ain't going to get in no big trouble over this, are you?"

175

"It won't be any trouble worse than a hairbrush whipping. Even that probably won't happen with everybody so excited over Daddy coming home tonight and Christmas tomorrow. If they miss them—well, they'll think maybe they got packed up someplace by mistake."

Lola pulled the gloves on and reached down and picked up the paper sack. "They feels toasty. This shawl's—you sure fixed Lola up like a eskimo."

They hadn't walked very far at all, it seemed to Honor, when Lola suddenly put her hand on her side. "Lola's got to set and rest a spell. I ain't used to all this bustling about. All this outdoor hiking in the cold wind. Kind of tuckers you out, don't it?"

Honor looked at her closely. "Lola, you got a long way to go before you come out on the highway. You sure you can make it? What'll happen if you miss your ride?"

"I don't aim to miss it," she said, getting up again. "He's going to wait till as late as nine o'clock. If I ain't there by then, then somethin's gone wrong."

17

After Lola's resting spell, they walked on in silence for quite a long time, the twigs and dry weeds crackling beneath their feet, the ice-coated briers in the low, damp places swinging out occasionally, catching hold of the maroon coat. It was a path Honor knew well. In summer she followed it frequently, sometimes taking the shortcut to Ruthie's aunt's house or the back way to visit Mary Sue Hembree, another friend of hers who knew where the holly grew thick and where to find a buckeye tree. Honor's mother considered Mary Sue white trash, and Honor had to sneak off every time she wanted to play with her.

"You good at crossing logs?" she asked Lola at one point.

"What you mean, crossing logs?" Lola had fallen behind some, and her voice came out deep and heavy sounding.

"There's a place, once we get past Ruthie's aunt's house, where you have to cross Frog Hollow on a log. But it's a big wide log. It's been there a long time. I'll carry the sack when we get there so you can balance good."

"That'ud be a fine howdydo," said Lola, puffing loudly, "break my leg falling off a log."

Honor slowed down, waited for Lola to catch up. "Why don't you catch your breath a minute while I find me a good place to squat. I never got a chance to go to the bathroom."

"I'll take you up on that," Lola said, sitting down on a log with one massive sigh. "All them years in the pen, puttering around doin' housework up on this mountain, I ain't in the shape I thought I was."

Honor hurried through the motions of pulling down her

leggings, trying to keep herself as dry as possible. When she came back to the log, she noticed that Lola was still breathing hard. She looked up through the prickly bare branches at the sky that looked spotty with cold gray clouds and a fuzzy sun too far off to warm up anything. "Lola, if you go straight down that old sawmill road and don't have to stop to rest for too long, I believe you'll have plenty of time to come out by dark. You can duck down low and wait for your ride if you get there ahead of time."

"Yeah, Suzie and me was talkin' about that. We got that part of it figured out. The man's going to pick me up. He's going to drive up and down and make sure he don't miss me for as far up and down the highway as a mile. That way, ain't no chance me coming out the wrong place." She took off one of the gloves and dug into the sack for her snuff. "I just got to fix me a dip. We can set a minute more."

Honor sat down on the log beside Lola. She kicked her feet hard against the cold bare ground, warming up her toes. "Lola, just say—well, what if maybe you did happen to stray off the sawmill road or get mixed up, you ain't scared of panthers, are you? The Northcutts said there was some black panthers down by the bluff. The bluff's close to where you'll be."

Lola threw back her head and looked up at the sky. "I ain't planning on seeing no black panthers." She pulled at her cotton stockings that were gathered in a gartered knot above her knee. "Lola aims to be mighty particular about the company she keeps going down that sawmill road."

"Well, they say panthers don't come out till past midnight anyway. You'll be already caught up with your ride by then."

"Yeah, I aims to be halfway to where I'm heading by past midnight." She reached down in the bag. "You said you brought Lola some cookies. I could use something sweet right now. Give me a little energy. This snuff, funny, but it's the first time snuff don't taste so good." She spit it out and wiped her mouth.

"Maybe you got a nervous stomach." Honor pulled out the round tin can and opened it for Lola. "The gumdrops and jelly beans are kind of old. I've been saving 'em for you a long time. The cookies are fresh. There's some divinity candy."

Lola picked out a cookie and a piece of divinity. She ate first the cookie and then the candy. Then she stood up slowly, stretched her arms up, and tied the wool shawl around her neck a little closer. "This wool feels awful good. My old joints don't take to the cold so good no more."

Honor had a sudden feeling of panic. "Lola, maybe you ought not go the sawmill road. Maybe we ought to cut back on to the main cinder road. Ain't that many people out riding around on Christmas Eve. I could go with you and we could make up something. I don't like you walking down that sawmill road all by yourself. It might be longer than we think. It might be thirty whole miles or something."

Lola patted her on the arm. "Honey, thirty miles ain't nothing compared to thirty years. Now come on, 'es get to stepping."

The path soon wound its way out onto the dirt road that would, after two more bends and a small hill, come in sight of Ruthie's aunt's house. "I didn't want you to think I was scared of black panthers or anything," Honor said after a moment of walking in silence.

"Aw, you ain't scared of nothing much. Lola knowed that the first time she ever laid eyes on you. If you was a fraidycat, Lola never would've got to make your acquaintance."

Honor stopped a moment and cupped her mitten to her ear.

"What's that?" Lola asked.

"It's the Freeman boys cutting wood over thataway. Nothing to fret over."

"That's good. And Lola ain't going to be fretting over no black panthers neither." She stopped, changed the paper sack to the other hand, adjusted the wool shawl again. "If I see some sneaky ole panther slippin' up on me, Lola's just gonna holler, 'go on, mind your business, nigger panther!'"

Honor laughed, made a little skip. "It ain't nice, calling something nigger."

"Seems to me like that'ud be the very thing I ought to call a sneaky ole panther." She put the sack down, balanced it on a rut in the road, and twisted at the armhole of the maroon coat. "If I'd had my scissors handy, I'd a made these armholes a little looser. They sure binds me where it hurts. Needs to be a little bigger through the shoulders."

Honor was trying to make up her mind about something. "Lola, I think maybe we'd better cut around through the woods behind Ruthie's aunt's house so we won't run a chance of bumping into the Freeman boys cutting logs. It won't be as easy as the road, but it's safer. And it won't take us but a little while."

"Lola's following you." She picked up the sack again. "These big old galoshes seem to weigh a ton on my feet."

"They'll keep your feet dry though," Honor said, seeing that Lola had on a pair of Dr. Clark's rubber hunting boots. For some reason she hadn't noticed them before. She had been too caught up in the excitement of everything else.

They pushed aside a stray branch from a bare oak and started a zig-zagging kind of path through the woods, skirting around the outer fence of the Freemans' place. "You know where you at?" Lola asked.

"I know all this like the back of my hand," Honor said. "I don't know anything about that sawmill road though except what I told you Buford said—and that it runs alongside the Northcutts' property and no matter what happens, even a black panther, don't step foot on their property."

"Suzie told me that too. Suzie said she went on that sawmill road one time. She said the same thing your brother said. I ain't scared, long as I get across it before dark." She stopped to rest again, putting her hand on her side. "This ole side of mine sure cutting up today. Feels like somebody stuck a thorn in it."

After a while, they came out just in front of a barbed wire fence that marked where the Freemans' land stopped and Ruthie's aunt's place started. Honor held up the loose wire while Lola ducked down and dragged herself under it, with Honor guiding the stickers of the barbed wire off the maroon coat.

"Why don't you chew a piece of Wrigley's spearmint?" she asked Lola, who had a kind of hurting look on her face.

Lola looked around for a place to sit. "That sounds like

180

a fine idea to me, mighty fine. I got a bad taste in my mouth."

Honor twisted the lid off the round tin can again and got out a stick of gum. "Why don't you chew that other one?" Lola suggested.

Honor was tempted. Her mouth felt dry, and all the walking had made her hot under so much clothing. "It's your Christmas present," she said, looking down.

"It's my present to you now," Lola insisted.

For a moment they sat in silence, chewing the gum. "That helped a lot," Lola said, getting up again, picking up the sack. "Looks like it's getting on. Them clouds seem to be picking up some snow up there."

Honor took one last worried look around. "Lola, we could still go on out the main cinder road."

"Listen, once you make up your mind that somethin' is the right thing to do, ain't no use in turning wishy-washy on what you made your mind up about. I done talked to myself about everything there is to be scared of. I prayed a little. I even took some special things and made a offering to something else I believe in—I got special powers with. If you want to call on that magic bluebird you told me about once, you can do that too." She laughed to herself. "If I was a bird, I'd done flown south for winter though. A bluebird'ud get his tail feathers froze off in weather like this." She gave Honor a hearty pat on the shoulder. "Now, whichaway? You going with me, or ain't you?"

"I'm going to get you onto the sawmill road and go as far as I can and still have plenty of time to get back before dark myself," she said. "I'm going to make sure you get across Frog Hollow."

"Well, Lola'ud sure appreciate that much. I never was no good crossing logs."

"I want to be sure and get home before Daddy does."

"Yeah, you ain't seen your daddy in a long time."

"I miss him," Honor said, as they walked along the path behind Ruthie's aunt's barn and disappeared down a slope that took them safely out of sight. "Daddy tells me stories all the time—poems. Once he used to write poems. He was going to be a poet and travel across the sea, all over the whole world, and visit famous places where other poets used to live. But he married my Mama."

"It happens like that sometimes. We get notions we can fly to the moon. When I was a little girl," she turned around and looked at Honor and stopped to get her breath, "when I was just about your size, I used to ask my Mama what I could do to turn my skin white."

"What'ud she tell you?" Honor asked, looking at Lola strangely, studying her dark skin.

"Well, she tell me, 'Lola, you say your prayers every morning when the sun comes up and every night when the sun goes down. You wash at least once a day behind your ears and scrub your body down hard and clean with soap. You go to church and you give regular gifts to the Lord. Then, if God wants you to be white, you'll turn white as snow, white as the little lamb of Jesus.'" Suddenly Lola threw her head back and laughed. "My Mama was a smart, good woman. I'm glad she didn't live to know her good little Lola ended up in the—" She picked up the sack. "What we standing around here talking like we got all day? Where's that Frog Hollow you was talking about?"

"It's coming up pretty soon," Honor said. Then she ran up beside Lola. "Your mama just told you that so you'd be good, didn't she? She knew you'd never turn white."

"My Mama knew all kinds of things, honey. And one thing my Mama knew best of all—she knew it wasn't no sin being happy with the way you was born."

"You mean, like being gawky, having big feet, being ugly?"

"You ain't none of them, if that's what you mean. Who told you, you was all of them?"

"Mama, I guess."

"Then your mama ain't so smart, or else your mama must think she's pretty ugly herself. Sometimes when people think they is one way, they try to make somebody else feel that same way, kind of remove it from themselves. But it don't work."

"There it is, Lola," Honor said, pointing out the gulch ahead. She hadn't been across Frog Hollow since last spring when she and Ruthie had gone looking for redbud and dogwood to fill up the schoolhouse for the Maypole dance celebration.

She walked up to it and looked back at Lola doubtfully.

182

"It's a good ten feet to the bottom. That might hurt if you fell off."

"Ten feet down is better'n six feet under." Lola was looking down at it, her eyes widening.

"Now don't be scared, Lola. We still got plenty of time. We're more'n halfway. You'll get to DuCasse with time to hide out before your ride comes along." Honor spit out her chewing gum so she wouldn't distract herself. She had never told anyone, but she was afraid of high places herself.

"I'll go first. I'll walk across first and show you how easy it is. Then I'll come back and walk behind you." Then she got another idea. "Look, I'll carry the sack across first and put it down out of the way. Sit down a minute and rest your side and watch how easy it is, okay?"

"I'll set if my creaky ole bones'll lower me down one more time. This cold is awful hard on my joints."

As Honor picked up the paper sack, she was listening to Lola mumbling behind her back. With her usual easy, light step, she jumped up on the footlog, held out her left arm for balance, and grabbed the sack with the other. "See, look at—"

That was the last thing she remembered. In one blinding, swirling turn, she was spinning off the log, falling down and down through the empty hole of air, like a dream she had had more than once in her life.

18

The maroon coat, the fur collar, and the flat palms of
Lola's hands spread out, all swirling in one dizzy, whirl-
wind motion, and the sound of Lola's voice, like some
deep-strung mountain wind coming through the tops of
far-off pine trees, were the first coming-to impressions
Honor had.

"That's right, come on. Come on back. Wake up. Lola's
got you here. Lola's taking care of you. But don't make no
fast kinds of moves. Something might be broke."

Honor felt herself being somehow rocked back and
forth. Then she realized it was Lola's arms tightly about
her and that bumpy uneven feeling beneath her was
Lola's lap, what part of it Lola could stretch her across.
She hadn't the vaguest notion, at first, where she was, beyond that.

Then she looked up through the bare, prickly treetops
rising like some weird, naked monster arms above the steep
banks of Frog Hollow. Through the branches, she could
see patches of a heavy, gray sky that reminded her for
some reason of a huge quilt rolled tight on quilting frames
that were beginning to sag from the weight and would
any minute come crashing down on top of them, bringing
tree branches and all.

Slowly, with Lola guiding her, she sat up and looked all
around, shaking her head in bewilderment. "Why're we
sitting down here in the bottom of Frog Hollow?" Her
voice seemed to echo in the cold, crisp stillness.

"That footlog done turned and tiwsted on you. You was
just a skipping up onto it, toting my sack across, and
showing me how to balance good." Suddenly, in one heav-

ing gasp, Lola began to cry. "I thought you was dead. The blood was running all down your face, and there you was spread out looking stone dead down there on top them rocks. I don't know how 'xactly I got down to the bottom myself. I kep' hollering and sliding and slipping and hollering some more. I just kep' hoping some of them wood choppers would be close enough to pick my hollering out of the noise of the woods. Wasn't nobody no place to hear, I reckon." She swiped hard at her face with the corners of the black shawl. "I washed all the blood off I could with my hands, spitting and wiping, and thinking how if Lola had come along by herself, if'n you hadn't caught me like that, off-guard, not 'specting nobody standing there with that scrawny-looking Christmas tree all decorated up with popcorn, I would've stepped on that log myself—and Lola ain't limber no more. Lola would've hit bottom, and it's a fact, wouldn't been nobody but the buzzards ever find me laying dead down here. You could holler till doomsday and ain't nobody but a echo going to answer you back from down here in Frog Hollow."

Honor pushed herself up slowly, feeling for the first time the throbbing pain above her eyes, bouncing from side to side all across her forehead and deep down into her ears. It felt as if Stuart had dumped all his quarter-sized marble taws inside her skull and somebody's big thumbs were shooting up the fastest games of marbles that had ever been played in Margate.

"I'm sorry, Lola, don't cry. It was my fault, butting in and being so gawky, falling over my own feet on that log. I was just showing off. Being smart-aleck. I know you're supposed to test a footlog before you go marching full across. It was all my fault."

Lola was trying to get up. Honor reached out and gave her a hand, but felt as though she was empty in the arms, that she had turned into a scarecrow with sawdust for joints.

"Lola's bones too stiff. I was fixing to carry you out and try to find us somebody. I couldn't even get you lifted up off the ground. So finally I just says to myself that if'n you was going to die, I wasn't leaving you down here by yourself to be picked off by the buzzards." She was breathing hard. "My big butt ought to have frostbite by now." She stretched out her arms and shook her hands around and

185

stomped her feet in Dr. Clark's big rubber boots against the rough, frozen ground. "I saw you was breathing and the blood wasn't gushing no place. But I've heard tell how people falls and get clots on the brain and all of a sudden die. You fell a long ways down. There's rocks everywhere. Wonder you didn't split your head wide open."

"I wish you'd gone on, Lola," Honor said, looking back up at the sky. "What time is it? How long have we been down here?"

"Ain't no way of telling," Lola said, shaking her head, pulling at her coat sleeves under the arms. "Seems like it might've been a whole hour, two whole hours, a whole lifetime. I kep' saying to myself, 'Don't let her have no broken bones. No clots on the brain. Don't let her die on me here.' Time to time, I'd get a notion I heard somebody tromping around up there in the woods, and I'd let in to hollering again. But wouldn't be nothin' coming back at me but a echo. Echoes sure sound lonesome. Woods take on funny kinds of noises all by themselves, don't they?" She seemed to be talking more to herself.

Honor was looking all about now, pressing on her head with her fingertips. She saw the scattered presents, the round tin can rolled over on its side against a jagged rock. Lola's clothes were hanging here and there from twigs and in lifeless heaps on the ground. "I'd better gather up your stuff, Lola. It's high time you—we get on down that sawmill road. It looks late. It's not too late, is it, Lola?"

"Now that I see you ain't going to die on me, you ain't got no broken bones, it ain't too late for nothing."

But Honor felt a sinking, deadening fear. "Lola, how you ever going to walk all the way down that sawmill road and come out on the highway before dark? Can't we go back home and try it tomorrow? I'll find us another way." Her fear, the pain, the confusion, and the guilt of having delayed Lola swam into one shapeless mass in the back of her head. There was no room inside left to hold back so much. She thought she would burst open in one popping-open explosion of all of it mixed up together. "Why didn't you leave me and get on your way while there was time!" she cried out as her crying caught hold and let off some of the pressure.

"Lola wouldn't a done that for nothing in this world. I wouldn't turn my back on somebody like you." She

186

seemed to be coming to some decision. "I 'spect it is getting on. But Lola's got to try to make it to the highway." She came over and put her arm around Honor's heaving shoulders. "Don't take on like that. You might get the blood started up again. You going to have a whopper enough of a headache—a black eye too, if I knows about people getting hit hard on the head. Lookit. There ain't no other way. Dr. Clark, he done told me last night how sorry he was, but they was going to take me back to the penitentiary because there wasn't nobody they knew, no place else to send me that the parole officers would agree on. Old Mamie, she don't give no time of day worrying 'bout it. The Doctor, he tried, I reckon, but there ain't nothing in this world can make me go back to that hogpen of a place unless they tie me down and carry me in. Even then, it'ud take a team of mules to drag me back inside and be locked up."

"Let's get going then," Honor said, starting toward the presents and the clothes.

"Leave them things. Maybe we'll hide 'em out of sight. Lola figures they weigh her down too heavy. This coat being so tight under the arms wears me out. These heavy galoshes. I ain't used to wearing so much that's heavy. Being cold in my joints, I'm cold down to the bone shaft. Something 'bout getting scared like that and sitting down on the ground so long, even being wrapped up like a Eskimo didn't seem to do much good."

"If you walk a little faster, maybe it'll warm you up," Honor offered, doubt tearing at her again. Lola looked so tired, and as if she were hurting all over. "That is, unless you don't think we could hide out and try it in the morning at daylight. Maybe we could hide in Ruthie Stinnet's aunt's barn."

"We ain't going to do nothing! Lola's going to haul her big froze-up butt up this here side of Frog Hollow, and you're going to get your little ass up that side over yonder." She was tying the wool scarf tighter under her chin and pulling the gloves back on. "I figure that if you don't mind Lola and walk real slow and steady-like and not do no fancy skipping or hopping or running, if you'll move just as easy as you can, you'll make it back to your house—to your daddy coming home for Christmas just about the time Lola here will be coming out the other end of that

187

old sawmill road, just like Suzie Daniels said I would. I got till nine o'clock to make it."

"But if it gets dark and you can't see, you won't know whichaway is the road and whichaway is the woods. It might be all grown over by now. Not many people use that sawmill road any longer. Let me go part way, Lola." She was crying again. "I won't be gawky-footed again."

"Lola don't never wants to hear you say that gawky stuff again. Ain't nothing wrong with you. You're a fine girl. 'Course, you look a little funny right now, your head puffed out like a goose egg lopsided and your nose blown up like a jellyfish, your face turning colors already. I'd just like to give some of that gawky business back to your mama who's done handed it out like she can't see good. You going to promise Lola one thing, you going to start thinking you are a pretty girl. You're a smart girl. Best of all, you're a mighty good and nice girl. It ain't in keeping with some starch you was born with to be getting like a turnip 'bout turning in on yourself and believing you one of God's uglies. You walk with your head tall in life. Be proud you the only one exactly like you."

Honor was embarrassed. Down deep, she had never felt so ashamed and clumsy through and through. She didn't know what to say back to Lola that would make sense and not come off the tip of her tongue the wrong way. "Can I help you get up your side of the bank?" she asked, looking up at the sky that seemed to be turning a deeper shade of gray.

"Thank you kindly, but I want you to climb up as easy as you can—thataway. I done picked me out a good place to climb up, down there by that thick sapling trying to grow up big enough to crane its neck out of Frog Hollow. I'm going to hide these things standing out like red flags. Hurry on now—shoo! We ain't got time standing aroun' fussing, making talk when we ought to be making tracks."

Honor helped Lola spread dried-out weeds and twigs over the clothes. "Okay, you take that side. Lola's going to ride this bucking mule of a bank all the way to the top." She waved her hand. "Go on, get! Don't you know the last one up is a—a dirty nigger!" Lola tried to laugh, but the sound of her voice sounded coated, or as though something was binding down her tongue the way the tight sleeves of the maroon coat were binding down her arms.

Honor went over, picking her way around, stepping over a rock, dodging a dead brier about to hit her in the eye. Every now and then, all of Frog Hollow seemed to take on a spinning motion, turn upside down, and then settle back into its rain-washed ruts now coated with ground turned as hard as chunks of ice and every bit as cold.

She had to concentrate on every move getting up the steep bank on her side. When she finally reached the top, she looked across at Lola, who was pulling at first one limb, then another: crawling up, resting, slipping, pulling herself up, until finally she too had made it. For a moment, she stood shaking herself inside the maroon coat that was torn up one whole side now, in a way that reminded Honor of old Lucifer coming up the bank after swimming out a long, long way in icy water to retrieve a duck, and holding the prize in his mouth, as proud as a dog could be.

"I told you I'd ride that old mule up!" Lola yelled out, brushing at herself, stomping her feet again.

Honor stood, somehow helplessly spellbound. "Lola, don't go!" she finally managed to screech out across the gap yawning out between them like some wide-open whale's mouth. "You might get frostbite all over. A panther might come along. You'll get lost maybe or can't see in the dark."

"Lola ain't going to do none of that. I'm going to hightail it down this old sawmill road lickety-split. I ain't going to look right or left or take no detours." She raised one arm and waved. "You go on home now. Go see your nice daddy come home. And Lola hopes you find your Christmas stocking stuffed full of lots of nice presents, just like all them you took the bother to fix up for old Lola. Ain't nobody never give Lola such a nice Christmas before."

"It wasn't enough—and then I messed it all up falling." She was unable to stop crying. The pain in her head was beating, thumping with the fear inside her chest. "Please come back. Let's hide in the barn."

"You mind me! You go on and do like I told you to do. You don't want a hairbrush whipping on top of all them bruises you done already got. I reckon you'll think up something to tell your mama." She looked up at the sky.

"Lola's got to be going, honey. I hates to—I hates to say good-bye. I sure hopes you grow up to be a fine happy woman now. And I hopes your family'll be all set up in that new place."

"I hope you get there on time. Don't miss your ride. Don't have any more bad luck, Lola." She tried to make her voice louder, clearer. It seemed to be going into an empty barrel. "I hope you find your people, that nobody never slips up behind you again and you'll—"

"Thank you. Maybe I'll find me that bluebird you was talking 'bout, by and by. You hang onto that bluebird, you hear? I 'spect it ain't out flying 'round right now—get its tail feathers froze off. Now get!" She was waving the way she might do if she was trying to shoo away some bothersome chickens coming too close to peck around. "Get on."

She was trying to think what to holler back at Lola, when suddenly there was no more Lola standing there. She caught a fuzzy glimpse of the slab of maroon color disappearing into the slit where the sawmill road picked up on the other side of the washed-out, long-ago-fallen-in wooden bridge and the place where the footlog had crashed down to the bottom of Frog Hollow.

"Be careful, Lola!" she screamed out, cupping her hands to her mouth. She listened to see if there was an answer. Even the sounds of Lola's heavy boots on the hard ground had faded in with all the muffled, shapeless sounds coming from the woods in a kind of drone. "It's too late, Lola, come back!"

For a long time she stood there, ignoring the pain, stabbing now, nearly blinding her. She tried to see clearly across the emptiness of Frog Hollow, into the deeper emptiness of the dark cave of the thick woods that seemed in their winter nakedness to look like mislaid, crooked skeletons of trees that had sprouted invisible monster eyes and ears and a kind of fretful, accusing voice mocking across Frog Hollow at her.

She turned to run. But as she wheeled around, the pain, and Lola's voice telling her to walk in slow easy steps, with no running or skipping around, made her start over again.

She felt as if the top of her head had a tight, tight

piece of leather cord wrapped around it, slowly cutting it into two separate parts.

As she lifted first one foot, then the other, trying to keep them in a straight even path, dead ahead toward the back of Ruthie's aunt's barn, which she could see coming into view now at the top of the rise of the hill, she thought her legs must have started to bloat up like a jellyfish—or else the sawdust was filling up the places where there used to be bones and muscles and shafts and joints and scabs and bony knees that kept bumping into each other.

She was stumbling along like that, groping with her arms outstretched around the edge of the barn, when one of the Freeman boys, who was stacking a half-cord of freshly chopped hickory wood in the barn to dry out and season for the rest of the winter, heard the noise. He came out just in time to catch her as she was falling down in a crumpling heap.

"I thought I'd been hearing somebody hollering. I could've swore it," he was mumbling to himself as he scooped her up in his powerful, big arms and started in a half-loping run, hollering at the top of his own full, booming voice, toward Ruthie Stinnet's aunt's house.

19

Inside Aunt Maggie Freeman's house, the two boys, Monroe Junior and J. T., had stretched Honor out on a bed in the front room and had chunked up the huge logs burning in the one-hundred-year-old stone fireplace. Honor felt something heavy and cold across her eyes and forehead.

"She's coming to, Ma. Come 'ere," the oldest, Monroe Junior, called out in a deep, rattling voice that seemed to boom across the top of her head.

The rag was taken off, and there stood Ruthie's Aunt Maggie with her snow-white hair and those funny round glasses that sat down on her nose. "What hit you? Who beat you up, one of them Northcutts?"

Honor lay very still, studying the situation as best she could and trying to bring her remembering mind around in full focus. This wasn't any time for her to be letting something slip off the tip of her tongue the wrong way.

"Maybe you ought'n ask her nothing yet," J. T. suggested.

"I fell off the footlog trying to cross Frog Hollow," Honor said, clenching the edges of the quilt that had been spread out across her. "Nobody beat me up. I just fell."

"That log is tricky. It turns on you pretty easy if you don't step on it just right," said Monroe Junior.

"I told you boys to get a new one put down." Their mother was glaring at them over the rims of her glasses. "I told you it was on our property and someday somebody was going to fall off and bust a leg or break their neck and then we'd have the law up here on us."

"I won't call the law," Honor said, wide-eyed. "It was my fault anyway. I know you're supposed to step up slow and test out a footlog before you go out on it."

"What in this wide world were you doing down there in them backwoods this time of day—on Christmas Eve?"

Honor thought quickly. "Well, it might sound funny to you, but my Daddy has been gone since last August. He's coming home sometime tonight. He's moving us all off to a big county seat town in Kentucky. Well, Mama's been so busy getting packed up—no man in the house . . ."

"I know what that means. My Monroe's been gone since J. T. was a baby."

Honor looked at all three faces staring down at her, waiting for her to finish. "Well, this being our last Christmas in Margate and all, and my Daddy liking to have the house all nice and decorated up, and Mama not doing much, I was just trying to find that big holly patch Ruthie showed me one time. I thought it was down there just across the footbridge. I was going to bring home a whole armload and surprise my Daddy."

"Why, that's the sweetest thing. I know what you're talking about, how you like to keep things the same. Even now, all this long time since Monroe was struck down by that timber and suffered on so long with his broke back and nearly killed us all seeing him laying there helpless and hurting so bad, every Christmas Eve I still fix us up a stuffed hen the way he used to like it. When we can afford it, I do a few other things he liked. That holly would mean a lot to your daddy, moving off to some strange place and all." She pointed at J. T., who was standing over by the window, shuffling his feet back and forth. "J. T., run over across that field and gather her up some holly with some nice berries on it. Get her some good cedar branches too. Hurry though. We want to get her drove home 'fore dark sets in. Monroe Junior, you maybe ought to finish unloading the wood before we carry her home in the truck."

"Won't it take the ruts, hold the road, and ride easier for her, with the wood left ŏn?"

"You just trying to stall off work, Monroe Junior, but I guess you're right about that. We ought'n to jar her up no more than she's already been jarred."

After the boys had gone outside, Monroe Junior to warm up the truck and J. T. to run across the field toward the holly, the old woman sat down in a chair by the bed. "I fixed up a good poultice and soaked that worst place on your head. I know how to fix a good herb root poultice my Grandma handed down, but you look like you ran into the side of the barn still. You got an awful nasty blow on the side of your head." She reached out and patted her on the hand. "Next time you looking for holly, come by here and let J. T. go get it. That Ruthie is so scatterbrained, she wouldn't know how to lead anybody to the well for a dipper of water. Not that I mean to say anything bad about my niece."

There was a silence in the room. Honor listened to the crackling of the logs burning. The smell of the roasting hen sifted through the small, ancient mountain house that had been in the Freeman family down through the years. After a moment, Aunt Maggie spoke again.

"Monroe Junior—I declare, I never saw him so bugeyed as when he came running in there with you, that is 'less'un he's looking at some new girl. He's got girls on the brain now. But anyway, he said he thought he kept hearing somebody out there hollering and hollering. But ever' time he'd get just about a ear on it, the wind would whip up. He just made up his mind it was maybe a hungry wildcat, maybe one of them panthers the Northcutts are always claiming they see ever' once in a while slipping up in wintertime from down under the bluff where they say they live." She got up and walked over to the window. "That J. T., he's the biggest slowpoke in Bragg County. The sky sure looks clouded up for a big snow. Looks awful threatening. I hope your daddy makes it up the mountain before the highway gets all slicky with fresh snow."

"Do you think it'll snow before dark—before nine o'clock?" Honor asked anxiously.

"You can't never tell when that old gloomy sky is going to open up and let it start coming down. Why, you worried Santa Claus ain't going to have snow for his reindeer?"

"I don't believe in Santa Claus. I'm too old for that."

"You know, it's a funny thing, but my J. T., and even Monroe Junior, they seemed to want to keep on believing in Santa Claus, even when they knowed better. They'd hold onto ever' little old thing we used to do when they was little—put out a glass of sweetmilk and a cookie, hang up their stockings. And I'd read out the Christmas story as best I could till Monroe Junior learned it by heart, and we'd sit there by that fireplace and they'd go to bed so wrought up and excited over what was going to be inside those stockings. I never had much to put in 'em, but I always managed to scrape up something I knew they'd like—that'ud be special. I see them get that kind of hungry look on their face ever' now and then about no more Christmas stockings hanging up. They're too proud to let on. They'd be bashful to admit that's what they'd still like."

She went over and picked up a long poker and rolled the log over. Sparks splintered and flew up the blackened, glowing chimney. "I reckon we're in for a long cold spell."

Honor's thoughts were whirling around now in a panic over Lola. "Do those wildcats—panthers—ever come up the old sawmill road?"

"Lord, I don't know, honey. It ain't often we see wildcats no more. Since the Northcutt boys got so hot on the triggers, we don't have much of nothing aggravating us around here. Ain't no telling how a panther slips his way around, what with me ain't never laid eyes on one. Mostly there's just whipped-up talk about panthers. Northcutt bragging."

"I guess that old sawmill road—well, does anybody ever go over it anymore? Is it grown up, covered up by weeds and things?" She watched the places in Aunt Maggie's eyes that would tell her if she was suspicious of anything.

"I reckon it's growed up some. Bound to be, ever since the bridge fell in and no wagons can get across it. But the hunters use it all the time during quail–rabbit season. In summer, Monroe Junior and J. T. go down it looking for things—blackberries, persimmons. Sometimes they chop wood off down thataway. You can ride into it with a truck from the other way, coming in off the highway from DuCasse."

"Oh, I see," said Honor, relieved a little.

"One thing I'm proud of—how I've raised my sons." She was looking into the fire as if she were seeing something there that no one else could find. "I never let them step foot down inside no dark coal mines to dig coal for a living. My Monroe would've been proud of that. He believed in being out in the woods, making your living off the land. The Freemans have always managed somehow. I tell my boys there's always somebody going to need a extra cord of good wood. You chop the best logs and season 'em right and you'll get steadies. Why, they was so proud they liked to died when they started getting answers to the penny postcards they sent out one year—all the way from down in Olympia. Townfolks who don't have no way of cutting good logs. If we can just save up and buy Monroe Junior a new truck. . . . The old flatbed's going to break down any day now. It's been mighty faithful though. Monroe Junior takes care of that truck. He's so good with his hands."

Monroe Junior came into the house, slapping his hands together over the fire to warm them. "It's colder'n Job's turkey out there right now, but I got everything ready, and J. T.'s tied down the holly so it won't blow off the truck bed. I guess we're ready to carry her home."

"Holler out there and tell J. T. I want him to stay here and watch the fires and keep a eye out on my roasting hen. I know he's too bashful to hold her up steady and keep her head from getting all moved around. I want to be sure she gets home to her daddy safe as we can get her there. I'll get on my things. You tell J. T. now."

J. T. was obviously disappointed he wasn't going to get to go along. "I'll bring you back a present maybe," his mother told him, as though she were speaking to a much younger boy. "You take your daddy's place while we're gone now." Then she turned to Monroe Junior. "Pick her up easy-like, and let me get set down good in the front seat of the truck so I'll be ready to hold her just right. Bring her out the minute you hear me holler. I don't want her getting no more chilled then she was already. Keep that quilt tucked in tight around her."

The truck bounced and shook in spite of Monroe Junior's careful handling of it. Honor was grateful for the support of Aunt Maggie's arm. As they drove up to the Whitfield house and he braked to ease over the cinder pile left by the road grader, Honor saw a strange shiny gray car in the alley. "Daddy must be home, driving a new car!"

"Looks like a brand new '38 Dodge to me," Monroe Junior said. "Someday, one of these days, I'm going to have me a new car. After I make us rich with our new truck."

196

"Carry her in just as easy as you got her loaded in the truck now, Monroe Junior."

As he scooped her up and tucked the quilt in around the edges, the front door of the house flew open and Honor heard her mother's shrill cry. "What's happened? Was she run over by a car? Is she dead?" She pushed the door open. "Did that nigger kill her?"

"What do you mean?" Monroe Junior walked in, looking puzzled and embarrassed all at once.

"Put her down on the daybed," Honor heard her father calling out from across the room.

"That nigger killer ran off today. We thought sure she had taken Honor along as a hostage, kidnapped her maybe."

"Naw, she fell off a footlog going across Frog Hollow. Hit bottom on a rock, looks like."

"She was just looking for some nice holly to surprise her daddy with for Christmas." There was a pause as Ruthie's Aunt Maggie stepped into the room. "I had my youngest boy, J. T., go out and gather up some, and it's out there on the truck bed. Monroe Junior, run out and bring in the holly and them nice cedar branches J. T. picked."

"Let me take your coat. Have a seat." Her mother was fluttering around, trying to get her bearings. "We've been out of our minds with worry, not knowing. I'm so glad Henry got here when he did. I was falling all to pieces."

"It's nice when the man's to home. My Monroe—"

"Honor Jane, you look *awful.* I declare, the stunts you pull. The things you don't get into."

"This is no time for that, Martha Jane." Her father's voice was taking over. Honor was glad to lie still on the daybed, to feel her father's arm across her, to smell the pipe tobacco—the Prince Albert can sticking out of his back pocket. Her head was pounding again. She rubbed it.

"Leave it alone now," her father said, gently pulling her hand away. "Buford, run up and tell Dr. Clark to bring his bag and come down immediately. It's an emergency. Tell him I'm afraid she might have a concussion."

"Stuart, why don't you go fix Mrs. Freeman and your mother some of that boiled custard—bring in a plate of cookies for our company."

"Henry, I'm just so thankful you're here to take over."

Honor's mother had stopped wringing her hands but was still walking about the room nervously.

"Sit down, Martha Jane. Be calm. It's all over now. We've got her home." He looked over at Mrs. Freeman. "I want you to know how grateful we are."

"It wasn't nothing. Monroe Junior found her out by the barn trying to grope her way to the house. He carried her inside and I fixed up a good poultice soon as I seen that awful lump on her head and all. She was out of it for quite a scary spell there. I was getting ready to send Monroe Junior for Dr. Clark myself, but I figured she was gaining color and looking better every minute and I decided to see if maybe it'ud be better to let her come around and then bring her home."

"You did just fine. We're much obliged to you. I'm going to make it up to you somehow." Honor had never heard her father's voice sound so deep and comforting.

Monroe Junior knocked at the door. Stuart opened it and helped take in the enormous batch of holly and cedar branches. "They smell so good—oh, they're lovely!" Honor's mother said, getting up. "Stuart, would you all mind putting them on the kitchen table and later on, after company leaves, we'll arrange some nice wreaths and decorate. What a lovely thing!"

"It was her idea," Mrs. Freeman pointed at Honor and smiled. "She's a nice girl."

"She's certainly going to have to learn to ask permission before she goes off on any more capers like that. I didn't have the vaguest notion—she was just suddenly gone, out of sight and hollering distance. And then Mamie Clark came down here telling me Lola had stolen some of her clothes and run off and asking me if I'd seen anything. Well, when we started putting two and two together, I guess our imaginations did run a little wild."

"Let's talk about it later on, Martha Jane. How's the boiled custard, Mrs. Freeman? My wife always did make delicious boiled custard."

"Oh, it's delicious. And this divinity candy—if you wouldn't think I'm being—well, would you mind if I took my boy J. T. a piece of this? He wanted to ride with us so bad, but I didn't want to crowd up the truck. I left him home by himself, and he ain't used to that."

"Stuart, go out in the kitchen again, please, and fix up a

whole box. There's a spare gift box on my sewing machine. Fill it up with cookies, candy, some of those oranges. I fixed enough for Cox's army. I'd be so happy to do that."

Buford came bursting in through the front door, breathing hard from his running. "Dr. Clark said he'd be here quick as he can. He's trying to put through a long-distance telephone call to the state penitentiary. He said for you to keep her perfectly still, on her back with no pillow. He said don't give her anything to drink or eat yet."

"That's why I didn't offer you any boiled custard, honey," her father said, leaning over. "Don't worry, you'll be okay."

"I hope they catch her," Honor's mother said.

"They've called the law down in Olympia. The county sheriff is going to be on the lookout."

Mrs. Freeman stood up. "Monroe Junior, I reckon we'd better be getting on back to J. T."

Honor's father stood up and reached in his pocket for his billfold. "I want to give you this." He took out a ten dollar bill.

"Don't you take that, Monroe Junior," Mrs. Freeman's voice shot out. "We don't take money doing neighborly deeds."

"It's not that. I want to give you something to show you my appreciation."

"We don't take money unless we earned it." She smiled at him. "This box of so many nice cookies and candy, that's the best thing you could give us. It's going to make our Christmas. We didn't want to spend anything on extrys this year with so many of the boys' steady customers moving off."

Honor saw her father, as he opened the door, slip the folded ten dollar bill into Monroe Junior's pocket. "You certainly have a fine boy here, Mrs. Freeman."

A glow seemed to spread across her face. "I tried to bring 'em up the way I figured my Monroe would've wanted it. He was so proud of being a mountain man. He figured digging coal was a disgrace, a mar on the land. Monroe wouldn't shed no tears over the mines' shutting down. His family was living off the land up here long before Black Diamond Coal Company came around and tore up so much of the woods and built up a town. Now they

199

say they're going to tear it down again, all except a few houses some folks is going to buy." She shook hands with them. "I reckon we'll be around here a long time after it's all tore down. I sure hope you'll be happy in your new place, in Kentucky. I hear it's a pretty state. A nice place to live. When you moving?"

"Well, if Honor's going to be all right, the truck will be here on the thirty-first. We'll be out by New Year's."

After the commotion of their leaving had died down, a sudden strange awkwardness seemed to spread across the room. It had been so long since August. They were looking at each other like strangers.

It was their mother, Martha Jane, who stood up. "While we're waiting for the doctor, I guess at least we can count our blessings we're all together again. Our family's back together. It's going to be a fine Christmas after all."

"It's snowing!" Buford said, looking out the window for any sign of Dr. Clark. "Big flakes. Looks like it's going to stick on the ground this time."

"Shhh," her father was saying, as Honor shut her eyes together in a tight clamp. She wondered how far Lola had gotten—if she had made it all the way out to the end of the sawmill road and caught her ride.

"Let's let her sleep."

"Come on, boys, we'll go arrange the holly and fix up some decorations in the kitchen. You stay with her, Henry. She'll be happiest with you there."

20

Honor dozed off, opened her eyes to the strange feel of Dr. Clark's fingertips pressing on the sides of her neck and to a tiny light beaming into her eyes from about an inch away as he peered down at her through some kind of instrument.

"How're you feeling? Your head hurt a little there?" His voice had that same wheezing sound she had heard before when he had asthma. She had heard him breathe that way once when he was lancing her stone bruise and another time when he was mopping her sore throat with swabs of awful-tasting medicine. He was kind of sucking at the air in quick, dry gulps, as if he was afraid there wouldn't be enough air to go around for everybody and he might come out on the short end of the stick.

"It hurts," she said, watching him. "How's your asthma?"

He took out his stethoscope and started unbuttoning her flannel shirt. "It's something I get this time of the year, something from the cedar trees I think that sets me off. This'll feel a little cold to your chest. Lie real still so I can listen to your heart and your lungs. Take a deep breath through your mouth . . . let it out. . . . Another."

She shut her eyes as tightly as she could. There was something about his hands resting across her chest, even if it was still flat mostly and not sprouted out enough to wear a brassiere yet, that embarrassed her.

He pulled the blanket back up over her chest, folded the stethoscope up, put it back in his bag, and pulled out a little hammer with a rubber end on it. "Let's have your foot there." He turned the cover back and pulled out her right leg and started tapping at her knee, then on her foot. "Her reflexes are good, pupils okay."

"Other than your head hurting, anyplace else hurt?" he asked.

"No." She tested herself. There was a knot riding on the inside of her stomach that felt as big as a baseball turned into lead. But she had felt that way lots of times before, when she was worried or scared of a hairbrush whipping. She decided it had nothing to do with having fallen off the footlog. He seemed to be waiting for her to say something. "I'm sorry you lost your free maid," she blurted out.

"Honor Jane!" her mother shot out.

She had let something slip out the wrong way again. "I mean I'm sorry Lola caused you trouble running off."

He shook his gray head. "I guess I shouldn't have told her last night about having to send her back. I was all for trying to keep her on with us. Where we're moving to is still out in the country. But Mamie—I don't know, lately, she's taken a turn against her. Doesn't trust her for some reason."

"I can understand that, from a woman's point of view," her mother said.

"How do you mean that?" Dr. Clark asked, wheezing again.

"Well, I mean the way you can't trust them, the way they revert and can't help stealing and all. A woman, being around the house all the time, picks up on things like that. That's all I meant—certainly you didn't think I was insinuating . . ."

"Of course not." He took out some cotton balls and moistened them with something from a bottle in his bag. "Here, this will sting a little, but I want to clean up that one place." Honor winced as he wiped the sore places on the side of her head.

"Did she steal anything valuable? Mamie said she took one awfully nice coat with a fur collar."

"Martha Jane, let him finish his examination." Her father sounded irritated, Honor thought.

Dr. Clark walked over to the fireplace and tossed in the used cotton balls. "From what I can tell you right now, she's going to be okay. That's a bad lump. You're right to be concerned, Henry. But it might not be much more than that. Let's keep an eye on her. Keep her flat in bed, except to sit up on the pot. Do you have a chamber pot handy?"

"We've got two old slop jars for when the toilet goes out of whack and don't flush," Honor volunteered. Her mother gave her a warning look.

"Well, that's good. Bring one of them in by the bed, and I think somebody should help her, stay with her when she's doing that." He was closing his bag. "I'd appreciate it, Henry, if you'd look in on her through the night, once or twice. Just see if you notice anything different. I trust your powers of observation. They've always been pretty keen."

"Thank you, Doctor, I'll be sure and do that."

Honor watched as her mother handed Dr. Clark his coat, scarf, and gloves. "You could get those clothes off her now. Put her in some warm pajamas. Maybe put some socks on her feet. If you see anything, if you're worried, send for me, Henry. I'll be right here."

"Well, you were just so nice to come down, interrupting your phone call and all. Did you get it through?" Her mother was smiling that puckered-up smile of hers.

"Not yet. I guess there's some trouble on the line. Pretty bad weather we're having. Looks like it'll be a white Christmas." He pulled on his gloves, tied his scarf. "I have to keep bundled up myself, this asthma and all."

"You take care of yourself now. I surely hope you won't get called out tonight—and that that nigger doesn't cause you any more worry." Her mother handed him his hat. "I hope they catch her right away."

Honor kept a steady eye on Dr. Clark's face. He had picked up his bag and was standing with one hand on the doorknob, ready to leave. "I don't know, I kind of hope somehow she makes it. She won't do anyone any harm. She's just homesick. I can't blame her, not wanting to go back there. Actually, I just wish I knew she was all right. I'm worried about her, out there unprotected on a night like this. I hope she's—well, I'd better be getting back. Merry Christmas to you."

"Why, I almost forgot, there's so much going on and all," her mother said, coming to. She had that look on her face as if she had locked up some kind of answer about Lola she had on the tip of her tongue. "Please tell your wife we send our best. I hope you like the cookies and the

203

brown bread I sent up earlier today." She laughed. "I think Mamie likes it."

"Sure, sure, Mamie likes your cooking." He waved his arm in the air, tucked the scarf in, and went out the door.

Buford, who had been standing quietly by the Philco radio said, "I bet she won't. I heard her throwing a fit and falling back in it while I was standing there waiting for Dr. Clark to hang up the telephone receiver. She was off someplace in the house yelling and throwing things around and saying how he'd promised to drive her to Nashville to be with Jerome and her mother, how she had the Packard all loaded down. I never heard such yelling and throwing."

"No wonder he has asthma," Honor's father said.

"You shouldn't be eavesdropping, Buford. That is not polite."

"I wasn't, Mama. I was just standing there with my cap in my hands waiting. I ain't deaf."

"I *am not* deaf, not 'ain't.'"

"That's enough!" her father broke in. "Now, boys, I want you to run off to bed early tonight. There's Christmas in the morning, remember. Get a good night's sleep, and your mother and I will tend to your sister, tuck her in. Then we'll have to be Santa Claus's helpers."

"But it's too early."

"Boys!" her mother's voice commanded. "Mind your tongues. Your father is home now."

After her mother had brought in the pajamas and a pair of Stuart's woolen boot socks, Honor's father sat down on the foot of the daybed and started putting the socks on her feet. He had her legs across his knees, and when he had finished, he patted her legs. "I'm glad you're going to be all right, honey."

Her mother swept in. "Here, let me help with those pajamas."

"You're being a little rough, Martha Jane," he cautioned. "Sit down. I'll finish." He helped Honor slip out of the flannel shirt and into the pajama top. "There, snug as a bug." He gave her a kiss, stood up, and walked over to the fireplace. "I see you've got the stockings up. The tree's pretty. I missed helping the boys cut it this year."

"Well, there's a whole lot different this year. This isn't exactly my idea of your homecoming." Honor tried not to look at her mother. "Having you sit up all night in here is hardly what I had in mind when—it's been such a long time, Henry."

"There's time."

Honor closed her eyes tightly. *Maybe she hates me*, she thought, feeling the baseball in her stomach grow heavier, bigger. *Maybe since I've messed up everything so badly, she just wishes I would have a blood clot and go on and die and not be around to mess up homecomings and be gawky-footed. Maybe she hates me because Daddy loves me, and is fussing around so much over me.*

But that didn't seem right to her either. Daddies were supposed to love their children in one way and their wives in another. Just as she loved Stuart and Buford different from the way she loved her parents, from the way she loved old Lucifer when he was alive, or the way she loved things like honeysuckle vines and birds singing and the way a lilac smelled, or the bluebird, her keepsakes, even the way she loved Lola out there maybe stumbling around lost or dead with frostbite by now. ... There were so many kinds of love. But most kinds of love, she guessed, sometimes got all mixed up with hate, and, like the branch water muddied up at rainy season, had to wait for enough run-off time for the mud to sift down to the bottom and the water to be sparkling clear again.

"I guess she's going to be all right," her mother said.

"We'll know by tomorrow."

Her mother was tapping her fingers impatiently on the mantel.

Honor wanted, all of a sudden, to be left alone. "Daddy's got me all fixed up now."

Her father sat down on the arm of the chair and put his arm around her mother's waist. "She seems tucked in. Maybe we should let her drop off to sleep. Honor, your mother and I—well, we have some things to unpack in the bedroom. I brought a lot of presents that still need wrapping." She saw him wink at her mother. "We'll stop in the kitchen first and have a little nightcap, some special boiled custard to celebrate everything being all right. I'll be back later on to check on you."

As her mother reached over and snapped off the floor lamp by the radio, Honor felt both a sense of relief and a fierce anger that they were leaving her. She tried to see clearly through the semidarkness as they headed for the kitchen, their arms around each other. She ignored Dr. Clark's warning and sat bolt upright on the daybed, propping herself up with her hands, fighting back the dizziness. "Well, when you get through *doing it*, would you mind bringing me the slop jar? I need to pee!"

It was her mother who appeared in the doorway. "Honor Jane Whitfield!" she rasped. "It's a good thing the doctor told us to leave you alone or I'd wash your mouth out this second! Your father is getting the chamber pot. Lie down there. You and I are going to have a whole lot to talk about sooner or later, young lady. Mamie told me about how she found a Christmas tree strung up with popcorn. I saw you stringing that popcorn up with that funny look plastered all over your face, trying to look innocent. I just knew you were up to something. But, you wait, I'll find out. Don't you worry about that."

They heard footsteps in the dining room, and her mother quickly shifted her voice into a different tone as her father called out, "You ladies ready for this?"

He came in with the enameled pot and lid. "Just put it there by the bed, honey," she directed. "I'll be with you in just a minute."

"Okay, I'll be in the kitchen. Call me if you need help, Martha Jane."

Honor put her legs over the side of the daybed, fighting back a strong urge to vomit. Her mother guided her by the arm. "Come on, please try to hurry."

"I'll do it myself," Honor said, fighting back tears. "I can't hurry when you're standing there watching. I can't go."

"I'll turn my back then. I'll stand over here by the fire. Tell me when you're finished. But try to hurry if you can. It's just that I've missed your father so much. . . ."

Honor went as quietly as she could, tilting the pot so that it didn't make any noise. Then she eased back under the covers and pulled the quilts up around her chin. "I'm all through," she said. "But the top needs putting back on."

Her mother slammed the top on and put the chamber pot over in the corner at the foot of the daybed. "I'll put this here where no one will stumble over it. I hate having it in the living room."

"Martha Jane." Honor heard the gruff sound of her father's voice that reminded her of the way Lucian Arnold had sounded that night when he crawled in the back seat of Tootie Farber's car with Mildred Matthews.

"I'm coming. Here, let me leave on this little sewing lamp by the machine. That'll give enough light for you to see by when you go in to check on her."

"Come on. It's been a long time since August."

"You mean, Henry, there wasn't another woman? Nobody like Mildred Matthews or anything?"

"I never laid hands on another woman."

They think they're whispering, Honor thought to herself, trying to blink back the hateful, salty tears that were stinging her face, sliding down the sides of her neck onto the edge of the pillow. But she could hear everything. She'd bet a dime she'd be able to hear them when they got the bed going the way Lucian Arnold got Tootie Farber's car rocking nearly off its brakes.

She didn't care what they did. Maybe she'd drop off to sleep and never wake up. Maybe she did have a blood clot. They could just bury her in Margate. She didn't want to move off to any big county seat town anyway. She'd move in with the Freemans—if she didn't die in her sleep. Ruthie's Aunt Maggie would take her in. She said she was a nice girl . . . and she knew all about poultices.

A dark, engulfing weariness took hold of her. She could hear her mother in the kitchen, giggling over the eggnog, but she wasn't awake to hear them when they did go off to bed. She was in a deep sleep, filled with nightmarish dreams that seemed to be screaming up at her, all the voices coming out in an echo from the bottom of Frog Hollow, echoes that spread out over miles and miles of freshly fallen snow.

21

All during the night Honor slept at fretful intervals, flailing her arms about now and then, striking out at the empty echoes, at other monster forces that seemed to gather in her nightmares in shapeless patterns that she could not recognize but that she knew were going to engulf her.

She remembered in fuzzy snatches her father's hand resting briefly on her forehead; a flashlight shining in her face, and quickly turned off again. Once she heard the poker hitting at a stubborn chunk of coal and smelled the thick black smoke that puffed out across the room from a back draft in the faulty flue.

Buford and Stuart, accustomed to opening presents on Christmas morning at daylight, had gotten up on schedule and dressed. They were standing impatiently around the kitchen table, uncertain as to what to do next with this break in their old custom. Usually, on Christmas morning all three children stood in line in the kitchen, the youngest first, waiting while their father chunked up the fire and turned on the Christmas tree lights in the living room, and their mother carried in a tray loaded down with boiled custard and brown bread and coffee for "Santa's Helpers." Only then did the children march in.

As she placed the last cup on the tray, fussing with the exact arrangement of everything, and placing a sprig of holly here and there, their mother turned sleepily and crossly to the boys: "You can just wait a minute. Your father was up and down all night long with your poor sister. She was so restless, he hardly slept a wink, and I feel as if I haven't even been to bed. We were both so worried over her, wondering if she had a concussion."

"Nobody but you ever touches that tray you fix up anyway," Buford complained.

"This Christmas tray is a custom I've had all my life, since I was a girl. If you don't like it, when you're a man with your own house, you won't have to have it."

Honor could hear their voices as she kept absolutely still, pretending she was asleep as her father tiptoed around the room, getting the fire going roaring hot and turning on the lights of the Christmas tree. She felt him kiss her lightly on the forehead, above the place that hurt the most. "Wake up, little lady," he said. "It's Christmas morning."

She sat up slowly and started to rub the eye that would not open.

"How do you feel? The bruises are coming out today. That swelling should start going down pretty soon though. Don't worry about how it looks or anything."

"I never look very good," Honor said, shivering. "I guess I'm just one of God's natural uglies."

"Not my girl! Don't let me hear my pretty girl say that. Okay, Martha Jane, I'm ready in here," he called out.

Honor watched as her mother whisked into the room, skirting around in her chenille bathrobe, her elbows stretched tight, bent back like turkey wings as she carried in the heavy tray and set it down on top of the Philco radio. "Merry Christmas everybody!" she beamed as the boys rushed in. "Slow down, don't shove and push, boys. Those presents aren't running off anyplace."

Honor tried not to look at her, wondering if she had found out yet about Buford's gloves.

But her mother swept in on her. "My word, Honor Jane, if you aren't the worst-looking sight I ever saw! Henry, look how black and blue she's turning, and her eye's swollen shut. I didn't know it was going to turn out that bad. Does it hurt, honey?"

"Not as bad as it did last night," Honor said, accepting the presents her father was piling in front of her from under the Christmas tree.

"I didn't mean to be so cross and cranky last night, it was just that—well, there was so much going on and— Henry, I declare, you went on a shopping spree. I never saw so many presents under the Whitfield tree before."

There was a general commotion of wrapping paper

being torn, ripped off, picked up by her mother, and burned quickly in the grate to "keep some of this mess cleared up," and a mixture of exclamations coming from this one and that.

"You still don't feel so hot, do you?" her father asked, sitting down by her and patting her through the covers. "Are you happy with your presents? Did you get what you wanted?" He was studying her closely. "I'm so used to you jumping up and down with excitement on Christmas morning."

Honor didn't have to answer, since at that moment her mother took out her own present. "Why, Henry, what a lovely housecoat!" She held up a pale lavender taffeta housecoat and turned around in mock grandness. "It's beautiful. Of course, it's nothing I can fry sausage or dip up oatmeal in."

"I thought you'd enjoy wearing it maybe for times like this, when you pour out your boiled custard. You might get more wear out of it in the new place." Honor thought her father looked a little disappointed.

"The new place—children, it all sounds so wonderful! That Nathan Dobbs, Mr. Dobbs, has been such a—well, a Santa Claus from Heaven to us: furnishing so much of our new house, providing your father with that lovely brand new car to drive up here and get us in, sending up a company truck to move us." She put the box down. "I'll be right back. I'm going to try it on." She held it up to her again. "You know, when I grew up in Maddoxville, every Christmas morning our house Negro, Rodessa Mae, well, she'd put on this special little frilly apron she'd drag out just for big occasions like Christmas, and she'd put this silly little ole hat on top of that kinky head of hers and come strutting in with the tray of boiled custard and brown bread that Mama always made, just like I make it today, same recipe. . . . Who knows, your daddy is acting so rich lately, maybe we'll even have us a house Negro down in Hartman one of these days. Now wouldn't that be something!" She fairly pranced out of the room.

"I've got a little special something for you too, Honor," her father said, reaching into his bathrobe pocket and handing her a tiny square box tied with a bright red ribbon. "I've been saving it for last. It's the first present I ever picked out for you all by myself. If it doesn't fit now, don't worry. The jewelry store in Hartman is run by the nicest people. They'll size it for you."

Honor felt her first genuine flare of excitement. She ripped open the package. She pulled out a small, blue, velvet-covered box and opened the lid slowly. Inside, shining up from a soft white satin lining was a birthstone ring—a garnet, deep red, and the most beautiful thing she had ever seen. Her fingers trembled as she put it on her right hand, shoved it over her knuckle.

"Does it fit?"

"My knuckle's a little swollen. It's fine. I love it!" Again, she felt the tears stinging, pushing out from under her swollen eye. She didn't know why she was always breaking out crying lately, and not able to stop herself.

"I'm so happy you like it. There, lie back down. You don't want to get overtired. I'll have the doctor look in on you again later on. We've got to get you up and well for the big trip."

"How do I look?" The lavender taffeta made a crisp, rustling sound as she turned around, pulling at the sash and running her hands down over her hips.

"Fine. It looks good on you."

"I'll look better after I get to a decent beauty parlor and get a permanent that won't frizz up. This material is kind of crawly-feeling. I'm not used to anything like it."

She picked up the tray and passed it to them. "I know those boys won't take anything. They're in there in the dining room putting their new sled together. Buford's tickled silly with his new gun. Will there be a place for him to hunt in Hartman?"

"Sure, out in the county. He's too good at it not to keep it up." He took the coffee, stirred sugar into it.

"Honor, do you feel like a cup of boiled custard? You haven't eaten. Don't you think it will be okay, Henry?"

Honor felt the empty gnawing in her stomach and reached out and took a cup.

"Why, look at that pretty ring on your finger! You didn't tell me, Henry. My, I should say we're getting rich. I never had a ring like that when I was your age. Is there a diamond in my stocking?"

"Someday . . . maybe someday."

"Buford! Don't you aim that gun in this house!" their mother yelled out.

"It's not loaded. It's brand new. See, the barrel's empty."

"One of these days it won't be. I still say, don't ever let me catch you aiming a gun inside this house, at anybody. That's the way people get their heads blown off."

Honor had been sipping on the boiled custard. At the sound of her mother talking about the gun, she felt a hot rising sensation of having to vomit.

"Quick! Hand me something. Honor's sick!" her father called out.

There was a rustling of papers. "Not all over everything, Honor Jane!"

"She can't help where it goes." Her father held her head and wiped her mouth with a handkerchief from his pocket. "There, lie back down. Get some rest."

"Here, let me wipe her off with this—"

"Martha Jane, don't be so rough. Her face is bruised."

"Stuart, bring me in a clean pair of pajamas or a nightgown out of Honor's dresser drawer, and a sheet, and—oh, what a mess. Never mind, I'll do it myself."

"I'm sorry," Honor said, crying again. "I didn't mean to mess everything up. I messed it up so bad, Daddy."

"Ah, that's nothing. Your mother always gets overly excited. She doesn't mean it the way it sounds. You didn't mess up anything."

"You don't know. You don't know."

Buford and Stuart, having finished examining their presents, had put on their jackets and hats, and Buford was pulling on his old gloves with the ribbing stretched out and a hole in the thumb. "Why don't you wear your new gloves, Buford?" Their mother was inspecting her taffeta housecoat to see if she had gotten any spots on it.

"What new gloves?"

Honor watched her mother closely. "I had a brand new pair under the tree wrapped up in some blue paper. Oh, well, they'll probably turn up. There was so much this year. I'll keep an eye out for them. You boys run on out now. But I don't want anybody getting their head busted in on that new sled. One banged-up child is enough for this Christmas."

"How deep did it snow?" Honor asked, her eyes widening.

"Nearly nine inches!" Stuart yelled out. "It's going to be

the biggest snow we've had in years. It'll stick a long time. Mama, we're going up to Black Diamond Hill where it's good sledding."

"Boys . . . Buford." Their father got up and went over to the front door. "Do me a favor and stop in at Dr. Clark's a minute. Just tell him that in case it means anything, Honor can't seem to hold anything on her stomach this morning. But tell him it was boiled custard and might have been too rich, that I just want him to know about it."

"Would you please shut that door," their mother yelled out. She crossed her arms and shivered. "There's one thing about this taffeta—it either sticks to you too close or you freeze to death in a draft. It's the funniest material."

"I can take it back if you don't like it."

"I like it, but it really isn't very practical. I could fold it back up and maybe we could get a—well, a washable one that would be just as pretty."

Honor leaned over and looked out the window at Buford and Stuart tromping around, making patterns in the snow, and throwing snowballs at each other. She heard the noise about the moment that Buford lifted his head and looked down the main cinder road. The window was frosted from the heat inside, and Honor wiped away a clean place to see better. It was Monroe Junior in his flatbed truck, easing in and out, slipping and skidding up the hill toward Dr. Clark's house. In the back, their legs hanging over the sides, were the Northcutts. It looked like the whole tribe of Northcutts.

Buford and Stuart burst into the room at once. "Please! Shut that door. And don't track in all that snow."

"Something bad's happened. Maybe a Northcutt has shot a Freeman. They usually don't even talk to each other, but they're riding in the same truck, Northcutts on the back and Freemans in the cab. Somebody's stretched out covered up—looks like how they cover up dead people. Just boots sticking out."

As the commotion whirled around her, Honor very quietly slid down under the covers. She wanted to slide on down and down and down, to end up in one tiny ball of an echo that nobody would ever find to see or touch again.

"Those ignoramuses. Those Northcutts are always so
213

smart-aleck with their shotguns." Their mother had pulled back the curtains over the Philco radio and was looking up the hill. "White trash. I'll be so glad to get away from all this—scum."

"Can we go look?" Stuart cried out. "Get a close-up look?"

"You most certainly may not! Standing around gawking—acting as common as they are."

"I guess I'll get dressed and go up to see what's happened," her father said, heading toward the bedroom. "I want to be sure Honor's vomiting wasn't something serious anyway."

"Then can we go on to Black Diamond Hill and sled?"

"Well, you're going to drive me crazy if you stay inside. But you march right on past that truck up there. You go straight on by, you hear?"

Honor still did not move. She clamped her eyes shut.

"We'd better keep our voices down," she heard her father say as he came back into the room. "I'm worried about Honor. Her color's turned to pale. She looks—different." He stopped at the front door. "Let her be, Martha Jane. Don't bother her about anything now. Promise."

"What in the world would I bother her about? You could hurry and close the door yourself, Henry. Oh, Lord, Henry, she's throwing up again. Get me something."

Stuart raced back across the porch and opened the front door. Honor could barely see his eyes; they were almost popping out of his head, and his skin was as white as a ghost. "It's her! It's that Nigger Lola shot straight between the eyes. Hardly no blood—he got her bull's eye! Thought she was a wild animal, a bear or something from down the bluff." He was talking so fast and breathing so hard that his words seemed to fall into the room like lumps of coal being dumped into a bucket. "Heard her prowling around his barn, the smokehouse over on the edge of the old sawmill road. . . ."

"Would you tone down your voice. You have got her at it again. And this time—oh, for God's sake! There's no exchanging of *this* housecoat. And taffeta will never wash out."

22

It was shortly past two o'clock that Christmas Day when Dr. Clark managed to get away from the commotion going on in and around his house—of waiting for the county sheriff to arrive and make out his reports; getting the long-distance telephone call through to the state penitentiary; trying to keep the curiosity seekers, the gawkers, at a distance; and, finally, administering a sedative to his wife, Mamie—so that he could get down to the Whitfield house to check on Honor.

"Hasn't this been some Christmas Day!" Honor's mother greeted him at the door. "That child, she has been throwing up, vomiting all blessed day long. Just about an hour ago she dozed off. Here, let me take your coat and things and hang them up."

"How's it going?" Honor heard her father's voice, making an attempt to speak softly. "Everything settling down?"

"It's been bedlam. I guess the main things are tended to." He bent over wearily and put his bag down. Honor could hear his breathing, the shrill high noises that sounded a little like static on the radio on a stormy night. She kept her eye that wasn't swollen slightly opened, but pretended to be asleep.

"Your asthma sounds worse. Say, how about me fixing you a good shot of Kentucky bourbon? I brought some up for the holidays. Fact is, I have a bottle I was going to slip to you, a fifth, the first chance Martha Jane wasn't looking."

"How's our patient, sleeping?"

"Finally dozed off. Poor kid, she's had quite a day."

"Yes, I rather suspect she has. I'll take you up on that drink. A double."

Honor thought a strange note had come into his voice.

As her father's steps retreated toward the dining room, Dr. Clark called out softly, "By the way, Henry, could you maybe keep Martha Jane—I mean, women do seem to carry on a bit. I've just about had it with Mamie today. I guess they don't bear up so well in crisis."

"I know what you mean." He laughed, his voice having that sound as if he'd already had more than a double bourbon. "That won't be any trouble. She'll stay put."

The room was very still. For a moment Honor didn't even hear the wheezing and wondered if they had both gone after the whiskey. She opened her eyes and turned her head to look.

"I thought you were playing possum," Dr. Clark said, smiling down at her. Then he sat down on the daybed and put his big hand over hers. She thought he looked the color of ashes, as if every part of him was ready to sink in under the heavy breathing. He reached into his pocket with his other hand. "Listen, Honor Jane, I want you to listen very carefully to me now. I *know*—and I understand. I don't want you to keep on blaming yourself. It's that, you know, that's making you do all this vomiting." He raised his head, listened carefully. "It was more my fault than yours. I could have saved her. I could have insisted over Mamie's objections. I didn't have to tell her—" He coughed, put his head in his hand a moment. "You only meant well. At least you were trying to help her."

She was staring up at him wide-eyed.

"Here we are." Her father came into the room, holding out the glass half-filled with whiskey.

"Henry, I'm sorry to bother you, but could you maybe take that back out to the kitchen and put in a couple pieces of ice, an icicle, anything?"

"No trouble at all. Sorry, I didn't think to ask you."

He covered her hand again and lowered his voice. In his other hand, he was holding the notebook paper, the map she had drawn for Lola. "I found this stuffed in her—in her underclothing." He got up, went quickly to the grate, threw it in, and chunked the fire with the poker until all traces of it were gone. He sat back down beside her. "It was a good map. You had the right idea. Nobody but

216

me knows. I want you to know that, and you've seen with your own eyes what happened to it."

"Mama knows. Suzie Daniels knows."

"Your mother is suspicious, but she doesn't know anything. I'll cover up her suspicions—in time. And Suzie—Suzie has her own guilt she's wrestling around with. She arranged the pickup, the contact. At least he got away."

Honor started crying. "I didn't mean to. She would've made it if I hadn't been so gawky and tripped over my own big feet crossing the footlog. She wouldn't go on and leave me. She said she was afraid I might've died and the buzzards would have picked me clean."

"Yes, Lola would've done that. That would've been her way."

"She wasn't a bad killer."

"No, she wasn't." He wiped her eyes. "No, she was—she was worth trying to help. And she saved your life."

"But I didn't mean for her to—"

"Look, Honor Jane, you would have saved hers too, if you could have. We're just lucky we didn't lose you both. Now, you quit this inside stewing you're—look, I want you to think about only the good side of it from now on. We've got to get you well for the big trip, you know."

"How's this? Hope it's not too much ice. Don't like to water down such good Kentucky bourbon."

"How's the drinking going, Henry?" He raised the glass toward Honor. "Have you eased up some?"

"Oh, Lord yes. This is just holiday celebrating, celebrating Honor Jane, my little girl there, going to be okay."

"I'll drink to that." They raised their glasses, and both took a deep, heavy drink.

"Sit down. Rest a minute in the armchair there."

"I could stretch out my feet a bit. It's been quite a day." Honor watched as Dr. Clark sat down with a big heavy sigh. His wheezing seemed to be letting up a little.

"It's different now—my drinking, I mean. Oh, I love to drink. There's no denying that. But there's something about—well, having Nathan serve me a nice highball in that big fine house of his, not having to slip around. You know how Martha Jane is about drinking."

"You still better keep down the amount. It's hard on your liver."

"Don't you worry, Doc. I've got a whole new future

217

ahead for this family of mine. Nathan Dobbs, he's saving my life, you know."

"Sounds like a nice man."

"The finest. He does have a tendency to kind of want to own me a little. But look—"

"I'm sure everything will be okay, Henry. I want it to be. I feel I have a vested interest in this family, having brought all three of your babies into this world." He laughed a hollow-sounding laugh. "The other day, I was figuring out I must have delivered about 457 mountain babies. That one over there is one of my favorites." He smiled across at Honor and got to his feet, draining the glass dry, rattling the ice around before setting the empty glass down. "She's a fine girl."

"I'm proud of her." He stood up. "I wish you'd stay longer. Visit awhile. We never had much chance to talk before."

"Always too busy. Being the only doctor up here kept me jumping. If I don't go now, I might fall asleep. It's so comfortable sitting in front of the fire. That's a nice chair."

"Well, we certainly appreciate your coming down to check up on our girl. You think she's okay?"

"She's going to be fine now. Some light soup, dry crackers. She ought to hold that down. By tomorrow she should be able to eat 'most anything."

"By tomorrow, maybe things will be finished up for you with that mess." He waved toward the door.

"I guess it will. We've still got to find out about the burial—if there's some reason why we can't go ahead and bury her here. Maybe there's some family somewhere who want to come and claim her body. I rather doubt it though." He was pulling on his gloves, tying his scarf. "In fact, I took advantage of some of that mountain muscle standing around the house and had them dig a grave, just in case."

"Where you plan to bury her? I mean, if you do."

"I figured there'd be some fuss stirred up if we mentioned the town graveyard." He looked down at Honor and smiled, giving her a special knowing look. "She always seemed to like that sycamore tree. Sometimes when I'd come in from a night call, I'd find her standing there just looking up at the Big Dipper. I think that would be a nice place to bury her, don't you, Honor?"

"I guess so," she said, barely able to speak.

"Well, I'll be getting on. I've got to drive Mamie to Nashville tomorrow. I'll get the burial over by then and shut up the house for a while. I guess you'll be gone by the time I get back."

"The movers are coming up with the truck on the thirty-first."

"She'll be able to travel by then," he said, reaching down and giving Honor one last pat on the hand. "She'll be in fine shape by then."

23

By eleven o'clock on the morning of the last day of December, the big yellow truck sent up to Margate by Nathan Dobbs, driven by two of the strongest men from the loading department of his farm machinery and equipment business, arrived to move the Whitfields' belongings to Hartman.

Soon after the truck had been pulled up as close to the house as possible in the side alley, the Freeman flatbed truck turned in and parked over to one side, out of the way. Monroe Junior and J. T., holding their caps in their hands, came to the back door and asked to speak to Mr. Whitfield.

Honor was up and about, the swelling almost gone by then, with only one deep blue-black circle under one eye and a few noticeable scratches here and there. Her mother had made her put on her best Sunday school dress stuffed down inside her woolen leggings for the ride to Hartman in the new Dodge. "I want your legs to stay warm. We don't need a runny nose on top of everything else."

Before the Freeman boys came, she had been wandering about the house aimlessly, from room to room, watching the men select which heavy pieces should be loaded up first, and then start hauling them out: the dining room table, the daybed, the armchair. Once she heard them mumbling to each other: "Beats hell outa me why they're moving this goddam junk. I bet when Mr. Dobbs sees it, you wait, I bet we'll be hauling it off to the county dump or to somebody's junkyard someplace."

"Yeah, he likes everything nice. Wonder how that man latched on to such a good thing."

"You want to know what I really think?"

"No, I just want you to haul ass so we can get out of this place before it snows us in."

Honor was in the kitchen, sitting at the table that had been pushed over in one corner out of the movers' path, when her father came to see what the Freeman boys wanted.

"Mr. Whitfield," it was Monroe Junior, taking charge, "Ma said we was supposed to help you move out furniture, do any kind of hard jobs to help you get moved off. We'll clean up after you've gone too. Sweep the house, do anything you want us to do."

"That's awfully nice. What a nice neighborly thing for you to do." He opened the door and asked them to step inside.

"Wasn't being neighborly. Ma said we can't take no excuses. She says we got to earn every penny of that ten dollar bill you slipped in my pocket or else we got to give it back, any part we don't earn rightly."

"But I wanted to give you that."

"She said money can't never be no gift. It's got some kind of strings attached."

"I promise, there's no strings attached whatsoever. It was just my way of showing you how grateful I was that you tended to my daughter."

"Ma said to ask how she was getting along too."

"Fine, just fine. Fully recovered just about, except a few bruises and scratches. Still a little puny, drags around, and—well, she's coming around. Tell her not to worry. She'll be just fine and dandy."

"What do you want us to do then? What things you want us to tote out? We're both strong. We can lift good."

"But it doesn't seem right." He put his finger on his chin. "I've got an idea, with one condition."

"What condition?" Monroe Junior asked, suspiciously.

"Consider that I hire both of you at five dollars each. You can pitch in and do whatever those two movers want you to help out with. After that, you can maybe haul off any trash, anything left laying—lying around. I want to leave the place as neat as we can."

"Sure, we'll be glad to do all that. We was aiming to anyway. But what's the condition?"

"Well, Monroe—"

"Monroe Junior. My pa was Monroe."

221

"Monroe Junior, I'm going to give you another gift. You see, I didn't know what, exactly, I was going to do with that old buggy of mine, the Oakland. It's got some problems, but with your way with machines, you could fix it up. You could still get some good mileage out of it. I'll give you the Oakland. That's the only way I'll accept your helping me out."

"I don't know if Ma'll like it. I'll have to ask Ma if that's okay."

"Look. Let's do it this way. When we get all loaded up and ready to leave, I'll have my wife drive the Oakland as far down the main cinder road as your side-road turnoff. I'll leave the keys under the—let's see . . . under the rubber mat in the back seat. I'll round up the papers for you."

"But Ma might not like it. She might not let us keep it."

"If she won't, then I guess you'll just have to let it rust in a heap, or give it to the Northcutts."

"Oh, Ma wouldn't want the Northcutts to have it," said J. T.

"Then I guess we've got a deal. Okay, you boys consider yourself working now. Go out there and ask the men what they'd like to have you do. If you find yourself out of work, come back to me and I'll give you something to keep you busy, to earn your money from. Actually, I'm pleased. We'll get out sooner now."

After that, Honor drifted back into the living room. All the furniture had been taken out. There was a strange empty, hollow sound in the room without the wool rug, the armchair, the daybed, and the Philco radio. She walked over to the window by the undecorated Christmas tree that was leaning to one side now with only a few straggly strings of popcorn tinsel left on its branches. Where the daybed had been, she saw a rectangular shape of light powdery dust. And then she saw the shiny blue of the broken ornament over in the far corner beneath the tree. She bent down and reached under for it.

It was the little bluebird ornament, the one her mother had sent away for a long time ago with coupons. Some of the blue color had worn off with the years, and when it had dropped during the undecorating of the tree, its tail feathers had been broken off.

For a long moment, she cupped it in both hands, like a wounded bird.

Then, she suddenly made up her mind about something that had been bothering her all morning.

She found her mother in the bedroom, checking out the vanity dresser drawers one last time and looking into the corners of the closet to make sure they were empty.

"Do you need me to help out with something, Mama?"

"Oh, Lord no, just stay out of the way. We'll be ready to leave in about—oh, just a few more minutes."

"Could I go outside for a breath of fresh air before we take off?" she asked.

"Well, if you'll stay in very close hollering distance—and not get your leggings all splattered up with that slush from the melting snow. Don't muddy up your shoes—if you'll put on your galoshes. A bit of fresh air might do you some good. Get a little color back in your face."

Honor took the back way up to Lola's little house. She stood for a moment looking all around at the boarded-up door on Lola's house, at the shades pulled down in Dr. Clark's house, at the porch where she and Lola had spent some time talking, at the iron pot sitting on the three bricks. Then, very quickly, she went over to the fresh mound of earth with the smooth stone placed at the head of it. She reached into her coat pocket and pulled out the shiny buckeye, her good-luck, light-blue marble taw, and the broken bluebird ornament wrapped in a soft piece of tissue paper.

She bent down and quickly scooped out a hollow place in the dirt beneath the headstone, using a sturdy piece of stick. First, she put in the shiny buckeye, then she carefully placed the marble taw alongside the buckeye, and exactly even with it—just in case it might bring some kind of good luck. "I should've maybe left these inside the round tin to start with," she apologized in a whisper to Lola. Then, nesting the broken ornament in her hands, she looked at it intently for a long time, wondering if she ought to try one last wish to the magic bluebird.

But instead, she quickly placed the ornament in its tissue paper at an angle in the scooped-out place and hurriedly threw the dirt over all three objects, packing it down with her hands.

When she stood up, there was a new, burning, hard glint in her eyes. They were very dry, even with the cold wind whipping at them. "The bluebird must've tried to help you out some, Lola," she said in a clear, brittle-sound-ing voice. "You said if he was out, he'd probably get his tail feathers froze off."

She tossed her head back and looked up one last time into the bare branches of the sycamore tree. "At least you got a good hex put on that crap-ass blue jay!"

Then, without another look back, she squared her shoulders, held her head as tall as she could, and took the longest way back down the hill, walking in full view of anyone who cared to look, down the front brick walk of Dr. Clark's house. She opened the front gate, let it swing back, creaking on its hinges. When the wind swung it open, she firmly clicked it shut on the latch.

When she reached the alley, she saw the men slamming the back doors of the yellow truck shut and tipping their hats to her father, signaling that they were ready to pull out.

She heard the deeper rattling sounds of the Freemans' truck, tuning up to move out of the way.

Parked alongside the main cinder road was the shiny new Dodge. She guessed it was as good a time as any to get her first bid in on the best seat, by the window behind the driver's seat.

She opened the door, letting it slam hard behind her. Then, she sat very still, her back straight, her chin up. She paid no attention to the interior of the new car, to all the plush new things—the fancy gadgets and domed roof and the strips of chrome that her brothers had been bragging about. To her, it was just a car to ride in. It was just a gray, empty new car, gray on the outside and a deeper shade of gray on the inside, every bit as hollow and as empty as an echo.